WHAT'$ ¥OUR NUMB€R?

L.R. Diaz

Published by Fly The World Publishing

FlyTheWorld.co

Contact or Follow the Author:
Email: Luis@FlyTheWorld.co
Instagram: @Wheres_Luigy
Twitter: @LRDiazAuthor
Lrdiaz.com
Lrdiazblog.com

Cover Design by Nusrat Abbas Awan
IBSN: 9781960603005

L.R. Diaz

For the modest degenerates,

PROLOGUE

A phone and a duffel bag stuffed with a hundred and forty thousand dollars in cash is all he had in his possession. Not too bad for most, but to him, it meant next to nothing. Luis looked down at his phone, it read 10:38 PM, as the private jet finally descended to an altitude where service was reachable. Time had been irrelevant for the last four to five weeks as he had crossed every time zone through some of the most luxurious cities across the world. Daytime and nighttime. Those were his two time zones. *Jet lag is for the weak,* he thought to himself, as he took another swig of Armand de Brignac straight from the bottle. He had become somewhat of a champagne enthusiast in that time traveling and was on his second bottle this flight.

Aboard the Gulfstream jet he rented just a few hours earlier from Las Vegas, he could finally see the coastline out of the small window to his left as it was lighted by massive beach houses on one side and by the moonlight reflecting off the ocean water on the other. "About time," he scoffed as his patience began to wear thin and his anxiety continued to rise. He looked inside his Louis Vuitton duffel bag which he had stuffed with his recent earnings at the blackjack table. Fourteen racks of ten thousand dollars each. He tossed the bag across the aisle in disgust. The flight attendant approached from the back of the plane carefully and asked, "Is everything alright, Mr. Diaz?" He flinched as he'd been momentarily startled by her and bluntly told her, "I'm fine! I specifically requested no flight attendant!"

"Sorry. Company policy. We're preparing to land, anything else I can get for you, sir?" He shooed her away as she collected the empty bottle and disappeared to the back of the jet.

His paranoia was running rampant since returning to the United States. "Why me?!" He asked himself before assuring himself, "I'm the man. I'll *always* be the fucking man." He checked his surroundings again to make sure the inquisitive flight attendant was not creeping on him. He took out his ID card to prepare his next fix and made two neat lines. *"Cleared for takeoff,"* he whispered to himself as he picked up the rolled hundred dollar bill and snorted both lines of cocaine from the tray table. "Wooooh!" he yelled sharply, instantly followed by a head shake and a one-two punch combination to the air.

The jet made a smooth landing at the Fernandina Beach airport near his home. He chuckled to himself as he thought back to all the times it would take him at least an hour from the plane touching down to then waiting for his luggage and finally getting to his parked car. In the economy lot. *What a loser. I'll never go back to that life. EVER!* He finished off the bottle, chucked it to the side, grabbed his duffel bag and walked off the jet.

Once he located his red Ferrari F8 Spider, he sighed a breath of relief. "I missed you, baby! Papi's home." He reached inside the rear wheel well to grab his key. His car being stolen didn't really concern him since only the affluent flew into this airport. Besides, if somebody had stolen it, he wouldn't have even cared, he'd just go out and buy another one and wish the thief well.

After jumping in the car, he pushed the button to start the car. The rush of adrenaline he thought had already peaked, due to his drug and alcohol consumption, just burst through the next threshold. He growled in sync with the motor. *Grrrrrrrr.* As he clutched the steering wheel and massaged the leather on it, he felt one with the car. All that raw horsepower surged through his body and he felt powerful, *invincible.*

Minutes later, he was speeding down the highway at over 110 MPH with the top down and Latin trap music blasting. He sang along to the lyrics and acted them out as if it were him they were rapping about. Luckily for him, cops weren't normally on this side of town this late. It was a small town with little police presence. Besides, he was on their good side since he had made a very generous donation to one of the cops not long ago. A good deed he'd hope to cash in later.

His phone buzzed and he looked down at it. *UNKNOWN.* He doesn't answer but he gripped the phone tightly and yelled at it in a fit of rage. "Leave me the fuck alone!" Then he tossed the phone up in the air and let the force of the wind take it until gravity took over and crashed it back down to Earth. Nobody mattered to him anymore, he was here for one thing and one thing only.

He reached over and checked his glove box. "There you are," he marveled at the Smith and Wesson revolver he'd purchased for protection. It was a beautiful piece depending on which end you were looking at. He knew close to nothing about guns, but it looked cool, so that's why he'd bought it. Then he looked inside his center console to find a fifth of Blue Label he must not have finished the last time he was in town, cracked it open and took a long swig. He didn't grimace, it was like water to him. Luis swerved lane to lane as if the dashed lines served no purpose to him, then reached under his seat. "Aha!" He kissed the gold plated tin he kept stashed which contained some of the purest cocaine known to man, unlike that trash he had been resorting to the last couple days. He opened it and brought it up to his nose. A sudden gust of wind blew most of the cocaine onto his face. "Fuck!" he yelled in a fit of rage, but a good bit managed to enter his nostrils and was now releasing vast amounts of dopamine into his brain. He clenched his jaw, gripped the steering wheel tighter, pounded the pedal to the floor and was laser focused on the road ahead, driving straight as an arrow.

As he rounded the corner to his neighborhood, his house became visible in the distance. He squinted his eyes for a clearer view to confirm what he thought he was seeing. A large moving truck and red Lamborghini Gallardo were parked in the driveway. The same one he'd gifted one of his life long best friends, Victor, not long ago. "That fucking asshole!" he yelled. "I'm gonna kill him!" He sped up on the driveway and slammed the brakes. Then reached in his glove compartment for the revolver, which he'd only planned on using as a scare tactic, but now things had changed. Voices in his head kept saying, *'You gave them everything.*

They're nothing without you. You're the fucking man.' As those last word slipped out of his mouth, he realized the words weren't in his head anymore. He was speaking them. He shook his head to regain focus and beelined to the front door. He rang the doorbell, secretly wishing his best friend would have the balls to open the front door to *his* house. The door opened slowly. Not the first person he was expecting to see, as his frightened little daughter looked up hesitantly at the broken shell of his former self.

"Daddy?"

CHAPTER 1

"American two-ninety-three, descend via the stockcar arrival landing north, Florence altimeter two-niner-niner-six."

"Roger, descending via..." the pilot responded.

Luis immediately turned to the side to jump back into the conversation with his co-workers. "Yeah man, you're right. Seven years in, and I'm *still* at the bottom of the seniority list. This is bullshit!"

He had been in the federal agency for seven years now but had been doing air traffic control for almost fifteen years. Entering that career had been unplanned and involved a little bit of luck. After a brief stint in college and a few years of jumping from one odd job to the next, he'd decided to give the military a shot. The Navy recruiter had him take the ASVAB and he scored well enough to secure just about any job available. In fact, he didn't even know what air traffic control was, but he'd been told they get paid well and that was enough to convince him. The recruiter was adamant about him taking the job, so thanks to him, here he was.

It wasn't an easy road though, as it may appear by his mostly chill and relaxed demeanor. He'd been told a few times throughout his career that he didn't have what it takes and he never forgot those individuals. It served him as fuel him to succeed. He had a drive like no other and when he said he was going to do something, it got done. After a four year term in the Navy, he contracted in Afghanistan for a few years as he waited for the call back in the states to work for the federal government. While working overseas, he began globe-trotting in places such as Australia, Thailand and all over Europe, where he'd learn to see the world through a different lens. As a single man, he'd wander and party recklessly from one city to the next, posting his wild and crazy lifestyle on his social media for friends and the rest of the world to see. But it wasn't always just the partying that gave him pleasure, it was being thrown into the unknown. From poor towns in Kingston, Jamaica to luxurious cities such as Dubai and Abu Dhabi, he developed an affinity of immersing himself in their cultures and traditions and would continue to do so until this day. Life was good.

Now, being in the agency, things calmed down

a bit. Life was more structured, the way was supposed to be according to society. The fabled American Dream. He always imagined bigger and more grandiose things, but he was more than content with this family life. Some envied him but most admired him, because he was the type of person to get along with everyone. Occasionally, strangers would inquire about what he did for a living and when he responded, they'd look at him either in surprise or disbelief like "Wow! *You're* an air traffic controller?" To which he would dish it right back like, "What? Hard to believe because I'm Puerto Rican?!" He lived for those awkward reactions. Funny at the moment, not so funny if you really think about it. But the military taught him how to have thick skin, so his ability to snap back at race sensitive jokes or work banter was at an elite level.

"All you young guys ever do is complain," said Pete, who was sitting across the aisle. "You make six figures, you punch in, punch out, don't take work home with you and you get a pension. Where else are you gonna—"

He was interrupted by two planes flashing on his radar scope.

"November One Victor Golf, descend and maintain flight level 2-3-0 immediately! Traffic 12 o' clock, 13 miles, opposite direction at the same altitude, an Airbus, not on frequency."

All the nearby controllers looked over his way.

No response.

Pete had been doing this for a long time and his colleagues always joked about his age and slowly diminishing skillset but in reality he was a very respected controller who's sarcasm was often mistaken for rudeness. At the moment, he was starting to panic though, something they were seeing more frequently from him. "TRAFFIC ALERT, NOVEMBER-TWO-NINE-ONE-VICTOR-GOLF, DESCEND TO FLIGHT LEVEL 2-3-0 IMMEDIATELY!"

The pilot responded calmly, "Roger, descending. Were you calling me earlier?"

"YES! THREE TIMES, SIR!"

"Sorry about that."

"Fucking pilots!" he yelled off frequency. The rest of the guys bursted into laughter.

"Maybe it's time to retire, Pete!" Luis suggested jokingly. Pete flipped him off.

"Speaking of retirement, ya'll seen that lotto jackpot?!" Ian asked. "Just played some numbers at the gas station. I'm feeling lucky this time around."

"What's it at now?" Luis asked.

"684 million dollars, one of the largest in history," Ian responded.

"Damn. I couldn't even imagine what I'd do

with that much," Luis said. "My grandma always said, you can't win if you don't play. I'll try to remember to grab a quick pick after work."

Javier jumped in the conversation. "Too much money for me. I like to play the smaller jackpots that nobody is going for. All I need is five million, that way I don't have to give anybody shit!"

"Man you're crazy! If you hit this one, just keep five and give the rest away then," Luis suggested, confused at Javier's rationale. "But don't forget about your boys!"

"See what I mean?!" Javier snapped back. "If I forget someone, I'll look like a dick. Not like I care, but all you peasants will come begging for some and I ain't trying to deal with that. Plus family. Then old cousins, friends, neighbors. I'm stressed just thinking about it!"

"I don't know man. Personally, I don't think it would be that tough. Set a strict budget for what you're giving away. Say fifty percent. Then set a house and car budget and all your necessities and let the rest sit and collect interest. I mean how hard could that be? You're filthy fucking rich! You can just pay someone to do it all for you," Luis tried to reason.

"Five million. That's my number and I'm sticking to it," Javier didn't budge. "Ok so tell me, what's your number?"

Previously, asking someone's *number* was asking them how many sexual partners they'd been with. Luis knew this was different, but he seized the opportunity for a joke. "Kinda personal, huh? I stopped counting a long time ago, lemme think." Luis started counting off his fingers. "There was Brenda, Latisha, Linda, Felicia, Dawn, Leshaun, Ines and Alicia—" he rattled off names from a well known DMX song. They rapped along with him once they understood the reference. Except Pete, he didn't get it.

"You're stupid bro," Javier laughed, "but seriously, the absolute minimum you'd need to win to say screw this place and go live your dream life?"

Luis did some math in his head. Ian answered first, "Enough for me to make a hundred fifty grand per year til I'm seventy. Soooo, five or six million? Somewhere in that range."

"So you're telling me that if you hit a couple million dollars, you're coming back to work?! Get outta here man!" Luis laughed. "I think two million and I'm out! Shit, maybe even a million. I'm sure I can somehow flip that into investments and live a simple life. I don't really need much. With what I have now, plus a million or two? I could sell my place, buy a small house on a beach, open a small bar and coast for the rest of my life. But now if I hit a *huge* jackpot, I'm going all out!," he pretended to slide money off his hand and into the air, better known as *making it rain.*

"Two million? Yeah right, dude! With these house prices? Inflation is sky high and your new president is gonna tax the shit out of you!" Somebody chimed in from across the radar room. Politics always found a way of infiltrating every conversation nowadays. The guys ignored him.

"Pete, what about you, old man? What's your number?" Luis asked.

"What number? There is no number. You'll see when you all grow up, *if* you ever grow up," he responded without turning his head from the radar scope. Then he turned to the guys and chuckled, "Actually the number is zero, because you guys are never going to hit the lotto. You're all idiots."

"Don't be so negative, Pete, it's hypothetical," Luis kept pressing him, not because he really wanted to know, but because he enjoyed Pete's unscripted reactions.

"I'll drop my retirement paperwork right now just to get away from you clowns."

It had been an interesting question that made everyone ponder. How much money would it really take to drop everything? What kind of lifestyle would you settle for and would you even tell anybody? Friends or family? Everyone has a number.

"Okay I'll tell you what. If any of us hits a big jackpot, above fifty million, we give each other *our number* so we can quit," Ian suggested. "Shake on it and give your word."

"That, I can agree on. Just need five," said Javier.

Luis followed, "I'm down! Five is a good number. Pete?"

"You millennials are so delusional," he rolled his eyes and shook his head.

CHAPTER 2

Luis got relieved from his position for the last time that day and headed immediately towards the exit. Pete was right in saying that once your shift was done, it was truly done. As soon as he crossed that door's threshold, he would be free and his weekend would commence. The increasingly bothersome con to his job was that his weekends fell on Wednesdays and Thursdays and not the typical Saturday-Sundays like the rest of the world. But he took the good things with the bad and his family had learned to adapt to it. The truth was that he quite enjoyed his job and his co-workers, but it was precious time he wasn't getting back. Time he felt was being taken from his family since he'd been working so many overtime shifts in the last few years. Luis wasn't alone in feeling that way. Most of his colleagues were at a tipping point as well, creating grand illusions as to what their 'escape plans' would be. For the time being though, he would just focus on what he could control, as he pushed open the exit door in dramatic fashion. *Freedom!* Tonight was pizza night at the Diaz household, the kids' favorite day of the week.

Luis jumped in his car and called his wife, Krystal. She answered right away. "Hey babe! You're off?"

"Yup, I'm on my way to the store. What do we need for tonight?"

"Pretty much everything for the pizza. I think the other stuff went bad."

"Okay, sooooo how about some wine for *later*?" He dragged out the question in a long sensual voice to imply he wanted something.

"Hmm, not tonight babe, dealing with a bit of a headache from work."

Damn, it was worth a shot, he thought. This was married life.

"Ok love, see you in a few."

They'd been married a little over ten years now and were parents to a beautiful set of twins, Mia and Mikey. He can truly say he married the love of his life. They'd met at a party through some mutual friends long ago. Then lost contact because of their distance but followed each other on social media for a few years and randomly bumped into each other while they were both vacationing in Aruba. Both were single and on vacation with their married friends as fifth wheels, so they instantly bonded over their shared misery and the rest was history. Soon after, they began to travel the world, falling in love all over again from one city to the next, learning new love phrases in each country and romantically saying them to each other. *"Je'taime, mon amour,"* Luis would recite in a terrible accent atop of the Eiffel Tower as they pretended to act out a scene in a French movie. Yes it was cheesy, but it was their thing.

After getting married in Cabo San Lucas a couple of years later, they got right to the family making. Luis wanted a huge family, she wanted two kids. Then they realized, having kids was not as easy as it seemed. It took years longer than they had expected and after coming home from a trip to the Dominican Republic, she thought she had eaten something bad or drank too much *mamajuana* and became very ill. Turned out she was pregnant with twins and beginning to experience morning sickness, except not just in the mornings. All. The. Time. It was a rough pregnancy and even worse labor but they had muscled through it all and were now parents to two wonderful children.

Everyone had told them that once the twins came around, they would never be able to travel again, but they were committed to defy those nay-sayers. Not even a year after the twins were born, they took a trip across Europe for a few weeks. Fast forward six years, the kids had more stamps on their passports than most of their friends. Combined. Luis loved watching their curious little minds trying to make sense of their foreign surroundings and languages. They'd even try foods that he was hesitant to try. Those kids were his whole world and he would do anything to give them everything he and his wife never had.

Luis arrived at the grocery store, and in less than five minutes, he got everything on the list his wife texted him. She had a thing for lists and his OCD had a thing about finishing lists, so they worked well together. After loading the groceries into his car, he remembered that he'd run out of beer a few days ago and his weekend was just beginning, so he went back inside for a twelve pack of his favorite beer, Coors Light. He grabbed a case and after seeing all the long cashier line, he opted to go over to the customer service line. Little known secret from a former cashier himself. The young, stoic-faced cashier asked him for his ID and he laughed. "Really? OK. Thanks I guess." She rolled her eyes as if to insist it wasn't a compliment, then barely glanced at the ID and handed it right back. *What's your problem?* he thought to himself assuming she was just having a bad day.

He looked over and saw the lottery machine, which took him back to the conversation at work. What *was* his number? He'd never really thought about that specific question but he'd had the 'what would you do if you hit the lottery' conversation at least a few dozen times at every other job he'd ever worked at. Not realistic but it was always nice to dream, right? Thinking it over again, he was convinced that anything over a million would be enough to quit his job. "Can I get a quick pick for the mega millions tonight?"

"Cash only," she responded as if she had to remind every customer that came through her line repeatedly that lotto can only be paid in cash. He reached into his pocket. Two singles, just enough. He paid the moody cashier, she printed a ticket and handed it to him, already looking past him and to the next customer. As he walked off, he thought, *damn, if you would've been nice, maybe I would've gave you a cut! But screw you and have a nice day.*

"Daddy!!" Both kids raced to him as he walked in the door. He raised the grocery bags up above his shoulders so they wouldn't knock them off as they wrapped themselves around his waist. "I want pepperoni and jalapeños on my pizza tonight!" Mia begged.

"I want cheese and extra cheese!" said Mikey.

"That's so boring!" Mia rolled her eyes in a way to tease her brother.

"You're boring!"

"You're both gonna be eating a huge bowl of broccoli if you keep fighting."

"No! Please! I'm sorry," Mikey begged apologetically.

"I'm only teasing, Dad, you know I love Mikey," she grabbed Mikey and hugged him tightly, kissing him on the cheek while he tried pulling back.

"Much better. Where's your mom?"

"She's outside laying by the pool," Mia responded.

"Okay, tell her I'll be over in a couple minutes."

The kids then ran outside while he put the groceries away.

After settling in and putting on some swimming shorts, he went to the fridge for a beer and walked out back. The weekend had just begun. His wife was catching some rays while doing work on her laptop. She'd been lucky to not only keep her job, but also be able to work from home now that the COVID-19 pandemic had changed everyone's way of life. Not his job though. He was slightly envious of that but there was no way to could control airplanes from home. So he carried on.

"Hola, mi amor," he leaned over and gave her a kiss.

She clicked and minimized a page quickly before he had a chance to notice. Not that he'd care anyways because they never hid things from each other. It was one of their strong suits. Luis' trust in humanity made him the type of person to give trust and allow them to lose it rather than not trusting someone until they had earned it. Although he'd been burned a few times.

"I'm finishing up here. I'll be done in a couple of minutes."

Out of the corner of his eyes, he could see the kids were up to something. Through their facial expressions, he understood they wanted to scare their mother and make a huge splash. He nodded in agreement, then signaled, *one…two…three*. They ran full speed towards him, he turned around and they did cannonballs into the pool. They laughed out loud, but Krystal shut her laptop appearing to be frustrated and walked away. A few seconds later, when the kids thought they had upset their mother and looked at him for suggestions, she turned around and ran straight at them, jumping in and splashing them all.

"Gotcha!!" she laughed.

"This is the best pizza EVERRR!!!" Mia said

dramatically as she devoured her pizza dripping with pepperoni grease, stringy cheese and jalapeños.

"Oh you think that's good, wait until we take you to Naples. The birthplace of pizza! Now *that's* the best pizza in the world, right baby?" He looked at his wife for confirmation.

"*Si signore, la migliore pizza!*" she responded and waved her hand in a very Italian-like manner before blowing a kiss into the air.

The kids yelled, "*Mama mia!*" and copied her hand gesture.

"Maybe we can go there this summer. Pizza and pistachio gelato!" he suggested.

"Pretty please!! And that place with chocolate and cheese!!" Mia begged.

"Switzerland! I'm surprised you remembered," Luis was impressed. Kids don't forget anything you promise them.

His wife looked at him with that *don't get started* look he'd been so used to seeing and quickly tried to change the subject. They would definitely be having a talk later. This was a common theme in their marriage, Luis wanting to do all these extravagant things and his wife trying to tone him down a bit. He'd get the kids all excited about new adventures and then mom had to be the mean one to shoot down the crazier ideas. Almost always though, he got his way. He'd long ago figured out his wife's number. He just had to ease into the conversation and not just bring it up suddenly because she wasn't much for spontaneity like he was. So he already knew they'd go to Europe that summer, he was just going to have to revisit the conversation later with a well-drafted plan.

"Okay kids, time to clean up this mess and start getting ready for bed," he said assertively, looking for support from his wife. The kids frowned looking for sympathy.

"You heard dad," she backed him up. "Go shower and brush your teeth. Especially you, Mikey." Luis winked at her, she winked back.

They made a hell of a team and he always cherished that. Their creed was simple, live by the golden rule. Don't lie, don't cheat, don't envy. Be a good role model and treat everyone as you'd like to be treated. Sure there's other cardinal sins no one should ever commit, but the point was to just do good and good things will happen to you.

After tucking the kids in to bed, he made his way to his liquor bar and poured a tall glass of bourbon over an ice ball. He felt a conversation brewing with his wife and he was arming himself for battle. *Deep breath. Patience. Here we go.*

He walked into their room, where she laid on her side of the bed with her reading glasses on and her eyes fixated on a book. *Okay, this is not the normal posture for arguments.* Krystal knew this was his favorite way to see her at night. Something about that nerdy 'oh let me innocently read a chapter before I go to bed' look raised his testosterone levels like a bull ready to buck. She pulled down her glasses and looked at him. He was ready for his prey. He squinted his eyes and stared straight at her, biting his bottom lip. He set his whiskey glass on the nightstand and took the book off her hands before she pulled back, laughing and shaking her head. "Oh you thought —," she continued laughing. "I'm sorry babe, maybe tomorrow."

Man down.

"I do want to talk though," she patted the side of the bed for him to lay next to her. *Here we go again*, he took a gulp from his glass.

"So I've been thinking," she took her glasses off and sets them aside. "I want to try and have another baby."

"Woah. Not the conversation I expected," he leaned back in surprise.

"What? I thought you wanted a big family?"

"Oh honey, I do! But after that last pregnancy —"

"Yeah but we had twins unexpectedly. What are the odds of that happening again? Besides, I was looking at our finances and we're doing amazing. Your little Bitcoin thing took off pretty nicely."

"Told ya," he smirked.

"You know I don't like to play with our money like that but I did some research and honestly, I still don't understand it. But whatever, that's all you. Just don't lose it."

He didn't understand it either, but it was making him wealthier, and that, he understood very well.

"I've seen people become millionaires because they invested in this stuff, who knows? Maybe it'll make us rich enough to quit and we can have all the babies you want."

"Yeah okay," she said sarcastically, rolling her eyes.

"We were just talking about that at work today. What our number is."

She interrupted, "Ew, I don't wanna know that."

"Not that number, babe." He laughed. He'd always avoided that conversation when they dated and it never came about later in life. He was hoping she wouldn't inquire now. "Like the amount of money you'd need to quit your job and live the life you always dreamed of. I'm curious, what's your number?"

"Hmm, two million, maybe?" she answered

after a few seconds of thinking.

"That's what I said! See, I knew I married you for a reason."

"You know I don't want much. I love where we're at right now. I'd just want to make sure we have money for the kid's education and enough to be able to travel from time to time."

"I think I'd be good with two million but if we hit five we could cop a few exotic cars and buy a small house on the beach in Puerto Rico."

"I'd be ok with that," she replied after pondering it over real quick.

"So another baby, huh? You sure?"

She innocently nodded.

"Ok well, let's do it…" He rolled over to kiss her on the neck and ran his hand under her shirt.

She slapped his hand away. "Third strike buddy, you're out. But try again tomorrow," she kissed him, "you might hit a grand slam." Then she rolled over and turned off her lamp. He turned over to grab his phone and immediately started looking up prices to go to Europe for the summer, plotting a way to convince her this time around.

CHAPTER 3

T he next day, Luis woke up to get started on his normal Wednesday routine. His wife would bring him coffee to bed and then disappear into the home office for the rest of the day, while he would take care of his weekly chores. She'd only reappear briefly throughout the day either looking to see if he'd made any food or to tell him to turn the volume down because she had an 'important' meeting coming up. *Must be nice,* he thought to himself as he pushed the lawn mower and thought of ways his job could become remote. *Controlling airplanes from the comfort of my own couch.* Not happening. It was hard to complain about a job that kept his family financially secure but he was reaching a point in life where he wanted to spend more time with the family now that the kids were reaching that age where they stayed busy in sports, music and school. Money wasn't everything, his family was.

Every few weeks, the thought of trading his high-demanding job for a lesser one that gave him more time at home would consume his mind. This time around, he thought the possibility was becoming more and more likely. The COVID-19 pandemic was rough to the majority of the world but they were fortunate enough to keep their jobs throughout and save aggressively since their travel and entertainment budget was at a near halt. They also invested a lot of that money when the market took a huge dive and benefited from some major crypto currency booms along the way, so he knew they'd be well off if he stepped down from his job and they managed their money right. People got by on much less. He doubted Krystal would budge, she was an accountant after all. The way her mind worked was to continue earning capital to meet quotas and balance budgets with any surplus being invested for their children's future. It was the better plan.

After returning from his daydream, he was brought back to the present as his lawn mower ran out of gas with just a small section of his lawn left to cut. "Shit!" The phone in his pocket then buzzed and continued to vibrate nonstop. He chose to finish up before answering to what was likely the guys' group chat being bombarded with raunchy memes or a debate about the newest victim to 'cancel culture.'

When he finished the lawn, he cracked open a

beer and pulled out his phone. Sure enough, over forty text messages from the guys at work. He scrolled quickly to see what he had missed.

Somebody in Fernandina Beach hit the lotto!

Holy shit!

Did any of you guys play?

How many winners?

It says just one winner.

If any of you fuckers hit, you better remember our pact!

What pact?

Not you Pete, you declined.

(Middle finger emoji)

How much was it again?

684 million!!!

Damn, Luis thought, *should've bought more tickets.* If it wasn't for that cashier's bad attitude and *cash only* policy, he would've definitely bought more. He still held a grudge.

Luis then went back inside, grabbed another beer and laid out back for some more day dreaming. This time about what he'd do if he had the winning ticket, which the odds deemed near impossible but it had hit nearby, unless the guys were just talking shit as usual. "684 million dollars…" he said to himself as he sipped his beer and thought about where would be the first place he'd want to take his family to before seeing the rest of the world. *Italy? Nah, been there. Maybe head west for once. Fiji, New Zealand, Bali, Singapore, Tokyo. Continue west, travel through Europe, then Africa. Help those in need along the way.*

He could go the opposite route and enjoy luxuries at home before traveling abroad. Purchase his dream cars, a house on a big property with his own lazy river and a slide for the kids. All kinds of exclusive material things, not because he was a material person but because he'd have enough money to do so, so why not? The possibilities were endless with a jackpot that size. He then remembered a show he'd watched about lottery winners going broke and their families being ruined, but he was sure that those people didn't have a strong marriage like him and Krystal did and they probably didn't know how to manage money because they'd never really had any. He would make sure to hire the right team to make sure that money worked for him via diversified investments, properties and so forth. In fact, it would probably be Krystal that would ensure that, as she would frantically tell him to stop spending so much money. He chuckled at the possibility of that argument.

As he finished his beer, he imagined how nice it would be to have a maid or butler bring him the next one at the snap of a finger. Instead, he had to accept reality. He would have to grab his own beer. Then wash the cars. Trim the shrubs. Pressure wash the driveway. Go back to work and repeat, until he'd be eligible to retire. If he's lucky, he'll have better days off in the next few years. He enjoyed daydreaming better.

Just like that, Luis' midweek weekend was over, just as his family's was about to begin. Friday evening shift. The rest of the world was getting ready to decompress from their work week or make memories with their families, he was going back in to work to make memories with the same miserable crew that shared his fate of low seniority. As he was getting ready for work, he slipped on his favorite pair of shorts and felt something in his pocket. A receipt and a lottery ticket. He made a mental note to check it in the car because he was running late at the moment. As he backed out of the driveway, his wife pulled in and the kids rolled the down their window.

"Where are you going daddy?" Mia asked.

"Off to work honey, you know that."

"I know, but can you just not go? We can go get ice cream and watch movies!"

This broke his heart. He always tried to leave before the kids came because of this exact scenario.

"If I don't work, we won't have money to do

those things. But I promise to take you next week."

"I can pay for it!" Mikey insisted.

If they only knew how much money it took to live their lifestyle.

"Next time buddy, I'm late for work. Love you guys!"

They waved him off and he was back to feeling low. He was going to have to miss his son's baseball game that night and his girl's first soccer game the next morning. He'd always imagined himself being the coach for these teams but now he didn't have the time or opportunity to even meet the coaches. He wondered, *what kind of things were they teaching them? Are they teaching them valuable life lessons such as winning and losing? Do they teach them about teamwork and how to handle adversity?* Kids were coddled and spoiled nowadays and sporting leagues were handing out participation trophies, lessening the value of being a winner. He remembered the agony of defeat as he cried watching the basketball team that beat them in the championship when he was a child. That made him want to train harder, day in and day out. He was obsessed with wanting to get revenge and the next year when the same two teams met for the championship again, his team dominated. They had become champions and it taught him a very valuable life lesson. Work harder than the rest and you'll achieve the success you desire. He doubted his kids would learn the same way he did but he would make sure to adapt to the new world and do his part in raising some tough, gritty kids. Right on cue, some Bob Marley came on over the radio telling him *everything was gonna be alright.*

Halfway to work, his phone vibrated and he reached into his pocket to find the lotto ticket he'd forgotten was there. Maybe he hits a few numbers and wins a free ticket. Maybe he doesn't win a damn thing and has to go clock in to work. He put his Tesla Model 3 on autopilot and unlocked his phone. He typed in the website for the numbers which took forever to load since the reception was slow in the heavily wooded backroads he drove to work. Finally, there it was, the headline for one lucky winner of the $684 million jackpot in Fernandina Beach, FL. "Wow! The guys weren't kidding for once," he spoke out loud as he again imagined what he would do if he really did hit. "Yeah right, I wish." He read the winning numbers.

4 - 21 - 36 - 42 - 56 and 13 for the Mega Ball.

He looked down at his ticket.

4.

21.

36.

42.

56.

And 13 for the Mega Ball.
HOLY FUCKING SHIT.

CHAPTER 4

Luis slammed on the brakes and pulled off to the side of the two lane road. He looked again to confirm the numbers. They matched. He checked the date. Another match. He checked another website just to be sure. Third match. It was real, he'd hit the damn lottery. Luis slapped his hands repeatedly on the dashboard and yelled at the top of his lungs in excitement, then pressed against the horn a few times. His mind was racing and rushing with all kinds of emotions. He didn't know what to do next as he tried to catch his breath. "Holy shit, holy shit! Are you serious?!" He put his hands on his head and wanted to tug at his hair from excitement, but he didn't have any, he was bald. He then looked up through the glass roof of his car as if he was asking a higher being for confirmation. "Thank you! Thank you lord!" He grabbed his phone to call Krystal, but decided he'd rather surprise her, so he scrolled down his list of recent calls to see who else he should call and pressed on his mother's number.

No luck. The call failed due to the lack of reception. Luis was bursting inside and was ready to race back home so he decided a u-turn was his next move as it was sinking in that he'd never have to make that drive to work again. "No more work!" He made one last fist pump before putting his car back in gear, then checked the rearview mirror for traffic.

"Shit!"

Amidst of all of his excitement, he hadn't noticed a police car was parked behind him with his lights flashing. There he was, in a small town country road with hardly any traffic or cellular reception. If the cop realized he'd pulled over the person with the winning lottery ticket, what's to stop him from shooting him and taking it? He was hispanic. They'd killed others for less. His paranoia was running wild. He shoved the ticket back in his pants, lowered his window and put his hands on the ten and two of the steering wheel.

Luis looked at his side mirror and watched the cop exit his vehicle. When he noticed it was a black cop, he breathed easier. *Phew*. He believed the chances of getting shot now dramatically decreased. He couldn't explain why that was the case, it was just a minority thing. The officer approached the window and in a stern voice said, "License and registration, please." As Luis reached over to get it, the cop asked, "Everything alright, sir? I saw you pull off suddenly and then you were yelling and honking the horn like a mad man." He pulled off his sunglasses and looked inside the car suspiciously.

"Sorry officer I just got some great news. My wife called to tell me she was pregnant and I almost lost it. It's just been a long process for us and I was overwhelmed with emotion, I had to pull over." He handed the documents to the cop.

The officer studied his license for a second. "Well Mr. Diaz, let me be the first to congratulate you then. I'll be sure to keep you in my prayers tonight." He handed the documents back to Luis. "I'll let you get on your way now but be careful driving now. Go celebrate the great news with your family."

Luis was overjoyed. "Thank you, Officer—"

"Jones. Derek Jones."

"Thank you Officer Jones, I won't forget this. Have a blessed day!"

"You do the same."

He closed the window and let out a deep breath. He almost felt guilty for lying to the officer, since the man had been so nice. He'd seen on the news that one of the local cops had been shot and killed while on duty recently and the whole tight knit town was affected by the tragedy. Cops only seemed to be in the headlines if they were either killed or if they killed somebody. All negative headlines, although the majority of them were good, like Officer Jones. He promised himself to surprise him with a nice gift from his winnings. A random act of kindness, a hundred grand or maybe pay for his kid's education, or both. He could imagine the gratitude and the local headlines. *LOTTERY WINNER GIVES COP THAT PULLED HIM OVER 100 GRAND AND PAYS FOR KIDS' EDUCATION.* Finally, a nice story about cops.

But enough of that for now, he thought to himself. "I'm fucking rich!!" He yelled out loud as he sped back home. What now? Who does he tell? Who does he need to hire? How does he tell his wife? He decided to call her to begin the setup. "Babe, I left my wallet at home, I'm on my way back to get it."

"Ok I'll look around for it."

"Thanks love. See you in a few."

684 MILLION!!!

Luis was still in shock. He wanted to tell everyone so it felt real, but then again, he didn't want anybody to come begging just yet. First, he had to get official verification before telling his closest family and friends. He'd obviously hook them up but he wanted to actually see that money in his account.

On the way home, he stopped at the same store

he'd purchased the ticket again to grab a bottle of his wife's favorite champagne and some flowers. He went back to the shorter customer service line again and sure enough, the same girl from the day before was there. "ID please." He handed it over and he knew that she knew it was him again. *What's wrong with her?* What she didn't known was that she sold him the winning lottery ticket and it brought him great pleasure to keep it a secret from such a rude person.

He paid and then asked for ten quick picks and before she was able to ask, he answered, "Don't worry, I got the cash." As she walked over to the lotto machine to print them, he walked off.

"Sir! You forgot to—" He ignored her and threw up a peace sign. If she only knew how close she was to receiving a hefty gift for selling him the winning lottery ticket. *Golden rule*, he thought.

He raced back to his car and his phone buzzed. "Oh shit…work." He picked up.

"Hey Luis, you were supposed to be here thirty minutes ago, everything ok?" It was Ian, the pact initiator. He would've loved to hear his reaction about him hitting the lotto but he didn't want the news to be out just yet.

"Yeah I'm sorry, my kids were supposedly exposed to COVID at school so I might miss a few days. I'll call you when I find out more."

"Ok no problem, hope they get better."
Another lie. He felt terrible. *Not really.*

As he pulled into his garage, he rehearsed in his head how he was going to break the news. He loved surprising his family because he enjoyed seeing their reactions. When he walked in through the door, the kids came running towards him and saw him holding flowers and champagne. He motioned them to be quiet so he could surprise their mother. They giggled quietly and led him to her.

"Babe is that you? I can't find your wallet anywhere!" she yelled from their bedroom.

"Sorry honey I forgot to tell you I found it in the car."

"Why didn't you tell—," she stopped mid-question as she walked out of the room and saw him holding the bouquet of red roses and her favorite champagne. "Baaaaabe!" She got emotional and walked up to hug him tightly and kissed him. The kids cheered and joined in on the hug. He absolutely loved these moments.

Krystal grabbed the champagne and put it in the freezer and then reached in the cabinet for a vase and some scissors. "Thank you, I needed this. Too bad you gotta go to work now," she pouted.

"Work? Yeah that's not happening tonight. I

want to spend the day with my family. Besides, we got some big news to share with the kids, don't we?"

She looked at him puzzled. "What news?"

He rubbed his belly, referring to her wanting to get pregnant again. "I think they should know."

"Tell us!" The kids begged anxiously wanting to be told.

His reveal was going according to plan.

CHAPTER 5

"Another baby?! Why?" Mia asked dramatically as she crossed her arms and wore a frown in disappointment.

"Yay! I hope I get a brother! Can you make a boy, please?!" Mikey responded.

"We can't decide what it's going to be buddy," Luis laughed, "but we talked last night and I think the time is right to grow our family."

"Ok...", Mia began to accept her fate. Luis knew her well and could imagine her thinking she might get another sister. Someone who she can not only help take care of but someone she could boss around. Although Mia was minutes younger than her brother, her maturity was years ahead of Mikey's.

"But wait there's more!" Luis brought everyone's attention back to himself as he tapped his fingers together like a magician ready to perform his next trick. "If you had all the money in the world, what would you do with it?"

"I'd buy ice cream!" Mikey yelled.

"I want a puppy!" Mia followed.

He looked at his wife and raised his eyebrow.

"Um, I dunno babe. Why, what's going on?"

"Tell us, what would you do?" he asked again.

"Yes mommy! C'mon!" Mia egged her on.

"I've always wanted my own coffee shop."

He looked at her confused, because he'd never known that before. "That's news to me. A coffee shop, really?"

She nodded back.

"I actually *love* that idea. Is that all though?"

"C'mon babe why are you asking? It's your turn anyways, what would *you* do?" She was getting impatient.

"Take my family on a never-ending vacation," he replied. "But *only* if we had all the money in the world." He made a sad face then reached into his pocket and pulled out the lotto ticket.

He placed the ticket and the phone showing the winning numbers on the table in front of them and walked to the fridge. The kids grabbed it, not knowing what was going on until Krystal snatched it from them like she was snatching their candy.

"Is this a prank?!" She grabbed her own phone to confirm the numbers. Then she matched the dates and looked up at Luis with her jaw dropped to the floor. "This is real?"

He nodded back with a huge smile.

"OH MY GOD!!!!!!!!"

POP! He opened the champagne bottle and sprayed it everywhere. The kids jumped up and down and celebrated with them without understanding what was going on. Krystal was freaking out and hugging Luis tightly. "Is this real? Don't play with me! This is a joke, right?"

He looked straight into her eyes and replied, "It's real baby. 684 million. And we're the only winners."

"My god, I can't believe this! How is this happening?! What are we going to do with all that money?"

"Oh, I can think of a few things." Then he whispered in her ear, "You ever made love to a millionaire?" and grabbed a handful of her butt.

"Go to your room kids!" she directed them right away. "Go make a list of ten things you each want to buy. Or twenty!" They ran off, screaming in joy.

Krystal then grabbed him by the shirt and pulled him closer to her. "Come here, Mister Millionaire."

CHAPTER 6

Later that night, after reality had finally sunk in, they went into their office and Krystal opened up a spreadsheet on her laptop. Because that's what accountants do. Luis knew those old habits would probably never die even though she'd likely worked her last day as an accountant. Then he thought about himself not going back to work again. No more Friday and Saturday night shifts, no more six-day work weeks. *Hell yeah,* he thought. He began to wonder how or *if* he should break the news to them? Does he follow through on his promise to give his coworkers 'their number'? That was their pact, but after further review, was it realistic to just give these guys almost twenty million dollars out of *their* pot? *Nah.* Simple as that. He knew his wife would take the blame if she needed to.

"Okay so 684 million?" She placed her hand on her forehead and shook her head, still in disbelief. She typed the number into a lump sum calculator she found online. "So we'll have almost four hundred million left. Wow. This is crazy!" She organized her rows and columns and started plugging away. "Where do we start?"

"Obviously, family first. Parents, siblings and kids are in the upper tier. We'll rank the rest of our family by favorites," he said jokingly. Not really.

She typed their names one by one. By her own ranking system, Luis assumed as he watched curiously.

"I thought about it and I want to start a college fund for the kids in our family and our closest friends," she said and he agreed.

"We can look at some charities to donate to," he suggested.

"I love that idea. Look into charities," she said as she typed. "What else?"

"Officer Jones," he said, expecting to give an explanation.

"Officer who?"

"Jones. He pulled me over on my way to work today after I found out I hit the lotto. Scared the shit out of me at first but he was a super nice guy. I promised myself I would give him a nice gift especially since the cops here have been having a rough time recently. It'd be nice to change the narrative for once."

"Aww, that's sweet baby. I'll see if the neighbors know an Officer Jones, it's a small town. Maybe we can make a donation to the whole department," she typed his name on the spreadsheet.

"Maybe. Let's revisit that later." He didn't want to get carried away with giving handouts just yet, he wanted to get to the fun stuff.

Krystal then looked up in thought. "Well I guess we can disregard the debt since it's not much anyways. We can pay off the cars if we decide to keep them, but knowing you, we'll probably be getting something new." She looked at Luis who now was grinning from ear to ear.

"You know me well, my lady," he leaned over and kissed her cheek, then took the laptop from her. "But first, I think we should put this house on the market ASAP and start thinking about where we want to live next. We can head south. West Palm Beach? Florida Keys? Maybe get some land and build a huge home with a badass pool?" Krystal let him continue. "Then get a vacation condo in Puerto Rico like we always talked about. So many options."

"Is that all?" she asked sarcastically.

"Oh definitely not, that's just the beginning. We can maybe find a place in London so it can be our middle place between here an the rest of the world as we travel—"

Krystal finally cut him off. "Ok ok, slow down babe. I love your ideas but I don't wanna move too fast yet. We gotta think about the kids and school. These are critical years for them and I don't want to end up raising spoiled little brats."

"Okay, how about we take a few days to think of places we can settle down at. You can research the schools and all that, and then we'll narrow it down. But just to be sure, we're in agreement that we need to move south, right?"

"Yes, and we'll be closer to family for once." She jotted down a couple of notes. "So what's next?"

"Back to cars," Luis rubbed his hands together, "you know I'm going straight to the dealership when this money hits the account."

She rolled her eyes. "I wouldn't feel right stopping you from doing that. Boys will be boys."

"And that's why I love you." His mind was going through cars like the Tinder app. *Chevy Corvette?* Swipe left. *Camaro ZL1?* Swipe left. *Ferrari?* Swipe right. *Lambo?* Swipe right. *Mercedes G Wagon for the family?* Swipe right. "I got a few cars in mind, but maybe we can make a date out of it and test drive a few."

She typed a few more notes on the computer as Luis tried to build courage for what he wanted to ask next. The anticipation made his legs bounce up and down under the desk as he waited for her to ask rather than insisting.

"What else are you thinking? I sense a bomb about to be dropped," she finally asked.

Damn, she's good.

"Okay, don't shoot me down right away, hear me out. I want to hook my guys up. You know they're like my brothers and we've stuck together since childhood." He shook his head in disbelief. "What's crazy is that we've actually talked of this day happening. I can't believe it's actually here."

"How much are you thinking?"

"I at least want to make them millionaires." Her eyes opened big and he tried to make his case before she got in another word. "We've got 400 million, it'll be a tiny dent. Besides, if we're giving so much to charity, might as well make our circle wealthier first."

She agreed. "Ok, just type their names here and we'll work out a splurge budget for your little friends."

Success.

"What if I took them on a nice boat trip to reveal the news to them all at once?" He played down the idea just a bit, hoping she would agree to it.

"That's not a bad idea. Maybe I'll take my friends on a little spa getaway to break the news as well."

"Deal. But I might need your help with the

wives."

She'd agreed to the proposition faster than he'd expected, which was likely a sign of great things to come. They were mega rich now, and could afford to do just about anything they wanted to do, within reason. Even if they spent a million dollars a month for the next thirty years, they'd still be loaded. The realization of that excited the hell out of Luis. So much was running through his mind.

"Who do you want me to call first?" Krystal picked up her phone.

"Annjulie." His best friend Danny's wife.

A moment later, she picked up. "Hey hun, how are you?"

"I'm good, but Luis sort of isn't. He's been a bit down lately with work and being far from all of you guys..."

They continued to catch up for a minute.

"Anyways, I was thinking of maybe setting up a fishing trip for him and the guys in a couple weeks. You think you can help me round them up?"

Luis and Krystal clenched their jaws trying hard not to laugh

"Of course mamita, anything for you guys!"

"Ok love, thank you so much. He's gonna be so happy when I tell him. I'll talk to you soon." Krystal hung up.

"I hate lying to her, why did you make me do that? She was really concerned," she frowned.

"We're about to make them millionaires, they'll be alright." He kissed her forehead and thanked her.

Now it was time to plan the ultimate guys trip. These were his brothers, he was going to do it right.

CHAPTER 7

Two weeks later, Luis stood tall and confident wearing a fresh *guayabera* shirt, some linen shorts and his newest pair of Prada shades. It wasn't a dream anymore, the money finally cleared and his new life was about to begin. The day had finally arrived, and it was a beautiful one in Miami without a cloud in the sky. He felt like a million bucks and soon, his best friends would be feeling the same. What a feeling it was to enrich your closest ones, whom were completely clueless as to what was coming. Luis was impressed word hadn't gotten out, especially knowing how terrible his wife was at keeping secrets. He always found that comical. But for once, he thought he would be the one to break first, because his friends kept calling him genuinely concerned for his mental health, further assuring him that these guys deserved every bit of this trip. It was 1 PM now as he waited anxiously at the dock he'd texted them the address to meet him at.

Luis spotted a rental van approaching and a

moment later he heard reggaeton music blaring through the open windows. *Yup, that's them.* He put his hands up, dancing to the beat as they pulled into the parking spot. If these guys were expecting a small charter boat, he wondered what they were thinking now as the dock behind him was lined with some of the most expensive yachts on this side of the world. Danny jumped out the van first and looked around in awe. Then the rest of the crew followed, Carlos, Victor, Cisco, Delwyn and Izzy. All seven brothers. Friends since grade school, about to have the trip they'd always dreamed of. All of them were dressed in their fishing gear except Delwyn, who had on a bold leopard print shirt. "Looks like I'm the only one dressed for the occasion! What's up Lou?!"

"Welcome to Miami boys!" Luis embraced each one of his brothers with a huge smile and hug.

"Rough time, my ass! What the hell is going on?" Carlos asked as he took Luis' shades from him and tried them on.

"We got El Chapo over here!" Cisco joked.

"My boy got money! Let me take care of it for you," Victor said as he reached for Luis' pockets. He was the banker in the group and managed most of their accounts.

"Sorry boys but this was the only way I was going to get ya'll to agree to come. I really appreciate every one of you and thanks for checking up on me. But for real, I'm doing good… actually I'm doing great! Just thought it'd been too long since we linked up and did something fun, so here we are." Luis put his hands up showing off the fleet behind him and waved them to follow him.

"I'm still confused," Danny asked. "Are we still going fishing? Cuz I don't wanna carry all this shit."

Luis laughed. "Just leave it all bro, follow me. Let's get on the boat and I'll let you in on what's *really* going on."

"This sounds like some Dexter shit. Luis is about to kill us and drop us off in the ocean," Izzy said suspiciously, still trying to grasp what was happening.

Luis responded, "Maybe."

Izzy retreated to the back of the pack and proceeded cautiously.

As they approached their ride for the weekend, the guys were going crazy in anticipation. Every yacht they walked past got bigger and bigger until they finally reached the end of the dock where a crew awaited them.

"Oh shit!!!" Danny yelled before making his way to the ramp.

"Welcome to the best weekend of your lives!" Luis revealed to the boys as they gawked at the luxurious 250 foot multi-deck yacht that looked like a cruise ship. The yacht was enormous, with multiple decks lined by reflective windows that made it that much more inviting. It was straight out of a drug kingpin movie scene. The captain welcomed them all in with a salute while a gorgeous blonde stewardess handed them each a glass of champagne, "Welcome aboard, gentlemen."

All the guys reverted to their classiest behavior as they took their glasses. They saluted the captain, said their "thank you ma'am" and boarded the ship. Luis took it all in. These guys had been through all the ups and downs of life and remained friends throughout. Sometimes they'd been half a world apart but they always stayed connected. It'd been a very long time since they all got together as a group and the fact that they all made it down here, to supposedly help a brother out, made it that more special. Luis boarded last as he watched the guys run around the yacht yelling and acting fools every time they rounded a corner, discovering a new feature to the yacht. The little bit of class they had just showed, was now gone. "You're the fucking man, Lou!!" someone yelled around the corner.

That made him feel good. Really good. He felt Jay Gatsby. The Puerto Rican version.

59

CHAPTER 8

The boys were now drinking and having a great time as the yacht was finally under way. When Izzy found out everything at the bar was included, he was quick to tell the guys. "Everything! Even the Blue Label. I don't know what Luis is up to, but I'm gonna take it easy, just in case." The bartender chuckled at his amusement while she poured shots for them all. She found it comical that he thought it was the best liquor on board. She'd introduce them to the good stuff later.

The champagne was flowing, trays of hor d'oeuvres were placed throughout and the weather was absolutely perfect. The day was off to a great start and the guys finally began to accept the fact that this was going to be a hell of a weekend. They stopped asking questions and just enjoyed the moment.

"Here's a toast to Luis!" Delwyn proposed as he raised his glass. "Wait, where the hell did he go?" They all looked around and right on cue, the stewardess approached them.

"Mr. Diaz is waiting for you all at the front of the boat," she said in a pleasant but monotone voice and directed them. "Right this way."

The guys looked at each other like, *that shit was weird*, but they followed anyways. They were ready to see what other surprises Luis had up his sleeve. So far he had not disappointed. When they got to the front of the yacht, they found Luis standing tall at the bow of the ship. He smiled and lifted his arms at his side. "Is this the life or what?" He raised his glass for a toast. "Enjoy my brothers! This is just the beginning."

"Hell yea!" said Danny.

"Is this a mid-life crisis? Because I'm all about it!" Victor said as he approached Luis and hugged him, clinking his glass.

Luis let them settle down for a minute in an attempt to build anticipation. This was it. They had no clue. Everyone dreams of this moment. *"If I hit the lotto, I'm taking my people with me!"* The odds are so low that all one ever does is fantasize about it. But not Luis, he'd always had that extra bit of luck. If you polled the guys as to who would be the one amongst them to hit the lotto, they would unanimously vote for Luis. It's as if he was destined for it. Maybe it was good karma, do good and good things happen to you. He would continue to pay it forward, starting now. He looked past the guys and waved two men over.

"Shit I knew it," Izzy said, with a look of surrender on his face.

Two giant men in black suits and sunglasses appeared from the corner carrying three large Louis Vuitton duffle bags each. They placed them in a neat row in between Luis and the guys and walked away without speaking a word. The boys looked and studied the bags from afar, as their optimism slowly started to take over during this uncanny moment. They knew Luis wouldn't go through all of this for nothing. Besides, nothing bad was ever in a Louis duffle.

"Alright boys, this is why we're here. Each one of those bags has a tag with your name on it. The combination to the lock is your birthdays. Go ahead."

They all ran to their bags, checked the tags and passed them around to the appropriate owner. "Damn this is heavy!" Victor said as he dropped the thirty-five pound bag on the ground and crouched over to try to open the lock. They shook and squeezed the bags trying to figure out what could be inside. Finally Carlos managed to open his first as the bag slipped from his hands, spilling bundles of hundreds all over the deck. His eyes opened so big, it reminded Luis of when Carlos used to wear huge eyeglasses as a kid. He looked up at Luis with his mouth wide open, speechless. Then he looked back down at the bag, shuffling through the rest of the bundles and started to get emotional.

"What the—," Danny said and also found himself at a loss for words.

"Holy shit!" Delwyn screamed as he grabbed a handful of stacks.

"This is for us?!" Izzy asked as he grabbed each ten-thousand dollar bundle, stacking them on a table while trying to keep count.

"How much is this Lou?!" Cisco finally asked.

"One point five million each! I HIT THE FUCKING LOTTO!!!" He yelled at the top of his lungs and pumped his fists into the air. It felt so good to finally let the secret out. Now he could truly enjoy his win, with his best friends.

"OHHHH SHITTTTT!!!" They all screamed. They started running in place and jumping up on the couches in celebration as if they were middle-aged women at an Oprah giveaway. Luis hadn't been the only one to hit the lotto, they all had. If the roles were reversed, he was sure they'd do the same. Izzy pulled out a black envelope with gold lettering from the bag and raised it in the air. "What's in here? Willy Wonka's golden ticket?"

"Oh yeah almost forgot. This was Krystal's idea so be sure to thank her. We also set up accounts for each one of your kids. For college or whatever future they decide on. Two hundred fifty grand per kid. *But* you can't access it until they turn fifteen."

"No way!" Izzy said as he clutched the envelope to his chest.

"I wouldn't lie to y'all," Luis replied.

The guys huddled up in a circle around Luis and started jumping up and down. They chanted his name. "Luis! Luis! Luis!"

Luis felt great. He wanted to cry because he knew this would change their lives for the better and they would be forever grateful. It felt good making others happy. Everything was going just the way he had imagined, but things were just getting started. This was day one of a trip he secretly wished could last a lifetime.

"Okay, I'll be the one to ask. Why the fuck didn't you just wire all this cash into our accounts?!" Carlos jokingly asked while laughing and wiping his tears with a hundred dollar bill.

"C'mon bro, that's boring! You know me," Luis winked at him. "But shit, I almost wish I had. It wasn't easy finding all this cash!"

"I bet! This would've taken me weeks at work," Victor said.

Luis looked over at Danny who had tucked a few stacks into his pockets and around his waistband.

"Um, I don't mean to be rude but," Danny sarcastically interrupted the celebration, "you still haven't told us where we're going? You did say this was going to be the best weekend of our lives."

"You're right. Head to your rooms first. Then meet me on the upper deck in an hour to find out."

The guys reached their rooms one by one in disbelief of what had just happened. Here they were, showing up for a friend supposedly going through a rough time but it turned out to be the complete opposite. There was no jealousy or envy amongst them, just pure love and joy. That's why they were here. Luis didn't expect anything in return, he just wanted to show how much he appreciated them and they were about to see what else he had in store for them.

Upon entering their rooms, they were treated to a fully stocked fine whiskey and scotch bar, a fridge full of Dom Perignon bottles from various decades and an assortment of the finest freshly rolled Cuban cigars. Mouth-watering charcuterie boards were neatly placed by the bar. On each of their beds, a custom tailored Italian suit was laid out alongside a few pairs of different colored Louis Ferragamo shoes. On the nightstand, Luis left them a Richard Millie watch that had taken him a few days to track down. These watches were not cheap by any means and were treated worldwide as another investment in people's stock portfolios. Next to their timepieces, an assortment of gold jewelry and Tom Ford designer shades were displayed. As if that wasn't enough, they would open their closets to find a wardrobe full of linen shirts and shorts along with some Gucci flip flops, because why not, right?

Luis could only imagine what each of his boys were feeling in their rooms. His recent splurges were all inspired by the latest hip hop lyrics hitting the airwaves. *WWJD?* The J stood for Jay-Z of course. All he needed was some Jean-Michel Basquiat paintings and the vision would've been complete. *Not a bad idea.* He made a mental note to research the prices on those later. He laid back in his bed and soaked it all in. It'd barely been a day and he was already getting infatuated with this lifestyle. Making others happy with his wealth was like a drug he didn't imagine he'd crave so much. He thought of his wife and kids back home and decided to FaceTime them.

"Hey love! What are you guys up to?"

"The kids wanted to go to the tiger feeding zoo so here we are," she said nervously. He heard the kids in the background yelling, "Hey Dad!"

"Lemme guess, her idea?"

Krystal rolled her eyes and showed Mia

running around aimlessly from cage to cage while Mikey stayed attached to her hip. "Yup, this daughter of yours is something else. How's your little guy's trip going? Did you break the news already?"

"Oh yeah! They're super thankful and thank you for letting me do this. They're in their rooms now probably freaking out over the gifts I left in there."

"Yeah well they better be, someone already exceeded their splurge budget and it's only day one." She gave him a fierce look through the phone.

"Sorry babe, we'll be alright. Besides, we agreed this is a one time thing."

"Whatever, just be careful. I gotta go, she's yanking on a baby tiger's tail. Love you, have fun."

"Love you too."

Shortly after, there was a knock on the door. He got up to answer and was taken aback for a second as he stared at the petite brunette woman who was smiling at him. She wore a collared shirt with a company emblem and some tight black jeans. He looked her up and down.

"I'm here for the massage you requested," the young lady said.

"Oh yeah, almost forgot. Come in." Luis was a bit nervous because he felt like he may have been caught staring at her long enough to make it known he was somewhat attracted. But she smiled at him and proceeded inside the cabin anyways. *Nice.*

She set the massage table in the room and after telling him to take off his clothes, he laid on it face down and she began her massage. He tried relaxing but he was somewhat annoyed. His wife's comment irked him more than it should've. Why was she being so uptight when they had so much money? They'd agreed on the number they were going to give their family and friends, the rest of the gifts hadn't cost that much more. If she only realized that the blank checks she was handing out to charities were most likely being used to buy the same stuff for their crooked CEOs. He wasn't going to let her make him feel guilty for spending money that he'd won. A near infinite amount, at that.

"Relax," the masseuse said softly. "You're so tense."

"Sorry, I'll try," he tried to clear his mind again. It didn't work. *Maybe you could help me clear my mind,* he thought, immediately feeling guilty about it. But would she? He wondered if other rich guys just asked bluntly or if the masseuse would initiate the move after finishing the massage. The famous *happy ending.* Ultimately, he decided to just relax and enjoy her soft oily hands rub all over his body.

He wouldn't make a move and risk making things awkward on the boat for the next few days so he loosened up and let his thoughts drift to the big night up ahead.

"Will that be all, Mr. Diaz?" she asked while rubbing his scalp. He didn't want her to stop.

"Yes. Thank you, I feel great. You were great."

He got up and slipped on his boxers while she folded the table. He could get used to this. Frequent massages to relieve stress or just to have another woman's hands on him. *Win/win.* As she was making her way to the door, she turned back one last time, looked him up and down and winked at him. "I hope I see you again, Mr. Diaz."

Damn it, he missed his shot.

One by one, the guys all made their way to the bar on the upper deck looking sharp as ever in their new custom tailored suits. They were the same guys as always, but with an inflated net worth. They were in the million dollar club now, with thousand dollar etiquette. The bartender poured them flights of some of the world's finest scotches so they could sample and they just knocked them back like cheap whiskey. The bartender grimaced each time but eventually joined in on the fun by pouring even rarer scotches and stating the price of each shot while the guys recorded themselves shooting them back.

Off to the side, Izzy studied each pour carefully as he swirled the glasses, sniffed them and sort of inhaled the scotch with his mouth. "Smooth. I taste oak. Some vanilla and a hint of sandalwood. Macallan 18?"

"Close! Macallan 30," the bartender responded nicely and somewhat impressed. "But spot on with the description!"

"Yeah that was my next guess."

They all showed off their new watches to each other and were mind-blown by the tiny details and features on them. Carlos and Victor traded watches, with Carlos not realizing he'd lost about fifty grand in that transaction. Cisco got the bartender to plug in his phone so he could play some music and went on to play some old school reggaeton they grew up listening to. "Now it's a party!" Cisco hyped up the fellas. "Where the hell is Lou? We always gonna have to wait on him now?"

Just as he said that, Luis walked in. The guys all shouted and celebrated his entrance, as he approached them doing some sort of dance before reaching in his pockets and throwing up handfulls of hundred dollar bills. He crossed his arms and mean-mugged as the bills rained all around him. The guys joined in on the rain dance by throwing their own money up. "All my boys rich!!!" shouted Luis and they got even wilder. He pointed at the bartender and mouthed, *the good stuff,* and gave her a thumbs up. She understood right away and reached into the cabinet for a bottle of Louis XIII. Luis corralled the guys over to the bar as they all looked at the bottle like a master work of art. Everyone knew what it was. Only one had tried it and posted the $400 sip on social media.

"Pshh…been there, done that. Y'all finally on my level!" Victor dismissed it jokingly.

Luis looked around. "Where's Danny at?"

"Who knows? He probably hit that liquor cabinet in the room and knocked out!" Delwyn laughed.

The guys turned to the door as it opened right on cue and in walked Danny, wearing his new linen attire and Gucci flip flops. "Oh shit, we're going with the suits?" He laughed because he knew that, but Danny does what Danny wants. "Sorry, I'm late fellas. That masseuse—" he started hip thrusting the air and the guys collectively burst into laughter. *Boys.* Luis couldn't contain himself and waved him over to the bar. "Getcha ass over here, *bellaco.*"

They were all present. The bartender finished pouring the Louis XIII in its special glass. The guys each grabbed one and fixed their eyes on Luis.

"Alright guys, I'm gonna make this quick. No emotional speeches. I just want to thank you all for being here. I fucking love you guys like brothers but you know that already. Make the most of your money and always be there for each other. And last but definitely not least," he raised his glass high. " Let's turn the fuck up!"

They shot the Louis XII back and the bartender cringed again.

"We'll be in Bahamas in about an hour!" Luis finally told the guys.

"Yeeeeeeeaaaaah!!!" They all started chanting and dancing.

It was time to blow some cash.

CHAPTER 9

A couple of hours after reaching the shores of Paradise Island, Bahamas, the guys had caused quite the scene at the Atlantis Casino. Before stepping off the yacht, they'd decided on a backstory of having become early crypto investors and now the brand new millionaires were injecting life into a what was sort of a dull mood that evening. An entourage of about twenty people from all walks of life followed them everywhere and they were more than willing to entertain them. Beautiful single ladies, a few fun couples, even some young guys on a bachelor party wanted to be a part of whatever Luis and the gang were celebrating. They bought everyone unlimited rounds of drinks and roamed the casino placing large bets at various tables. The night was off to a great start.

After being noticed by the casino boss, Luis was invited into the high-roller section of the casino. "Only if all of my new friends can join us," Luis demanded and the boss allowed it. He asked the pit boss for two hundred fifty grand in chips and sat at the $10,000-a-hand blackjack table. Prior to this, the most he'd played for was $25-a-hand one time in Vegas and he remembered thinking that was that was pretty steep. Not tonight though. He was going to put on a show for these people and his confidence was sky high. This was his show and he was the star. *Let's give them what they want.* He grabbed a few chips from the top of the stack and shuffled them as he contemplated how large of a bet he would make. Ten grand? A hundred? He was a high-roller now. *Fuck it.* He pushed the whole stack of chips into the pot, all two hundred and fifty grand. The dealer looked back to the pit boss for approval, who responded with a thumbs up. After a few *oohs* and *aahs*, the crowd squeezed in to see what the commotion was about. Luis heard the whispers.

"What is he doing?!"

"Holy shit! He's crazy!"

"Who is that guy?"

"I think that's Pitbull."

He laughed at the chatter but then turned to the dealer and let her know he was ready for the cards.

First card, she dealt him a King of clubs.

Then she flipped a card face down in front of her.

Next, she dealt him another King. The crowd

gasped.

She flipped a ten of clubs on top of her face down card.

"Easy money!" one of the spectators yelled out.

Luis sat back and looked at the two Kings. He had twenty. She had ten. The odds favored an almost guaranteed win or a push at worst. But he wasn't here to play it safe, he was here to put on a show. After not thinking too hard about it, he announced, "Split." He gave the pit boss a thumbs up to assure him he had the money.

"What are you doing bro?!" Victor approached him, but Luis didn't budge.

Half a million up for grabs on a single hand of blackjack. Luis didn't break a sweat, this was chump change now.

She flipped over a Jack of clubs. *Twenty.* He waved his hand over the cards. *Stand.*

Then she flipped a seven of diamonds. *Seventeen.* He took a deep breath analyzing the numbers in his head. He waved his hand over the second pair of cards. *Stand.* Worst case now, he'd win one hand and lose the other which would bring him back to even.

She flipped herself a three of spades. *Thirteen.*

Then a Jack of hearts. *Twenty three.*

Bust!

"Let's go baby!!" Luis roared as he stood up

and pounded his chest like King Kong.

The crowd went crazy. He doubled up half a million dollars, just like that. He tossed a $10,000 chip to the dealer and she winked back. Then he told the pit boss to cash him out. Everyone was praising him and giving him high-fives for the gutsy move.

This is the life! He could picture himself getting used to this lifestyle. Maybe this was his calling. In five minutes at the blackjack table he was able to make nearly four years worth of his previous income. There was no way he'd ever go back to working for someone else, he would be his own boss from here on out.

After deciding it was time to continue the celebrations, Luis grabbed everyone's attention. "Tell the club we're on our way and to put every champagne bottle they have on ice. Everyone is drinking on me tonight!" They all cheered again, feeling lucky to be a part of his circle for the evening. He had them all at his fingertips and he loved the feeling. A few feet away, a strikingly gorgeous woman whom he hadn't yet seen, caught his eye and smiled at him. She had a mixture of exotic, as well as plain features. Her long jet black hair dropped to the small of her back and she had piercing dark eyes that radiated tons of sex appeal. She was slim and had just enough curves, wrapped in a tight black dress with the perfect amount of shimmer to where it wasn't overbearing. The woman was what Luis and his friends would often refer to as *baaaadd*.

At the moment, he was feeling very sure of himself, practically unstoppable. Everything was going for him and he could do no wrong. As more and more strangers introduced themselves to him and lingered around to remain in his presence, his ego began to inflate. So much so that he knew it was just a matter of time before the ladies approached him, and that they did. One by one, they made their moves on him with cheesy pickup lines or desperate pleas, but his eyes were fixated on one. She sipped on her drink and chuckled every time Luis found himself trapped by another sleazy woman throwing herself at him. He kept an eye on her as she turned back to chat with the guys doing their best to impress her. She stood tall and confidently, laughing and drinking amongst the crowd. Not pretentious or clingy like he was used to seeing, but fun and humble, just like him. *She's worthy enough*, he thought to himself before weaving his way to her.

Luis approached the lady and interrupted her conversation with some of the bachelor party guys. "Sorry fellas, you mind if I steal her real quick?"

"Of course, Luis! Anything for you! This is the

best night of—"

The man's voice went monotone as Luis was no longer listening to him. Instead, he had been hypnotized by her eyes and was quickly put under her spell as everything around him began to lose focus. He was lost in thought as he pictured himself as a millionaire hunk with unshakeable confidence, easily swooping a woman that was way out of his league off of her feet with just a glance. She snapped him out of his trance, offering her hand delicately for a handshake with a tinge of confusion on her face. "Luis, right?"

"Oh yeah, sorry." He snapped out of it and came back to real time, wondering if she'd noticed. "Let me just tell you, you have the most mesmerizing eyes I have ever seen. What's your name?"

"Jasmine," she blushed slightly and took a sip of her champagne, "and thank you."

"Here let me take a closer look." He opened his eyes big while moving in closer to examine her eyes with his mouth opened in awe before bursting out in laughter. "I'm just messing with you."

"You're silly," she replied.

"I try. So what brings you to the Bahamas?"

"Work. And a bit of pleasure I suppose," she responded in a foreign accent. "How about you?"

"Just here for a little weekend fun with the

guys."

"Seems like a special occasion," she looked around at the crowd.

"Guess you could say that. So…the accent?"

She sensed it coming based on his reaction after she had spoken. "I'm Chinese but my parents immigrated to France when I was a teenager. But now I like to consider myself a citizen of the world." She said it so eloquently with a hint of sarcasm. Luis was intrigued.

"Citizen of the world? Wow, I like that. How do I apply for citizenship? I'm quite the traveler myself and I've got a few plans coming up."

"Oh yeah, where to?" They had yet to break eye contact.

"Can't decide whether I should go to Italy and drive from one end to the other, explore Basque Country in Spain or maybe check out the Swiss Alps. I guess I really don't have any plans set in stone yet, just a lot of places I want to see. But I'm open to suggestions, and now that I have a new friend from France, maybe I'd consider going there again." He wants to go where she goes next.

"Oh I'd show you a good time," she replied with a cheeky smile as she took another sip of her champagne. "What type of traveler are you?"

"I love exploring and getting lost. I know it sounds cliche nowadays, but I will literally leave my phone and get lost. But I also like to splurge from time to time and enjoy the finer things in life." She nodded in approval and raised her glass to that. "My next mission is to do a bit of networking around the world and invest some of this hard earned wealth so I don't have to work anymore," he lowered his voice as if he was letting her in on a secret.

"Like at the blackjack table?" She joked back.

He laughed, "Oh, you saw that?"

"I thought it was sexy," she looked him up and down. "A man who takes risks."

"That was nothing," he winked at her.

He was making an attempt to impress her by letting her know he was a wealthy man, without trying to seem too cocky. It'd been almost a decade since he tried to charm another woman and he felt like he was playing his cards right. Luis was hooked. Her beauty, her accent, those eyes and she was a little mysterious. He wanted her. And between the alcohol and the overall mischievous atmosphere they were surrounded by made it that much more difficult for him to resist his temptations.

The pit boss approached them and kindly excused himself. "They're ready for you and your party, Mr. Diaz. If you'll follow me." He led the way and Luis reached for Jasmine's hand. She grabbed it and immediately felt a rush run up his arm as he touched her soft cool hand.

As he walked across the casino floors with his lovely new friend at his side, the rest of the raucous entourage followed them. He looked back at the guys as they pointed and made all sorts of hand and facial gestures to indicate the obvious. They approved of Jasmine, and they wanted him to...*go eat ice cream with her?* Probably not what Victor was referring to as he swirled his tongue in the air. Luis laughed and did a quick head count, realizing one of the guys was missing. "Where's Danny?"

Danny was over in the corner with his arm draped over the soon to be married bachelor. "Don't do it man, look at this!" He pointed at all the gorgeous women around. "This is how you wanna live, you don't wanna be tied down! How old are you? You know what...it doesn't matter, you're young. Don't be stupid. Go travel the world!" The bachelor was looking for a way out but Danny kept pulling him back. "I'm telling you man! You'll remember me when you sign your divorce papers!"

The next morning, Luis rolled over in his bed hoping to have found Jasmine at his side but instead he found a naked man lying on the ground. Izzy. He shook his head laughing wondering how the hell he had gotten there, but he couldn't remember much. One thing was for certain, it was the best night they'd ever had, and probably the most expensive one, too. He knew he'd have some explaining to do when he got back home and he was already dreading that conversation. Bits and pieces of the night flashed through his mind but he couldn't recall much after the shots of tequila Cisco kept lining up for everyone. He remembered dancing with Jasmine and sneaking off to the bathroom with her. *Did I do drugs?* He tried to think hard but decided to roll out of bed instead. This was his new life, one where he didn't have to submit drug tests so he could do things like that now. Might as well have some fun when there's fun to be had.

He slipped on his shorts and flip flops, and on his way out of the room, he smacked Izzy on his bare ass and said, "That was fun bro but let's keep that between us, ok? I don't want the guys to know." Izzy looked up terrified as he looked down to realize he had no clothes on. Luis blew him a kiss and walked out.

As he reached the dining area of the boat, he was surprised to see Danny awake already. He was struggling, trying to position his hands up to block the sun light. "Fuck bro. I don't remember shit from last night and my head is pounding. Did one of y'all take two hundred grand from my cut?" Danny asked, counting all the stacks of cash he'd laid out on the breakfast table.

"You don't remember telling that kid you'd give him a hundred grand to hit up his fiancé and call off the wedding?" Luis laughed hysterically. "I can't believe he actually did it! You ruined that kid."

"Oh shit I thought I dreamt that," he said in realization of what had happened. "What about the other hundred?"

"You put it all on red because we all put our money on black," Luis was cracking up realizing that Danny actually didn't remember anything. He seemed coherent at the time. Somewhat. Or maybe he'd been so infatuated with Jasmine that he hadn't been able to tell.

"Shit, oh well. So what are we doing today, big money?" Danny asked as he chucked all of his money back in the bag.

"I got a few plans but I gotta make some calls first. Get some food and go recover a bit," Luis helped a lethargic Danny throw the rest of the money in the bag. "Oh and if you see Izzy around later, tell him you know what he did last night and it's ok to be himself. I'm playing a prank on him."

"Wait—" he looked up at Luis, "are you playing one on me too?"

"Nah that shit happened."

"Damn. I figured."

Luis opened the fridge in search of some water but found it fully stocked with champagne, so he decided to grab a bottle of Moet instead. He walked over to the sun deck and laid back on a lounge chair, popped open the bottle and sipped right out of it. The sun had just risen and the light was reflecting beautifully off the calm blue waters. The morning breeze flowed through his body and it felt like it was taking away all of life's pressures and stresses he'd been dealing with recently. He was starting to live his dream. *Four hundred million dollars*, he still couldn't believe it. He replayed the conversation at work from just a few weeks ago about how he'd be set with just five million. *No way*. That definitely wouldn't be possible, he'd spent more than double that since he hit the lotto and he was just getting started. *Maybe twenty million? Nah. Four hundred is perfect.*

He took another swig from the bottle as he tried to regain focus and remember the night prior. *What happened after the bathroom? How did we get back to the yacht?* He couldn't remember if Jasmine had gone back with him and he hoped he hadn't done anything stupid or embarrassing, so he reached into his pocket to check his phone. And there it was, a text via WhatsApp from a foreign number.

Pleasure to meet you Luis, text me in the morning. Wink emoji.

He was relieved to know he hadn't messed up but now he wasn't sure if he had been unfaithful to his wife. *If I can't remember, it didn't happen, right?* There were a few times that they were dancing face to face and he wanted to go in for the kiss so bad, but he restrained himself, for no reason other than he wanted her to make the move. He was *the catch* after all. As he scrolled through his phone, he saw a text from Krystal.

We miss you!

She'd sent a picture of his daughter snuggling with a medium sized tiger and another one of a selfie of the three of them with a boa constrictor wrapped over their shoulders, with Mikey looking terrified. He laughed and started to miss them but Jasmine kept pushing her way back into his thoughts. He couldn't wait to see her again. She was so classy and kind, unlike the other women that tried vying for his attention throughout the night. He was sure he'd never met a woman so interesting, yet so mysterious. So simple, yet so exotic. He decided to check in on her so he posed for the camera and took a selfie, making sure it showed that he was aboard a mega yacht. *Gotta keep up the appearance.*

He typed, *you should be here*. Send.

…

And you here.

She responded almost immediately with a photo of her in a black lace lingerie under her bed sheets. He pulled down his sunglasses to take a closer look. *Holy shit*. She wanted him, too. All his doubts were erased and the temptation was now eating him alive. He texted her the address to where the yacht was docked and asked, *see you at 3?*

I remember where the yacht is silly. See you at 3.

Oh shit. Maybe he had been unfaithful. Well if he'd already done the damage, what more harm could he do? He felt a small sense of guilt but promised himself it would be a one time fling. He'd just make sure to remember their encounter next time.

CHAPTER 10

The yacht party was now in full swing. Luis thought only a few guests would show but apparently he and the guys had invited anybody and everybody they had made contact with previous night. The bachelor from last night spotted him and gave him a big drunken hug. "Your boy Danny was right! I'm so glad I met you guys last night, you saved me! And to be honest bro, she was kind of a bitch." The kid confessed, slurring his words. He'd dropped everything for a hundred grand, which he'd probably blow in a few months. Luis wondered if he would regret it when he went back home and explain to his fiancé what had actually happened. Maybe go on a nice honeymoon and place a down payment on a house with that money and all would be forgiven. Or if he really had been saved from a marriage that wasn't promising. A hundred grand was apparently his number for love. *Kinda cheap*, Luis thought.

"No problem man, enjoy the party." Luis patted

him on the back and continued to make his rounds. He found himself squeezing by groups of strangers because of how many people were on board partying. He hoped the money handlers he hired secured all of the cash in the safe in his room like he'd asked them to. As he sipped on his drink and roamed the boat looking for a familiar face, he passed one beautiful model after the next. *This is crazy.* Somehow the guys got the DJ from the club to agree to host their party and he was now deep into his set and had the whole crowd grooving. Victor rounded the corner and bumped into Luis.

"There you are! Here bro, put this on." He placed a captain's hat on his head, and not one of those cheap flimsy ones. "So they know who we are." *Clever.* He looked over to the crowd and sure enough, all of his boys were rocking a captain's hat and the ladies flocked around them like seagulls ready to swoop in on their bait.

"This is crazy, huh?" Luis said, looking around the yacht. "Who would've thought? From college parties in our tiny apartment to massive yacht parties." Victor had been his best friend and college roommate all them years back and they were notorious for their Tuesday night parties. Every time they reunited, they reminisced about it and it never got old. "This might be a good business opportunity for us, what you think? Organize yacht parties, hire the DJs, models, boat staff."

"Shit, I wish! As much as I love the idea, you know our wives won't have any of that."

"Yeah you're right." They laughed at the thought of their wives' reactions. But for a second, Luis thought he might be on to something. Live in Miami, a hotspot for VIPs and celebrities. He already had enough capital to do whatever he wanted, unlike the usual person going into that business to try and earn a living wage. He'd probably lose some money at first but after word got out about how insane his parties were, his list of clientele would grow to include athletes, actors and actresses, music artists and maybe even royalty from the Middle East. He knew those guys really liked to party, he'd seen them in action a few times while visiting Dubai. Imagine the kinds of events he could put together. People from all over would want Luis Diaz to organize their next soiree and then he could take his business worldwide.

"Yo!" Victor snapped him out of his fantasy. "Where's the girl from last night?"

Luis shrugged. "She said she was coming, I haven't heard from her since this morning."

"She's baaaadd bro, but be careful. I know your ass likes to fall in love quick." Victor pressed his finger onto Luis' chest.

"Nah man, you're crazy. I'm not *that* stupid," he

laughed because he knew Victor was right. "It's just a one time thing. Promise. Besides, tomorrow we'll be outta here and back to our *regularly scheduled lives*." He spoke sarcastically and then pulled Victor in closer. "But of course with a whole lotta money! C'mon, let's go take some shots."

His mind kept wandering between Jasmine, business ideas for the future, his wife, the kids. He wanted to clear his mind and enjoy the moment but he was having a hard time doing so. He checked his phone once again. No response from Jasmine. Honestly, it was probably for the better. He was starting to obsess over her and that would only mean trouble for him so he decided he wouldn't text her anymore. *Fuck it, plenty of women here*. And now after putting on the captain's hat, the same women he walked past earlier that ignored him were now trying hard to grab his attention. He joined the rest of the gang who were having the time of their lives as they timed every beat drop and jumped up and down with the crowd. It was time to unwind and let loose.

The DJ paused the music after seeing Luis approach the crowd. "Attention everybody! The man of the hour has arrived. My main man Luis! Let's give it up for him one time for putting this together for all you crazies!" The DJ played a couple of horns and the party goers went wild.

"You wanna say a word? Come on up man!" The crowd cheered him on as Luis proceeded over to the DJ booth, receiving pats, high fives and a couple of butt grabs. He looked around feeling like the man for being able to set up this party with some of the most beautiful people he'd ever seen. They were on a yacht, off the coast of Bahamas, with the sun setting off in the distance. The golden hour. It was an incredible feeling. Luis felt powerful, like he had control of everything and everyone around him. He could end the party now before it got too crazy, but that wasn't him. The party *must* go on.

"Thank you beautiful people for coming! Ya'll having a good time or what?!" They all cheered. "Well, my name is Luis and I've got a problem." He looked down as if he was ready to admit something. "I *like* alcohol…" A cheer followed. "I *loooove* women…" The single ladies raised their hands and wooed. "But most of all, I love to fucking party!!!" He chugged the beer in his hand, spilling half of it on his chest and the crowd went nuts. "Anyways, I want to give a special shoutout to my brothers, you can identify them by their sick captains hats," they each waved their hats in the air to draw attention, "make sure ya'll show 'em some love! *Ladies…*" He insinuated as he pointed at a few gorgeous women around the crowd while they nodded in agreement. "DJ can you keep this party going another couple hours?"

"You kidding me?! I can take this til the sun comes back up!"

"Well then prove it!" The DJ dropped the beat and everyone started dancing again. As Luis walked back to his boys, he received even more handshakes, fist bumps, and now crotch grabs. Jasmine was the last thing on his mind now, he was back to where he wanted to be. Again, he noticed Danny missing. "Where's Danny?" He laughed when they all shrugged their shoulders. This was common pattern behavior by Danny that always led to a wild story. He couldn't wait to find out what it would be this time.

The music was blasting and Cisco huddled the guys in close. "It's gonna be hard going back home after all of this! But we definitely gotta do this again! At least once a year, boys' trip."

"Cheers to that!" Luis said as they raised their drinks and chugged what was left.

It was just past 11 PM and the party showed no signs of slowing down. Luis' full attention was now on Maya. A stunning tall, slim but curvy model from the Bahamas with gorgeous curly hair and dark caramel skin tone. He had a thing for the al-natural look. They'd spent about the last hour chatting by the bar, joking back and forth, taking shots and talking about places they'd been. He was really enjoying getting to know her, but she made it clear "she wasn't one of those girls" even though her flirtatious mannerisms would've hinted otherwise. But he was fine with that. He'd learn to appreciate good company and good conversations over the satisfaction of conquering a woman sexually. Besides, he was now thinking of getting back to his family the next day and that excited him more than it did a few hours ago.

Maya was easy to talk to. She listened, asked great questions and was quite the open book herself. *She's so cool*, he kept thinking to himself. She was someone he'd love to be friends with. He'd had many female friends before without the expectations of something more than a friendship and he prided himself on being able to be a good male friend. A few drinks later, he was opening up about himself but keeping the secret of hitting the lottery was burning him up inside. He wanted to tell the world! What harm could it do if he just told Maya? She apparently wasn't into him after all. After pondering it over, he decided he'd tell her. "I actually won the lottery," he whispered in her ear and she pulled back in shock and awe. When he told her how much money he'd won, she didn't believe it at first. So he showed her a few pictures on his phone of the winning ticket, the big check and of all the cash he stuffed into his friends' duffel bags.

"Wow that's incredible! How lucky is that?" Her mouth was agape in disbelief. "What are you going to do with all that money?"

"Well this was my first expense. I wanted to treat my best friends to a fun trip, so here we are. Who knows what's next?"

"Wow. I'm…speechless," she laughed and looked at him amazed.

"Believe me, I know the feeling."

"Well lets take another shot to that! But first, will you wait for me here? I gotta step to the ladies' room."

"Of course, go down a level. There's cleaner bathrooms down there. I'll have the tequila waiting." He winked at her as she walked off.

Luis was feeling good, tipsy enough to be loose, but not drunk enough to be annoying. He rubbed his face and decided to go check himself out in the mirror, just in case he did have a shot with Maya later. He'd been around long enough to know what the *'girl going to the bathroom'* usually meant. *You never know.* He told the bartender to hold their spot along with a couple shots of tequila and got up to go to the men's room. As he walked past a few people making out along the hallways of the yacht, he wondered how many people were on board. There had to be at least a hundred. Luckily the yacht company was able to provide more staff and security to accommodate their impromptu party and he took mental notes for his possible future in the industry. *Bigger boat next time.*

While in the restroom, he took a good look in the mirror splashing some water on his face to freshen up. "Damn, Luis. You look good!" He told himself in the mirror. "You're killing it out there, papi!" Then he grabbed a towel to dry off. Suddenly, he felt someone grab his hips and forcibly turn him around. He tensed up, ready to defend himself, but it was too late. He had a tongue down his throat and arms wrapped behind his neck. But it wasn't Maya's, as he'd initially assumed. It was Jasmine, just what he wanted.

"Where've you—"

She shushed him with another kiss. "I'm sorry, but some business came up and I couldn't get away. Please forgive me. I'm so happy to see you again."

Those eyes did it to him. He was hooked again. She wore a one piece black bikini that covered less than a two piece would have and a see through cover up that really didn't cover much up at all. She had a phenomenal body and he wanted to put his hands all over it.

"Looks like I've been missing quite the party."

"Actually, my night has just begun," Luis said as he stared deep into her eyes.

"Oh yeah?" She reached into her clutch and pulled out a small gold tin and opened it. He looked down at the powdery white substance inside, and before he realized what it was, she'd already taken a hit up her left nostril. Then the right one. She offered it to him and he hesitated slightly. "Don't worry, same stuff from last night. My connect has the cleanest stuff in the world." Guess he had done some drugs after all. It'd been at least a decade since he'd touched any hard substances. Back to his partying years, before Krystal, and he'd promised her that that time was long behind him, never to be done again. He'd been completely honest about it. He didn't see the need for it anymore as a married man and father, especially now with the rise of fentanyl. It was scary out there, not worth the risk. But there he was, between a rock and a hard place, or more precisely between Jasmine and the bathroom door. He wasn't gonna punk out especially after watching her in her tiny frame take two hits like nothing. She didn't fall back into a seizure so he assumed it was safe. He grabbed the tin and the small tool she used to scoop it up and prepared a fix. *Sniff.* He took a hit and immediately felt the rush and his whole body shivered. The effects of the alcohol he had been consuming all day had instantly vanished and he was now alert and ready to party again. All night.

"That's some good stuff," he validated and reminisced to the last time he had done that. "I might need that contact of yours." He thought about needing a reliable and reputable drug connection if he was ever going to start a business for his future VIP clientle. She put the tin back in her clutch and grabbed him, pulling him back outside to the party. In the amount of time he'd spent at the bar with Maya and in the bathroom downstairs with Jasmine, the guests seemed to have doubled on board the yacht. This is exactly what he'd imagined for the weekend with the boys.

As they reached the main deck, Luis looked around to find the place was at near capacity and the party was at its peak. The DJ increased the intensity of the music and had full command of the party. Luis looked out into the crowd and found Victor on top of one of the tables pouring alcohol into people's mouths straight from the magnum bottles. Carlos and Cisco were standing on the couch spraying champagne into the air and onto people willingly accepting the showers with their mouths wide open. Izzy was at the bar still chatting with the bartender and sampling every bourbon and scotch on board. He looked up and made eye contact with Luis before awkwardly looking away. And of course, Danny was nowhere to be found. Jasmine sipped her drink and joined him watching what was happening. "I love your friends."

"Yea me too. This is everything I expected it to be."

The last one of the guys, Delwyn, walked up to them in his bold zebra print shirt, a gold bottle of Ace of Spades champagne in hand and noticed the two together again. "Jasmine! Bout time you got here! Lou's been waiting all day." Luis wished he hadn't admitted that, even though it was true. He had tried everything to get her off his mind and when he finally had, there she was again. But he wasn't complaining.

"Best thing comes to those who wait." She leaned up and kissed Luis on the cheek.

"Can I grab him from you for a sec?" Delwyn asked Jasmine.

"Of course. *Weezy*." She called him by his nickname and winked at him.

She walked off to the bar to grab some more drinks and Luis stared at her the whole way. Delwyn waved his hand in front of his face to snap him out of it. "Holy shit bro, you're sprung! What happened to that other girl you were talking to? I saw Jasmine giving her a mouthful and she left."

"She probably saw her sitting at the bar with me and got jealous. I dunno."

"Well go enjoy the rest of the night papa, back to real life tomorrow." He took a huge swig from the bottle and handed it to Luis. *Real life? This was real life.*

"Thanks bro, you too."

He finished off the little bit left in the bottle before Delwyn lowered his Gucci sunglasses and looked at him directly in the eyes. "Don't be falling in love."

Luis laughed out loud. These guys knew him too well.

The night had just passed 1 AM and to nobody's surprise, the party hadn't slowed down a bit. In fact, it had elevated a notch. Luis was able to distinguish the new guests by their evening attire as half of the crowd was now wearing cocktail dresses and suits while the other half was still in their shorts and bikinis. It looked like a battle of the middle vs upper class. They didn't mingle with each other but they also didn't mind each other. He was laying next to Jasmine now on the uppermost deck where they'd spent the last half hour lounging on the beach chairs alone, drinking champagne and chatting. She reached into her clutch and pulled out a joint. "Wanna join?" She placed it gently between her lips and lit it up. Very smooth and extremely sexy. He stared at her in admiration as she inhaled the marijuana smoke and slowly released it through her nostrils. Then she took a deep breath and looked as if all the weight she ever carried on her shoulders had been lifted. She looked free and he wanted to be as free as her. He wanted to be free *with* her.

She looked over at Luis, tossing her leg over him and sat on top of him, straddling him. He couldn't take his eyes off of her, she was one of the most beautiful women he'd ever seen. Her jet black hair blended in with the night sky and her eyes reflected the bit of light the moon provided. It was a dream he wasn't hoping to wake up from. She took another hit, holding this one a few seconds longer, then looked deep into his eyes and pressed her lips against his. He opened his mouth with her and she exhaled the smoke into his lungs. As the THC infiltrated his body, he felt the same sense of calmness he'd just witnessed her having. He was now free. *With* her. "How bout we take this back to my room?"

"Thought you'd never ask."

Luis wasn't sure if it was the drugs or the alcohol, or maybe having bitten the forbidden fruit, but the passion they'd shared for the last hour was unlike any he'd ever experienced before. It was better than drugs, better than all the money in the world. He was hooked, he wanted more. But would *she*? It had only been two days but the chemistry they shared was electric, it made him feel alive again. As she walked back from the bathroom, she purposely left the light on. Still naked and not hiding anything. She wanted him to see her and his eyes were fixated on her. If this was the last time he'd see her, he'd remember this image forever. As she crawled back into bed next to him, she said, "You know, this doesn't have to end just yet. You can come back home with me and we can sail around the south of France. Ever been?"

He shook his head.

"Oh you must go. Nice, St. Tropez, Cannes. I would love to show you around."

"I...I just can't." He responded, sadly. This fantasy would soon end, and his reality awaited back home. As tempting as it was to go and travel the world with her, he wouldn't actually throw everything away for the opportunity even though he contemplated it seconds before climaxing.

Luis sat up as he heard someone jiggling the door knob to his room. It sounded like someone was trying to pick the lock. "Shit, all the money is here in the safe," he said as he threw the covers over Jasmine. Now looking back, he thought the idea of bringing all that cash onboard was a stupid idea after all. The yacht was full of strangers and he hadn't thought about the possibility of someone trying to gain access and robbing them until now, so he grabbed the empty champagne bottle from the nightstand and stood up, ready to swing on whoever broke in. The door opened slowly and he immediately recognized the face. It was Danny, stumbling in and looking up at Luis in shock.

"Oh shit, my bad! Is that Jasmine?" Danny leaned over to look behind Luis. "Heeeeeeeey Jasmine," he said flirtatiously.

"Hey Danny," she laughed.

"Umm, Luis. Sorry to interrupt by the way," he leaned in close and whispered louder than he probably imagined, "I need like two hundred thousand from the safe."

"For what?" Luis asked, confused but trying to hold in his laughter.

"This rich asshole wanted to bet me twenty grand in a beer chug and he pulled the cash out. So I told him I'd be back with the money," he slurred his words as he became more animated. "I'm gonna bet him two hundred k to see how rich he really is!"

"That's probably not a good idea, Danny."

"C'mon man, you hit the lotto! You can just front me. You're my brother, right?!"

Shit. He'd just let his secret slip and didn't even

realize it. Luis opened the safe, chucked a hundred grand in the duffel and gave it to him before he said anything else. "Here's a hundred. Now go show that rich prick what you're about."

Danny embraced him. "I love you, man." Then he kissed him on the cheek and stumbled out of the room.

He opened the fridge to grab another bottle of champagne, hoping to distract Jasmine from what Danny had just slipped. He poured her a glass and kept the bottle for himself. It made him feel more dominant drinking straight from the bottle and he was starting to get used to it. He slipped back into bed and handed her the glass. "Lottery, huh? Cheers to that," she said, raising her glass.

"Sorry, he's just drunk. I made some good investments and got some even greater returns. That's why he said that, he thinks I got lucky."

"Oh ok, well cheers to *great returns*. I know all about those." She took a sip, "That's how I make my living."

"Oh yeah?"

"You won't find many women involved in the crypto scene but since I travel so much for my modeling gigs and my nonprofit work, I got the inside scoop many years ago. So I was very fortunate to get in pretty early and I've made out quite nicely."

Luis was very impressed. What *didn't* this woman do? She was special indeed and as he thought that, he remembered what his friends kept reminding him. *Don't fall in love.* They kept reminding him for a reason, because they knew him too well. He was a sucker for love but he wasn't an idiot. No way he'd leave his family for a woman he'd just met. And now he had all the money they'd ever need to live a pretty exciting life. He looked forward to that. Not to mention the possibility of Krystal allowing him to have guys trips every now and then if he behaved well. She'd always had full trust in him, this was the first time he'd ever slipped. Guilt started washing over him as the moment began to sink in. The love of his life and his two children, he'd betrayed them.

"I'm sorry, I just can't keep doing this. I'm married."

"I know that, Luis. You told me last night. And two beautiful twins. Don't you remember anything?" She looked at him confused.

He shook his head.

"This is just two adults having a bit of fun and living a little," she assured him. "Believe me, I understand. But if you ever decide you want to have some more fun, you know how to find me. I really do hope I see you again. I like your vibe and I'm a sucker for bald men." She rubbed his head.

"You know, I can be discreet. It'll be our little secret." She kissed him on the cheek and got out of bed. As he watched her get dressed, he was fighting his conscience. She knew he was married and it didn't faze her and she made it clear she wanted to see him again. He felt lucky but also felt some shame. *Is this too good to be true?* A minute later, she walked to the door. Jasmine turned back one last time and said, "You've been a pleasure." She blew him a kiss and left.

The final day had arrived and it was probably about time. As Luis made his way around the yacht, he was having to wake up strangers who'd fallen asleep on couches, inside some bathrooms and a few stragglers outside on the sun deck. He watched a topless woman covering up and looking around for her belongings. She looked up and smiled at Luis and thanked him for throwing a great party. *Phew.* That was a relief, last thing he wanted was any lawsuits or anything else following him back home after the wild weekend. Except for Jasmine of course, he might make an exception for her sometime in the future.

The yacht was an absolute mess, but the company assured him all incidentals were included in the price. It still made him feel uneasy, he was the type to leave a hotel room clean before checking out. He then went over to the breakfast area to see if the boys were there. He spotted them eating from the buffet, replenishing life back into their bodies after draining everything out of them for the last forty-eight hours.

"I can't believe I'm gonna say this, but I'm glad this weekend is over. I might die if I stay another day!" Victor said as the guys all nodded in agreement. "But damn what a great time. I'm telling the grand kids about this one. This is one's for the history books!"

Luis felt the same. This life was too fast for them, they were all in their late 30s now and their party days were way behind them. But it did feel great to share this weekend with his best friends. No doubt that any of them would have wanted it any other way. Luis noticed Izzy chomping down on his food, quieter than usual. "Hey bro, you good?"

"Yeah man." He didn't look up, he just continued to shove food in his mouth.

"You know, you don't have to tell your wife anything about us."

Izzy looked up at him with his mouth full and made a facial gesture, which Luis understood to mean, *not here, not in front of everyone.*

"Nothing happened that night bro," Luis finally confessed. "Jasmine said she saw you coming out of a shower butt ass naked and you were looking for your room. You probably just walked into my room and passed out."

"Are you serious?!"

The guys bursted in laughter.

"Oh thank god!" He looked so relieved. Luis hadn't imagined Izzy really being convinced that they'd fooled around. Now he wished he would've kept the prank going longer.

"I do have one last surprise for you all though," Luis said with a big smile.

The guys all shook their heads and pleaded.

"Please no…"

"Take me home!"

"Nope…I'm out."

"I will not drink anything else…"

They were done with the surprises, except one.

"Try me, what you got?" Danny walked in with his duffel bag.

"I'll make y'all wait til we get back to Miami. How much you got in that duffel?"

"Like three hundred. Where'd I get this from?!"

Once again, he couldn't remember, but this time he'd more than doubled up.

The guys laughed in disbelief.

"What?!" Danny laughed in a way that either he did know and he was messing with them, or that he really was clueless. Most likely the latter.

"Nothing bro, that's all yours! Anyways, the boat is gonna be under way as soon as they kick everyone off so we should be back in Miami in a few hours."

Later that afternoon, they arrived back at the port in Miami, exhausted and ready to see their families. They all debarked the yacht with their duffel bags, new attire and a few souvenir bottles of alcohol they snatched from the bar while nobody was looking. As they reached the parking lot, they all thanked Luis for the weekend and were extremely grateful for the trip and the life changing amount of cash he had given them. It wasn't enough to set them for life but it was enough to have a good one. All of them were fairly successful before this trip, but a couple million dollars never hurt anybody. After Luis embraced the last one, he called the other guys back as if he'd forgotten the last surprise. "One last thing."

He reached into his back pack, and pulled out a handful of keys. Actually, key fobs, these cars didn't take keys. They were emblazoned with Lamborghini, Ferrari and Mercedes logos. The guys gasped and the bit of energy they had left, was enough for them to jump up and down in excitement. One last surprise for his brothers, their dream cars. That put him way over the budget that he and his wife agreed to but he'd find a way to ask for forgiveness later. This moment was everything and he would cherish it forever.

109

CHAPTER 11

What. A. Weekend. Luis reminisced as he shifted his mind to the future, with the more pressing matters at hand worrying him the most. He wondered what his wife would think of the brand new Ferrari he was about to pull up in. As he drove around the corner, he could see his kids playing outside with some of their own new wheels. That made him happy. They looked in his direction and quickly got off the street and onto the sidewalk, not recognizing it was him in the car. Mikey's jaw dropped as he saw the car pull up on his driveway. Then realization hit. "Daddy!!" The kids yelled and ran up to him, attacking his lower body with vicious hugs. "Is this Ferrari ours?" Mikey asked.

"Yes it is! Jump in buddy."

Mikey jumped in as Krystal walked out of the house to see what the commotion was. Her mouth dropped just as their son's had. "Going for a spin honey! Be right back!" Luis was grateful for the extra few minutes he could burn before seeing where his wife's head was at. He helped his son buckle up, having never seen him so happy that he couldn't even speak. They'd obsessed over Ferrari's before and his son owned at least two dozen toy replicas. That's why he had chosen this one, for Mikey, and his reaction was priceless. But of course it wasn't all for the kid. He knew the kinds of heads the car would turn on the streets, and he loved the idea of getting that attention. He strolled around the corner onto the interstate and asked his boy, "Ready to go fast?" Mikey's eyes were locked on the road ahead. He looked nervous and excited at the same time, and when he was ready, he shook his head up and down vigorously with his teeth-bearing smile and jaw clenched. "Here we go!" Luis yelled as he pressed the gas to the floor and in a few short seconds, they were going over 100 MPH. "Woooooooooh!!!"

Then Mikey joined in, "Woooooooooooh!!! This is the best day ever!!!"

This is just the beginning, kiddo, Luis thought. He'd live for these 'best day ever' moments. They'd be able to give their kids everything him and his wife never had, plus more, although they were already sort of doing that prior to hitting the lotto. This was different though. This was multi-generational wealth. If they managed it right, their family lineage wouldn't struggle again for generations to come. His name would live on forever as the man on the family tree who started the Diaz empire. *That has a nice ring to it.* He snapped back to the present, as he drove back to the house and thought of how he was going to approach Krystal. First, ask for forgiveness and then start planning for their future.

He pulled back onto the driveway and Mikey immediately jumped out and ran to her. "Mom that was so awesome! Your turn! C'mon!" He grabbed her hand and pulled her towards the car. She was reluctant at first but he kept pressing her and she finally gave in, taking a seat in the Ferrari. She looked around the interior, swiped her hand across the smooth leather dashboard, checked herself out in the mirror, then turned to Luis and said, "I like it. Good choice, baby. Now get out, my turn to drive." Not the reaction he expected, maybe she hadn't seen how much he'd spent yet. But this is exactly who she was, fun and adaptable to his craziness. He felt bad assuming she'd receive him in a negative mood, because she very rarely did. It could just be the guilt he felt.

He stepped out of the driver's seat and walked around to the passenger side of the car. As they passed each other, she grabbed his butt and winked at him. *What the hell is going on?* he thought. But this was exactly why he loved her. He regretted doubting her and jumped into the passenger seat.

Luis buckled up and told the kids to go inside, before turning to Krystal. "Okay, this is the button to—"

But it was too late, she'd already pressed it and was in gear to reverse it.

"You think you're the only fun one in the family, huh? I went on a few test drives myself this weekend. This was my second favorite car."

He was impressed. "Oh yeah? What was your favorite?"

"The Mercedes AMG GT. The Black Series."

His mind was blown. She'd never cared or been interested in anything vehicle related, he made all of those decisions for her. Now here she was, gripping corners and speeding down straightaways in their brand new Ferrari. The thought of adding that AMG to his new fleet of cars excited him and he would try and find a way to convince her that she *needed* it. "Well what my wife wants, my wife gets."

"No sir. Not so fast. We gotta talk about all this money you spent first."

Shit. He thought he'd gotten off easy.

Once again, he found himself sitting next to Krystal. But this time in their office, staring at a spreadsheet. Again. They literally had enough money to never worry again, but there they were, *budgeting?* He didn't understand why she couldn't just loosen up a bit. "Between your *little* guys' trip, handouts, donations and expenses we've already spent about fourteen million." He was getting annoyed by her constant jab, referring to his trip as *little* guys' trip. If she only knew how *little* it actually wasn't. She clicked a few boxes and typed in some numbers. "Plus what we planned on giving our family, let's see. About thirty million gone. That's almost ten percent. It's only been a month since we hit!"

"Okay well we got our major expenses out of the way. We'll still have over three hundred seventy million! An insane amount of money! I don't know what the big fuss is about."

"The big fuss is that I know you, and if I let you, you'll continue to spend it recklessly like you always do. Then we'll be staring at nothing in a few years. You know they have a show about people who win the lotto? I watched a few episodes and guess what? They all end up broke and miserable!"

"These are people that had nothing. You can't compare us to them. We've been living a pretty good life already, it's not like we're seeing nice things for the first time in our lives."

"So what do *you* suggest we do?"

"Well I'm definitely on board with making a plan with you, but it's summer and the kids are out of school. I want to put this house up for sale and go fly off somewhere. Away from everything until we figure out our next steps. Maybe Italy or Spain. Then we can decide what we'll do with the kids' schooling. Maybe home school them and hire tutors? Private school? Depends on where we decide to live, I guess."

"See that's what I mean. You *guess*. You can't create a solid plan. You just want to figure it out as we go but that's not so easy to do with kids. They need structure, they need friends and their family. I know these things, I was a military brat and I don't want my kids to go through that."

"Ok, so what do *you* think we should do?"

"We need to speak to a financial advisor, maybe a lawyer too. This is a lot of money babe, we have to protect ourselves. Our kids' future. I want to do all that traveling and live on a beach somewhere but we have to be patient. I don't understand your rush."

"My rush is that we're already rich! We have the money in hand. We can do anything we want but here we are arguing over nothing!" He was getting heated, tossing his hands about.

"I'm not arguing, you are. I am simply trying to make a reasonable plan. For our lives. So you can lower your tone." She snapped back. "I'll tell you what, I'm gonna let you cool off a bit. I think you're still on a high from your *little* guys' trip since that seemed to be your first priority. I'm gonna take the kids and spend the weekend at my parents' since they need help selling the house anyways. When I get back, we can try this again. I won't let this money ruin us."

"Fine," he responded without complaint. Maybe he did need some time to cool off and slow down. Too much was running through his mind and none of it was any good. He knew he was ultimately in the wrong, but still, he felt trapped at a time he thought he'd be free. *Looks like money doesn't buy freedom after all.*

Later that evening, he was all alone lounging in his back patio and staring off into the sky. It was Friday night, his family was gone and he was starting to feel pretty empty. "I don't get it," he talked to himself as he reached for the bottle of Veuve Clicquot next to him. "Guess it's just us two tonight." He spoke to the bottle as if it was his new best friend and took a nice long sip. He wondered what his friends were all doing with their new riches and what their wives' reactions had been when they got home. Almost certainly they wouldn't have run off with the kids and left their husbands alone like his wife had done. Maybe he deserved it, maybe he didn't.

He decided to check his phone and browse social media out of boredom. "What are the guys up to?" As he scrolled through, he noticed Victor showing off his brand new red Lambo with the caption 'Work hard, play hard'. Luis chuckled to himself and said, "Or maybe have rich friends." He kept scrolling and saw Danny posted, 'On my way to Puerto Rico with the fam...may never come back!' "Damn, already?!" That's exactly what Luis thought his life would be like! He still had well over three hundred million and Danny just did it with two or three million, he couldn't remember how much he ended up with after the weekend. Surely, Delwyn put all of his cut into crypto, why not try to double up or more? The rest of the guys kept their lives pretty low key on social media but he was sure Cisco, Carlos and Izzy weren't dealing with the same drama he was dealing with.

He then closed his eyes and pictured Jasmine. She'd been on his mind constantly ever since he got back from the Bahamas. After they had said their good-byes, he was convinced he'd never see her again. She was trouble, and he was smart enough to know that, but he craved another bite of the apple. He looked up her profile on Instagram. After scrolling through a few Jasmines, he came across her profile. There she was, Jasmine Li, Citizen of the World, 10.5 million followers. *That's a lot of followers*. She did mention being a model and doing some nonprofit work so it was reasonable. He creeped through her pictures carefully as to not click 'like' on any of them by accident. He'd opted not to reach out just yet, but he was curious as to who this woman was. "Oh shit." He looked at her latest post. 'Captain's Orders.' She must have snuck a selfie of them two while they were kissing on the yacht. His face was mostly covered by the angle and dim lighting but he knew it was him by the captain's hat. He looked through the comments section and everyone was inquiring as to who the 'lucky guy' was.

Luis did feel lucky. Here she was somewhat showing him off to her ten million followers, even if just the back of his head. Maybe she liked him more than she led, even though that's not the vibe she gave him when she left. But to broadcast this to the world, usually meant something. Then he came across another comment. 'Luis was so sweet!' Posted by a Maya_Bahamas. *Shit!* Were they friends? Maybe that's why she had left so suddenly. Jasmine must've seen them flirting and she told her she was there to see him. Girl code.

The more pressing matter was that his name was out there now and in this age of cyber stalking and internet detectives, it could just be a matter of time before he was exposed. Luis started freaking out so he put his phone away and finished off the bottle of champagne. There's no way this could get back to his wife, right? She had so many followers, though. Hopefully nobody in his or his wife's circle would come across her post and connect the dots.

He walked over to the fridge in search of more champagne, but no luck. In the spur of the moment, he decided that he was not going to spend his Friday night stuck in the house alone. The solitude would drive him crazy, so he decided to book a few nights at the Ritz-Carlton nearby on the beach. There he could have all the premium cocktails he wanted and would be surrounded by folks of his stature. Rather than dwelling in sorrow, he wanted to enjoy this newly upgraded life. He was a multi-millionaire now, he was going to live like one.

CHAPTER 12

L uis woke up the next morning to a pulsing buzz which he assumed was his phone, but ignored it anyways. He'd met some guys at the bar the night before and set up a high stakes poker game in the penthouse suite he'd reserved for the weekend. The bartender offered to set them up with a dealer and a cocktail waitress for the evening for a fee under the table. It turned out to be a pretty decent night, and he made about seventy grand in the cash game that lasted five or six hours. *Takes money to make money.* He'd always thought he could be a professional poker player or gambler, but decided on a more secure lifestyle instead. When he finally rolled out of bed, he saw the gold tin Jasmine had left in his room on the yacht, which was now his special souvenir and small reminder of her. He had done a little coke to keep him awake last night and it actually helped him focus more on the card game, even though he didn't like how much it made him talk. Every now and then he'd have to bite his lip to shut himself up before giving away any poker tells. When he finally rolled out of bed, he opted for a swig of the Blue Label scotch that sat on the nightstand and walked to the bathroom, where he found his phone sitting by the bathroom sink. "Holy crap!" He realized it wasn't morning, it was just past 1 PM.

MISSED CALL

MISSED CALL

Where are you?

Are these your charges at the Ritz??

MISSED CALL

Call me, I'm worried.

All the missed calls and text messages were from his wife. He walked back to bed, chucked the phone to the side and laid back down. It seemed like all of the fun he'd been able to have since winning the lottery was when his wife wasn't around. That's not what he had imagined when he read the winning numbers on his way to work a few weeks ago. They should be out in Italy exploring which region of the country had the best cuisine and who made the best pizza and gelato. Instead, there he was, in the most comfortable luxurious bed, alone at the Ritz-Carlton. He started building some resentment towards his wife. *It's all her fault*, he was convinced. She could've easily gave in to his ideas just as she had ever since they started dating, he'd never steered them wrong, at least in his opinion. The phone buzzed again.

"What?!" He was agitated as he reached for it. Except this time it wasn't his wife, it was Jasmine.

He opened the message to a selfie of herself in an evening dress with a gorgeous background. The sun looked like it had recently set and the full moon was glowing bright, highlighting the cliff-lined coast with its illuminated buildings. Amalfi coast? Maybe Greece?

You should be here, she texted with a winky face emoji.

He zoomed into the picture and finally recognized the place. Monte Carlo, Monaco. He'd known of the place from the Formula One races he loved watching with his son. Matter of fact, it was race week and he was now a little envious he wasn't there. He stared at her picture just a bit longer and started to reminisce about their passionate sexual encounter a few days prior, then closed his eyes to try and replay it, only to be interrupted by his phone vibrating in his hand again. This time the screen saver he had for his wife appeared on the screen. Her and the kids sticking their tongues out. He picked up.

"Thank god, are you ok?" She asked in a worried tone.

"Yes babe, just decided I couldn't stay in the house alone so I checked myself into the Ritz."

"Alone?"

"Yes, alone. Made a few guy friends at the bar and played some poker. Nothing crazy."

"Okay well I felt guilty leaving you like that so we're on our way back up. My parents found someone to buy their house already. I can't believe this market! But now they want to know where we're moving so they can buy a house next door and I dunno how I feel about that." She laughed nervously.

"Yeah I guess I didn't think about that. Both of our parents as our neighbors? That wasn't in the fine print of the lottery ticket." They laughed in unison at the thought of that. He didn't think he'd be laughing during that call. That's why he loved his wife so much, she always caught him off guard. Here she was apologizing to him when it clearly should've been the other way around. He needed to just suck it up and be patient as his wife had been insisting since the very beginning. Maybe it could work out after all. "Well drive safe honey, give the kids a kiss for me."

"I will. See you in a few hours. Love you."

After hanging up, he saw Jasmine's photo on the screen again. Luis felt disgusted with himself for thinking of taking the easier route and chasing her. He wished he hadn't slipped into temptation with her, as selfishly satisfying as it was, because it was playing tricks with his mind and his marriage. But he could't blame her, it was him. She was a nice woman, he'd been the fool. Nothing he could do about it now, except go back and be the husband he'd always been.

"No thanks, Jasmine. Maybe in another life," he said to the picture on the phone and put it away. He got up, stashed his cash winnings from the poker game in his backpack and made his way to the door. As he reached for the door knob, he remembered something he almost left behind. He doubled back to the nightstand for the gold tin and threw it in his back pack. "Just in case."

Luis' drive back home was a rather positive one. He had an epiphany about why his wife had been so against all of his ideas these last few weeks. He was bringing them up suddenly instead of easing them as he had done hundreds of times before, *stick to the playbook*. Now that some time had passed, she seemed more receptive to his random ideas but obviously she wanted to take care of her family first. Rightfully so. She had her own process and he wasn't giving her the time or space to do what she needed to do. He made his mind up. As soon as he got home, he would apologize and tell her that he would be patient like she had asked. It felt like deja vu. Next, she'd feel bad for rejecting his dreams and she would succumb to his plans.

Within a week or two, they'd all be in Italy just as he wanted. Guaranteed.

As he rounded the corner of the street to his house, he noticed a large black SUV in his driveway. He hoped it wasn't the IRS trying to collect, they'd made arrangements for that already. A couple hundred feet away now and he recognized the vehicle by its boxy shape. A Mercedes G550, black on black on black. "Damn she's good!" He slapped his Ferrari's steering wheel in excitement and pulled into the driveway. He stepped out of the car and checked out their new ride sitting on what had to be at least twenty four inch rims. His wife walked out the front door.

"I opted for a family size vehicle, you like it?" She asked flirtatiously.

"I love it! The G wagon?! Black on black? My baby's gangsta!" He'd been obsessed with these SUV's since he was a teenager watching them in every hip hop video ever made. It was a status symbol and every time he saw one on the road, he imagined someone famous riding in it. Now it would be them driving the G wagon, while others looked curiously to see who was inside. She probably had no clue, but he would educate her on the topic later on.

"I figured it would be great for road trips. Plus, the kids fell in love as soon as they jumped in."

"This is perfect, but why are you spending all this money without asking me?" He asked jokingly, raising his eyebrow.

"It was only a hundred fifty grand," she did her best impression of him and then pouted like a little girl asking for forgiveness. Except she wasn't asking for forgiveness, she was back to using her sense of humor again. All was good.

"Let's get these cars in the garage before our neighbors think we started selling drugs or something." They were the only Latinos on the block, the assumptions would be warranted.

"Good idea," she replied.

They hadn't told their neighbors yet about winning the lottery and when some asked about the Ferrari, they lied and said they had gotten it for a good deal at an auction and were planning on renting it out as another stream of income. They bought it for now, not sure if they'd still believe it with the new addition to the fleet.

Keeping it a secret was much harder for Luis than for Krystal, and that was normally not the case. It'd been four weeks now and besides their closest family and friends, nobody knew of their winnings. Except for the officer Luis had promised to fulfill his good deed with. They dropped off a $100,000 check in an envelope at the precinct with a nice letter thanking Officer Jones for his service.

Luis mentioned that it was the guy 'he pulled over who was having another baby' and apologized for the lie, but that he hoped he would understand due to the circumstances. Initially, he wanted to make a public display of the good deed so the police could get some good recognition, but then thought twice about it. He didn't want everybody else coming to ask for money, his co-workers mostly, so he asked the officer to keep it low-key and enjoy this present with no strings attached. But that was all, nobody else knew. Putting their house on their market sooner rather than later would be very wise.

Later that evening, the kids were off to bed and Luis poured himself and his wife a glass of wine. He'd suggested pasta for dinner and bought Krystal her favorite Chianti so she would think back to the time they roamed the streets of Trastevere. It had been one of their favorite vacations as they ate their way through the city and downed bottle after bottle of Chianti while mingling with locals. That part of Rome made such a lasting impact on the way they traveled now. Although it was more touristy now, it hadn't been when they went. Locals didn't even bother learning English, so Luis and Krystal found themselves communicating via their very limited Italian, or trying to communicate in Spanish which was kind of similar. Add some exaggerated hand gestures and they blended right in. By the end of their two week stay, they had learned so much about Italian culture and were so appreciative of the opportunity, that they promised themselves to come back someday when they had kids. Hopefully the older lady they came to know as *Nonna* would be at the same small corner restaurant, making her delicious family recipes.

"I know what you're doing," she said as he handed her the wine glass. "You think you have me all figured out, don't you?"

"I actually do," he smiled back.

"Okay what's your plan now?" Krystal took a sip of her wine and prepared herself for another one of her husband's wild ideas.

"We put the house up for sale, hire movers to pack what we want to keep and we donate the rest. While they do that, we eat our way through Italy with the kids." He drew a map in the air with his finger. "Start in Lake Como, make our way down through Cinque Terre. Florence. Go introduce the kids to *Nonna* in Rome. Follow the coast down through Naples and Amalfi and end in Sicily."

She was smitten by him and his imagination. "You've put a lot of thought into this, huh?"

"I've been *dreaming* of this."

Key word: Dream. He emphasized it because he knew she didn't like to shoot his dreams down.

The bait was cast.

She was giving in. "Can you give me a couple days to think about it?"

Hooked.

"Of course honey. I'm in no rush. I'll be *patient*," he made air quotes over 'patient' and she gave him the side-eye. He needed to tread lightly so he leaned in halfway for a kiss, waiting for her to meet him in the middle. She leaned in and kissed him.

Catch!

CHAPTER 13

"Daddy daddy, can we go for a ride!" Luis was in such a deep sleep he couldn't tell if he was still dreaming or if it was real life. He and his wife stayed up pretty late drinking wine and looking through photos of their past adventures and he couldn't recall what time they had gone to bed but it was definitely too early to be getting out of it. The stinky breath his son breathed on his face confirmed that it was in fact real life. "Wake up daddy!" Mikey climbed up on top of him and half hugged, half wrestled his neck.

"Okay buddy, I'm up. But no rides til you brush your teeth and eat some breakfast."

"I already had breakfast! I cooked a bowl of cereal."

He wanted to ask him if he had also eaten a bowl of shit, but decided to save that joke for when he was a few years older. "Okay well go brush your teeth then and let me get my breakfast first. Then we'll go out for a spin."

His son jumped off the bed and ran straight to the bathroom. Then he heard the sink turn on in the distance and some aggressive brushing and gargling. Luis turned over to see his wife still in bed pretending to be asleep so that he would handle the kids. She slowly opened one eye and said, "Your turn." Then pulled the sheets over her head.

"Our kid has a serious breath problem, we should get that checked out."

She just nodded her head, not wanting to be bothered.

After breakfast, just as promised, he would take his son out for a spin. Mikey put on his favorite Formula One driver's shirt, Lewis Hamilton, a cool pair of sunglasses and a Miami Heat ball cap. Luis laughed to himself, wondering how long he'd taken to put that outfit together. The kid had swag. Not something he'd inherited from his father.

Luis stepped into the garage with Mikey and handed him the key. "Here, press this button for three seconds."

He studied the key, pointed it at the car and pressed it. "One, two, three" Then he jumped back as the loud roar was deafening. "Woah!" After the brief scare, he started trembling in excitement and couldn't contain himself. Luis picked him up and raised him over the door and onto the seat. He didn't even need to tell him to buckle up, as he muttered to himself, "safety first" and clicked his seatbelt on. He was very aware of how fast they were about to go. As his dad slipped into the driver seat, Mikey asked, "Is this for me?" He picked up the backpack full of cash that Luis had left behind.

"No buddy, that's daddy's. Leave it there, ok?"

"Ok," he responded, slightly disappointed that it wasn't a gift and put it back down.

"I hear there's a racetrack at the airport on the island, you wanna see how fast we can go in this car?"

"Yeah!!!" Mikey yelled excitedly.

"But you can't tell mom," Luis looked at his son in the eyes, waiting for confirmation.

"Pinky promise," he stuck his pinky in the air and Luis locked pinkies with him.

When they got home a few hours later, Krystal greeted a very ecstatic son who had very messy hair. "What happened to your cap?"

"Oh it flew off at the race track." He quickly covered his mouth with both hands, and looked up at his dad, having realized he let the secret slip one second after entering the house.

"Oh really?" She questioned as her gaze went up to meet Luis'.

He tossed his backpack on the countertop and

breathed in deeply. "Don't worry, we took all precautions. It was a closed course."

"Well I hope it was fun," she said in a serious tone. "But next time, you better take me!" She then grabbed Mikey and squeezed him tight, kissing him all over his face.

"MOM!!!" He tried escaping her grip from embarrassment but was unsuccessful.

She covered Mikey's ears and looked up at Luis and whispered, "Damn! His breath really does smell like shit!"

"I told you," he replied.

"Nice bag babe. What's in it?"

"A couple grand I made last night playing poker. Well more like seventy or eighty, I gotta count it again."

She shook her head. Then she unzipped the top and looked inside. "Wait what? How?"

"Playing poker with a bunch of rich old guys. Chump change to them, I don't think two of the guys even knew how to play. They were just there to have fun."

"Well, great job honey. Just don't make this a habit."

"Don't worry babe, I'll deposit it tomorrow."

His daughter finally popped out of her room. "Hey daddy!" She gave him a hug and he bent over to kiss the top of her head. "Nice backpack! Is it for me? I need a new one for next year."

"It's daddy's, not yours," Mikey responded and made a silly face directed at his sister.

Before Luis could respond to her, she'd already grabbed the bag off the counter and as it slid off, a bunch of the cash spilled out onto the floor. "Who said you could touch that? Give me that." He said in a tone that she knew meant she was in trouble. Mia panicked and tossed the bag to him and as Luis tried catching it mid air, the bag snagged and all of its contents were now airborne. The golden tin he'd forgotten that he put in there was flying through the air and crashed on the ground. About ten grams of fine Colombian cocaine was now scattered across the tile floor and on the kids' feet.

"Is that candy?" Mia asked as he hurried to to lift her off the ground and straight to the bathtub.

It was as if time had slowed down while Krystal connected the dots as to what had just happened. She went from looking puzzled to being alarmed, then scared before her face was dressed in a fit of rage that was almost impossible for her to contain in front of the children.

"Honey grab Mikey and bring him too, we have to wash this off!" Luis tried to snap her back into the unforgivable moment.

Without hesitation, she rushed Mikey over to the bathtub to splash some of the already running water on his feet. She was increasingly getting more and more agitated to the point where Luis noticed her face turning red. He'd never seen anyone this angry before. How could he be so stupid to forget he put that in there? This was not going to be pretty. All hell was about to break loose.

"What the fuck, Luis?!" Krystal yelled furiously after sending the kids to their rooms. Luis knew he was in deep shit because his wife rarely dropped the 'F-bomb'. He'd never seen her this angry before. He had no defense. He messed up. Again. "You hit the lottery and think the rules don't apply to you anymore? Bringing drugs into our home?!" She paced back and forth and put a finger in his face. "What kind of shit bag father are trying to become? Cocaine! On our kids?! You better pray to god there's no fentanyl in that! Ugh!!" She put her hands on her face in disgust and looked up at the ceiling. She could no longer bare looking at her husband. "They could die with just a fraction that! I swear, for your sake, you better hope they didn't ingest any." She was fuming, and he was speechless.

He tried motioning for her to lower her voice so the kids wouldn't hear them from their rooms. "Don't tell me to lower my voice!" He should've seen that coming, she snapped louder than she had before. "How about you man up and put your family first! Out here partying like a desperate boy looking for attention. If you didn't get the memo, you're thirty-six years old and you have a wife and two kids. And don't think I'm stupid enough to think there weren't any women on that boat with your *little* friends. Guess what? They were after your money. Not some old balding men with dad bods going through a mid-life crisis." She was coming at him with everything.

"What are you talking about?" He managed to ask, hoping she hadn't been made aware of Jasmine's Instagram post with him in it.

"I talked to one of the wives, don't you worry about it. I was willing to give you a pass for that but I'm running out of patience with you. And then you pull this stunt?!"

"No babe, one of the guys left it in the room last night. I couldn't leave it there and let the cleaning crew find it. I just forgot to throw—"

"BULLSHIT!!!" She cut him off. "I'm tired of your shit! Everything that comes out of your mouth, 'Oh, money won't change me. We won't be like those people.' Yeah fucking right!" She continued mocking him and the words he had said after hitting the lottery. "I just had a feeling this would all happen. You don't have self-control. You want to be all high and mighty and now you think because you have all this money, that you really are. Well, you're not! You wanna do something good? Donate all of the money. Let's see what really matters to you."

He tried closing the gap between them, reaching for her hands. "It's not about the money, babe. I made a terrible mistake. I'm sorry! I never meant—"

He tried to get another word in but she didn't allow it. She slapped his hands away. "I don't wanna hear anymore excuses!" She yelled frantically. "You crossed the line. Now get the fuck out of my house!" Krystal pointed out the door as tears streamed down her face. "Go figure out who the hell you wanna be."

As he walked away from her, his anger began to fester. She continuously tried to put him down without hearing him out. "I'll show her," he mumbled underneath his breath as he grabbed his backpack and keys. The gold tin was on the counter with some contents still in it and he grabbed that too. Sure, he felt guilty for what had happened but he wasn't perfect. Nobody was. He was still the same old Luis. Generous, fun, adventurous. She was being the complete opposite. He was convinced the money hadn't changed him, it had changed her. Now she'd kicked him out of *his* house. He'd be back. But she would have to beg him to come back. For all he cared, she'd given him a free pass to 'figure out whoever he wanted to be.' And he was going to do just that.

He jumped into his Ferrari and texted his buddy Victor.

Meet me at the Ritz, need some help with something.

He responded quickly, *Roger that, give me an hour.*

CHAPTER 14

"Damn bro. I'm sorry to hear that. Maybe just give her a few days to cool off and go back." Victor suggested after Luis explained why he had gotten the boot. "I mean the coke is kind of a big deal. You gotta admit, that was pretty stupid bringing that in the house."

"Yeah man, I totally forgot it was in there. I'm such an idiot," Luis shook his head at his stupidity.

"Put yourself in her shoes. My wife would've probably stabbed my ass! You're lucky to be alive!" He laughed as he took a sip of his beer. He grabbed the bartender's attention and threw up two fingers. "Your finest scotch please. His tab." He looked back at a pensive Luis. "C'mon man, this will blow over like it always does. Just take this time to relax and come up with a plan."

"That's what I'm doing now. Coming up with a plan."

"Okay, see! A couple more drinks and you'll be good bro. You know I always got your back." He raised his beer bottle and clinked it against Luis' as he finally got him to crack half a smile.

"Well, that's why I called you here actually. I need a pretty big favor." His tone changed a bit, he now looked and sounded nervous. "You didn't quit your job at the bank yet, did you?"

"I thought about it. That was a lot of money you gave us but you know me, I'll spend that shit quick. Wifey is already breathing down my neck about it."

"Believe me, I know how it is," Luis said in agreement as the bartender handed them two glasses of neat scotch.

"Dalmore 64 Trinitas 1946. One of my favorites," the bartender said.

They each sniffed the contents, as if they could actually differentiate the distinct flavor notes. It was more show than anything. You can't order expensive drinks and not take the time to appreciate them or you'd look classless. They took a sip and swished it around their mouths. Neither grimaced because showing weakness would make that person look inferior. "Smooth," they said in unison. In reality, they could be drinking cheap scotch and not know the difference.

"Anyways," Luis continued. "I'm thinking of leaving for a bit, a small break away from the family. Me and Krystal keep butting heads. I didn't think she'd kick me out like that, and to be honest, I don't feel happy or sad about it. I'm indifferent." He took another sip of the scotch as his remorse began to fade. "Ever since we got the money, it's been nonstop fighting. I'm sick of it. I'm just tired of the negativity." He looked off in the distance and took another sip to process each thought running across his mind. "You know, all that money can't buy happiness talk is B.S. You can literally do anything you'd ever imagined. How can someone be so upset with so much money in the bank? I just don't get it."

"They also say money is the root of all evil," Victor interjected to try to kick some sense into Luis.

"Evil people are gonna be evil. Money or no money. I like to think I'm a generally good person, what do you think?" Victor nodded in agreement. "Believe me, I would love to give a lot of this money away for the greater good, but is it selfish of me to want to enjoy it for myself first? Shit, I hit the fucking lotto! Let me live a little and then we'll figure out the rest afterwards."

"Yeah bro I get it. But you can't just leave like that, what about the kids?"

"I'll stay in touch. They're still young, I'll be back before it's too late. My pops left for ten years and I still gave him a chance." He paused for another sip. "I'm sure I'll have time to explain myself and hopefully they'll understand one day. Krystal is one hell of a mother, I won't take that from her no matter what happens between us. Besides, with all the money they have, they'll have plenty of distractions. I'm not abandoning them and leaving them high and dry like my father did. And unlike him, I actually plan on coming back."

"I dunno man, I'm all about living it up and all but I think you should reconsider. I really feel like you'll regret this and in a few months, I will bluntly tell you that I told you so."

"You know Krystal. I love her to death but she can't live without me. It's just a matter of time before she calls begging for me to come back home. Trust me, it's all part of the plan. I've thought about it and this is what I want to do," he said in a definitive voice. His mind was made up.

"Okay so what do you need me for? Keep an eye on them?" Victor asked curiously.

"I need you to open an account for me and transfer half of the winnings over."

Victor almost choked on his scotch and his eyes opened wide. "What?! That's not that easy man, how much are we talking?"

"Two hundred million."

His jaw dropped. "What the fuck?! I had no clue y'all hit that big! And that's half?! I don't know if that's even possible. Shit, it might get me fired."

"I thought about that, too," Luis scooted his barstool closer to Victor to better explain his plan. "So my proposal is this. I'll pay you a million if you can do it discreetly before she blocks the account. Put it under my name and don't allow her any access to it."

"You know if Krystal or my wife find out I helped you with this, I'm a dead man, right?"

"Don't let them find out. Maybe open a separate account for yourself."

Victor took a minute to think about the proposition. "When do you need it by?"

"Wednesday. I still gotta figure out where the hell it is that I'm going."

"And if I actually do get fired?"

"Add another million," Luis responded without hesitation.

"Shit. How can I say no? I can't turn down that money, that's life changing. How many opportunities do we ever get like this in life?" Luis knew he wouldn't be hard to convince. "I mean I think you're making a huge mistake but I'm not gonna tell you how to live your life. You always manage to figure it out." He was right. It never mattered how many times Luis failed in life, he always came out better. Like a phoenix who rose from the ashes.

Ultimately, he was glad Victor felt concerned because that's what real friends were for but he was here for business and not to be lectured. "So do you think it's possible?"

"For a million, you better believe I'm gonna find a way to do it. Shit I hope they fire my ass too!" They laughed out loud and knocked back the rest of their scotch. "Hey bartender, another two please! The most expensive thing you got."

Later that night, Luis was laying back in the same bed as he had been two nights earlier. He originally booked the whole weekend but when his wife called him home, he didn't think he'd be back again and he didn't bother getting a refund. Too much hassle. But there he was, all alone once again. He finally felt at ease for once since winning the money. Krystal hadn't even tried to communicate with him and after the rage he witnessed from her, he was certain she wouldn't reach out for at least a few days. Maybe once the kids started crying for him. By then, who knew where he'd be.

He briefly thought about going to Thailand but after second thought, maybe Dubai or Abu Dhabi would be more fitting. He could hang alongside wealthy folks, like those oil sheikhs and celebrities that frequented there, and he could dine in some of the finest restaurants in the world. Or he could try and see what Jasmine was up to. It wasn't his first preference to go run off with another woman so soon after getting the boot from his wife, but she didn't seem the type to fall in love and want to run off happily ever. She was more of a free spirit, total opposite from his wife. He could picture them globe-trotting with no itinerary. And once they'd had enough of each other, they would shake hands and part ways amicably, with no strings attached.

The more he thought about it, the more it excited him. He unlocked his phone and scrolled through her Instagram page again. Her new post showed her in an elegant blue dress aboard a yacht in Monte Carlo. "What a life," he whispered to himself, slightly envious but mostly fascinated. He swiped over to his messages to find hers from a couple days before. He stared at her picture for about a minute before deciding he was going to do it. "Fuck it."

How about Wednesday?, he replied to her text.

A few minutes later she responded, *Took you long enough.*

He smiled, *How do I get to you?*

I can arrange your flight through a friend of mine.

Monaco?

Yes. Here for race week, hope you like Formula One.

I do.

She sent a selfie of her in the mirror wearing a bathrobe.

Hope you like this, too.

He was immediately turned on and zoomed in to get a better view. She had to have just rolled out of bed as it was morning there and she already looked flawless.

I'll see you Wednesday. I'll send you the deetz later, she responded before he could think of a clever response to her picture.

See you then.

Can't wait, followed by a winky face emoji.

Perfect, he thought. He didn't come off as desperate and he felt rather cool, like he still had game even after being off the market for over a decade. Now all he needed was Victor to come through with the transfer and he'd be good to go.

CHAPTER 15

Wednesday morning had come and he was all packed and ready to go after splurging for a few days at designer stores like Gucci, Dior and Balenciaga on a new wardrobe. Again, brands he knew from watching his favorite musicians on social media. Add a few watches, shades and accessories and he was feeling like a reincarnated version of the man formerly know as Luis. He also picked up a new phone with a different number so he couldn't be reachable unless he wanted to be. He hadn't heard from his wife or kids and thought it would be easier if she didn't know what he was up to until he set off on his trip to go 'find himself.' *Easier to ask for forgiveness than permission.* That had always been his motto.

Now he was anxiously waiting on a final confirmation from Victor so he could catch his flight to France from the local private airport. Jasmine set him up in a private jet through a friend's company and hadn't asked for a dime yet.

He knew it wasn't cheap to fly private and he'd never flown other than economy class so he wasn't sure what to expect. Would there be other passengers or would he have the jet to himself? He was excited to find out, but in the meantime, he cruised up and down the coast of Amelia Island admiring his newfound freedom.

Riding around in his Ferrari with the top off had been just as satisfying as he'd always imagined. He was getting looks from everyone that drove past. Gorgeous ladies trying to grab his attention, men trying to race him in their measly Mustangs and Corvettes, teenagers trying to snap a picture for whatever reason and his favorite, older white guys seeing a young Latin guy with tattoos and a backwards cap driving around in a quarter-million dollar car. *Has to be a drug dealer or a rapper,* he imagined them thinking. But he didn't mind the labels, instead he cranked the volume up on a Rick Ross track and pretended he was a *gangsta* as he would flash his bottom teeth to anyone who stared longer than they should. *Thug life baby.*

His phone finally rang and he pressed the button on his steering wheel to answer. "Talk to me papi!"

"We're all set bro. Where do you want me to meet you?" Victor asked.

"By the private airport. I'll send you my

location when I get there. I'm close-by."

"Sounds good. I'm about fifteen minutes from there."

"Roger."

Exactly fifteen minutes later, Victor pulled up in his red Lamborghini and parked next to Luis. "Damn, I almost forgot I got you one of these!" Luis said as he drooled over the car. He walked around the Lambo to take a closer look at it. "I hadn't got a chance to check any of the cars out, I just cut Tony a check to have them brought over to Miami for you guys."

"Best present I ever got! Well, besides the couple million of course," Victor laughed and greeted Luis with a hand shake and a hug. "How you doing brother? You change your mind yet?"

"Nah man, the complete opposite. In fact, I'm flying out on that jet over there in an hour." Luis pointed towards the hangar.

"Damn! In the Gulfstream? Where you headed? I mean, who cares, take me with you. Screw it." Luis could see Victor fighting his conscience. "Shit. Who am I kidding? I can't go but maybe I can find an excuse to meet you up for a weekend. Just tell me where you'll be."

"I rather not tell you bro. I'm gonna disappear for a bit and I don't want to be traced. It's probably better that you don't know so you're not in a position to be the bad guy."

"Too late for that!" Victor reached inside his jacket pocket and pulled out an envelope. "Just a matter of time before I get that call from Krystal asking me what the hell did I do. Then I'll have to hear it from my wife." He rubbed his hand across his head.

"That's why I paid you what I paid you. Figured it would ease the pain." He put his hand on Victor's shoulder to make him feel better.

"Oh it definitely does. I just have a bad feeling about this man. But you're gonna do you no matter what. You meeting up with that Jasmine girl from the yacht?"

"Nah man, I'm flying solo. We'll see where the wind blows."

Victor brought Luis in closer by grabbing him behind the neck and looking into his eyes. "Ok bro, just promise me you won't abandon those kids. I would feel like an accomplice if you did."

"What are you talking about, man?" Luis backed up somewhat offended. "Those kids are my life! It's my wife who decided she didn't want me around for the time being. So I'm taking that cue and I'm leaving for a bit. When she decides she wants me back around, then I'll be home. But until then, I'm gonna go live." He snatched the envelope from Victor's hands. "Thanks for this. Enjoy your cut."

"Yeah man," Victor's tone changed. "You got everything you need in there. I went through a buddy of mine that works at another bank so it couldn't get traced to me so easily. Your card, account number, his phone number, everything is in there. I'll be here if you ever need anything."

"Thanks Vic, sorry I snapped." He felt bad considering all the trouble Victor had gone through in order to pull this off. Without him, none of it would've been possible.

"It's all good brother. Safe travels." They hugged one last time and parted ways.

CHAPTER 16

As the jet began its final descent into the Nice Côte d'Azur airport, a beautiful blonde flight attendant approached Luis to let them know they were about thirty minutes from touching down. During the seven hour flight, he'd managed to have a whole culinary experience that included one of the best filet mignons he'd ever had along with an array of charcuterie with meats and cheeses from different regions of Europe. For the first time ever, he'd also been introduced to a selection of caviar served on blinis paired with different champagnes. He wasn't yet sold on the fish eggs but he wasn't going to admit that to anyone yet, as each ounce of these probably fetched over a grand. Jasmine sent him a message shortly before he departed. *Enjoy! xoxo-Jasmine.*

She set the bar high, having arranged this flight with him being the only passenger along with the lone flight attendant and two pilots. This was by far one of the most luxurious experiences of his life and he sensed there would be many more to come. He raised his glass at the flight attendant. She propped up from her seat right away, approached him with a bottle of vintage Moet and topped him off. She moved so eloquently and spoke so gracefully, that Luis wondered if she ever broke character.

"May I offer you anything else, Mr. Diaz?" she asked with a bright smile.

"Actually yes. Do mind giving me a foot rub? These corns on my feet are killing me!" he said as he kicked off his shoes.

The edges of her mouth started to twitch and she bent down to take a knee until Luis started laughing out loud. "I'm just kidding! I wouldn't make you do that!"

She sighed deeply as if she'd finally been given permission to be human again. "That was good," she said as she laughed and straightened back up. "But you'd be surprised at the strange requests I get on these flights."

"Oh yeah? Like what?" He welcomed her to sit across from him and she did so while also letting her hair down. He got up to grab another glass for her. "I'm listening."

"The people who can afford to fly private are some of the weirdest people on the planet. I've seen everything from the whole cabin being full of marijuana smoke to these very old wealthy women with their young boy toys doing it right there where you're sitting. Sometimes it's their own husbands who set the whole thing up just to keep them happy or distracted." She grabbed the glass Luis poured for her and took a sip. "You don't seem like the typical private jet customer, what's your story?"

"Well first, I'm glad you don't think I'm weird," he smiled. "Probably not a story you hear often, but I hit a pretty big lottery jackpot back home."

She's was stunned. "Oh my god. How lucky!"

"Depends what you consider lucky, I guess."

"So you're off to see the world then?" she asked, amused and intrigued.

"Yup. Meeting a friend in Monaco for the weekend and we'll see what happens from there."

"Jasmine, I presume?"

"Yes, do you know her?"

"We do business with her often, she's quite a lovely person." She gulped the last bit of her champagne and got up suddenly. He doesn't think anything of it, but he was glad to have at least made her laugh and not be a rich prick like she was probably accustomed to dealing with.

"Well thank you for being so kind and letting me put my guard down a bit. I'm going to prepare the jet for landing. Can I offer you anything else?"

she asked nicely, back in character.

"That'll be all, thank you for everything. It's truly been a pleasure."

She bowed, flashed her smile and walked away.

The southern coast of France was now visible and Luis began to wonder what was in store for his near future. He was about to embark on a new journey where he didn't know what the possibilities could lead to. The more he thought of Jasmine, the more he got excited about exploring new places with her, and *of* her. He was in that puppy love phase everyone goes through when they first start dating someone new. Sometimes it gave him chills, other times the nerves made him sick to his stomach. What if they didn't hit it off like they did in the Bahamas? Surely she had to have a high standard of men if she was out here flying him in a private jet to meet her. Did she do it because she knew he also had money or was it because she actually liked him? What if he wasn't good enough? After all, he made his fortune by playing the lottery, not by earning it. It's something he hadn't shared with her yet or planned on doing anytime soon. She bought into the lie that he was an early investor in crypto and he knew enough about that industry to stick to that script. At the end of the day, winning the money shouldn't subtract from the fact that he had worked hard all of his life and that he was doing very well for himself and his family. Luis was a bright man and given some different opportunities, he knew he could've earned all of this wealth another way.

CHAPTER 17

"Bonjour, Monsieur Diaz. Bienvenue en France!" A slim young man in a tuxedo and a tilted chauffeur hat approached him as if he'd recognized him. He was a bit younger than Luis with a neatly trimmed beard and a tattoo creeping out of the sleeve of his right arm onto his hand. He cheerfully greeted him and took his luggage. "How was your flight, monsieur?"

"It was great, you can call me Luis," he reached his hand out for a handshake.

"Luis! Nice to meet you, my friend. I'm Charles, I'll be your driver for today. First time in Nice?" He was very upbeat and his English was a bit better than he imagined him having, although he still had the distinct French accent.

"Yessir! I've been to Paris but not here."

"Ugh, Parisians," he made a face of disgust. "You'll like it here a lot better, much nicer people. That's why it's called Nice!" He laughed at his own recycled joke as he loaded Luis' luggage into the back of the sprinter van. "Jump in, my friend. Make yourself comfortable!" He slid open the door for him. The inside of the van looked like a rockstar tour bus with all sorts of neon lights and speakers visible throughout. There were four massive reclining seats inside and a fully stocked bar that covered the whole back panel of the van. "There's champagne, beer, whiskey. You Americans love whiskey, I know. I love whiskey too! Jack Daniels." He made a fist to show how strong it made him feel. He got closer to Luis and whispered, "You want anything else? Mary Jane, blow, molly?" Luis couldn't tell if he was serious or not but before he had a chance to respond, Charles said, "I'm just kidding, my friend! Or not. Anything you need, I'm your man. Very discreet." He winked at him and smacked his shoulder.

Luis laughed and thanked him. "I appreciate it, but I'll just open some champagne for now."

"Pop champagne, oh! We pop champagne! I like that song, you know?"

"Of course! I like your style, Charles," Luis loved his energetic vibe.

"I love hip hop, very big influence in my life," he admitted as he looked through his phone for a song to play.

"Actually, me too."

Charles turned around from the driver seat and

pointed at Luis, "I like you, Luis. You're a nice American. Anyway, Mademoiselle Jasmine said she was very busy today with work. She's always busy busy. She said take you to her condominium in Monaco later. I have the keys. And she asked if you have tuxedo for tonight? You have to dress very fine if you're going to Casino in Monte Carlo with her. She's very very beautiful. Everybody wants her. You're a lucky man, my friend. I'll change shoes with you if you want. Not too late."

Luis cracked up again. This was going to be a good time, he just knew it. Instead of sitting in the back of the van, he jumped up to the front seat next to Charles and opted for a bottle of Jack Daniels instead of the champagne. "I'll tell you what. Let's both get some new tuxedos, maybe buy some watches, and then you can show me your city. And take me to your favorite restaurant, too." He took a swig of the Jack Daniels and offered it to Charles. He took it and poured about two shots worth of whiskey into his mouth. He pressed down on the brake and yanked the gear handle down and put the van on 'Drive'.

"Let's turn it up, as you Americans say!" He pressed play on his phone and 'Jumpman' by Future and Drake came on over the speakers. Charles started dancing in his seat as he checked his side mirrors before pulling out of the parking spot. Luis laughed as he was sure Charles meant to say 'turn up' but he was also impressed by the sudden song selection, so he let loose and danced along with him. It was the right track for the occasion.

By the time they drove into the city and to the tuxedo shop, they were feeling pretty good. A combination of good music and whiskey along with a never-ending debate of who was the NBA's GOAT, or greatest of all time, had kept them busy for most of the ride. Lebron or Jordan? Of course, neither side won. You couldn't ever convince the other side to change their mind. It was more about who could recite more stats about their favorite player and who did more of what in their careers. That's it. "Okay man, whatever you say," Charles said as he reached for the bottle again. Luis pulled it back as if to say he'd had enough while driving but Charles assured him, "We're already here my friend, don't worry!" He pointed at the store and grabbed the bottle for another swig.

Once inside, it didn't take more than twenty minutes to get fitted into the right tuxedos. Like Luis, Charles made his hatred for shopping known and wanted to get out of there as soon as they got in there. After the older gentleman rang up the pair of tuxedos, two pairs of shoes for each and the last two Rolex watches he had on hand, the total came out to just over €25,000. Luis didn't break a sweat at the price until he reached for his wallet and realized he hadn't used his card yet. When he pulled it out, he didn't even recognize the bank that was on the card and hoped it was activated. He actually started to get nervous now because this was it. This was the moment where he would begin to spend the money he had taken for himself from his joint account. He thought about his wife and what her reaction might have been after realizing half the money was gone. Then he thought about Victor. He knew there was no way he would be able to deflect responsibility. That was his only friend who worked at a bank and he'd handled most of their accounts throughout the years. But then again, Luis had given him a whole lot of money, it was the least Victor could've done.

As he slid the card across the counter, he thought to himself, *what's meant to be, will be.* The gentleman plugged the card into the computer. Luis' anxiety was rising. If it was denied, he was screwed. Krystal most likely locked him out of their other accounts in retaliation and he hadn't thought to create a back up plan. *Idiot.* Every second felt like a minute. The man adjusted his glasses and stared at the computer and after a few seconds he stroked away at the keyboard. He reached behind him to pull a paper out from the printer and placed it in front of Luis. "Sign here, please."

Approved! He wanted to yell out loud but decided against showing any emotion. Instead, he signed the receipt and put his card away like it was just another day in the life of Luis Diaz. "*Merci*," he thanked the gentleman. Charles grabbed the bags and they walked out the door.

Before entering the van, Charles gave him a hug out of nowhere and patted his chest. "Thank you so much, Luis! You're too *nice*, maybe this is a good place for you. You understand joke? *Nice*?" He tried again. Luis laughed this time, but mostly because of the effort he kept putting into the same joke, or maybe it was the alcohol.

"Here's my number, my friend. Anything you need, you call me. No matter what time. I come fast." Charles hugged Luis again as he was ready to exit Jasmine's apartment. "Americans are not so bad as they say. Maybe because you're Porto Rican, like you say."

"No, thank you! That *daube nicoise* was one of the best things I've ever eaten. Thank you for taking me there. Today was awesome man and I won't forget it. I'm sure I'll see you again soon, my friend. You call *me* if you need anything."

Charles closed the door behind him and

disappeared. Luis was now in Jasmine's condo as a wave of fresh lavender scent hit his face. The entrance was lined with abstract art paintings and dim lighting. When he got to the living room, the sunlight beamed through the massive glass doors overlooking the Mediterranean. Dozens of yachts and super yachts lined the coast as far as he could see. He also had a clear view of the starting line for the Grand Prix race. "Daaaaaamn! This is what I'm talking about!" he said aloud, not quite believing what he was witnessing. Then his phone buzzed in his pocket. It was Jasmine.

Make yourself at home. Mi casa es su casa.

Gracias señorita. I absolutely love your place! What a view! he responded.

Yes, it's probably my favorite place but I'm always so busy when I come to Monaco.

No worries, I'll see you tonight?

Yes. Meet me at the casino around 8 PM. Car keys are in the kitchen, choose one and leave it at the valet. So sorry I couldn't pick you up but we will make up for it tonight.

I'll hold you to that.

There's beer in the fridge and plenty to drink at the bar. Not much food since I'm not there much. Can't wait to see you.

He decided not to text back. *Keep her waiting,* as she had done to him. He kicked off his shoes and placed his luggage aside and found the fridge. Inside of it were a few Peroni's and a couple of boxed leftovers, nothing else. Seemed about right for a person who was constantly on the move. He grabbed a beer and continued to explore the condo. On the living room wall, he saw a stunning nude black and white portrait of a woman he believed to be Jasmine covering her more intimate parts with vivid red hand fans. He stared at it for a minute imagining who this lady could be and how did she manage to become so wealthy that she owned a condo in Monaco. This was the land of millionaires and billionaires and to own a decent place in this tiny country, you'd have to shell out at least ten million euros. He'd watched a documentary on it. And she mentioned it was one of her favorites. How many other places did she own around the world? It was still a mystery to him. One he hoped to crack in the near future, but one thing was for certain, she wasn't one of those girls who would be after his money, she had her own. He realized that maybe he was the one in the position to take advantage of her wealth and enjoy these escapades while she kept insisting. Except that wasn't the kind of person he was, he disregarded that thought quickly.

Luis noticed a few family photos on a shelf. An elderly couple dressed elegantly with her and a tall man who looked kind of similar to her in features and age. Parents and brother, he assumed, a very beautiful family. Had she inherited the money? Maybe.

Luis then walked out to the balcony with his beer and looked down below and watched the city come to life. There were crowds spectating from balconies and rooftops, party goers aboard yachts. He'd seen it all on TV before and now here he was. He could hear the Formula One cars approaching, and a split second later, they zoomed past less than fifty meters away. He felt the rush and let out a 'woooh' as the cars disappeared around the bend. At that moment, he began to think about his son, Mikey. He wished he was here with him to see this. They'd always talked about coming to this race when he got a little older and it was a promise he would still keep. He pulled out his phone to record the next time the cars drove past so he could show him once he got back.

After having fallen asleep on the patio from what was most likely jet lag, he woke up about two hours later to get ready for the evening. He helped himself to one of the many Dom Perignon bottles Jasmine had stocked in her wine fridge and put on his brand new Dolce & Gabbana tuxedo. "Sharp," he complimented himself as he looked in the mirror. He opted for his Richard Millie watch since it had a much heftier price tag than the Rolex and bent his arm upward from the hip to form a gun with his fingers, like James Bond. "The name is Diaz. Luis Diaz." Then he winked at himself in the mirror.

He recorked the remaining champagne and went to the kitchen to look for the car keys he was supposed to 'choose from.' He found two pairs hanging in the corner. One with a Mercedes emblem and the other with a McLaren emblem. *Easy choice.*

CHAPTER 18

Aboard the all black McLaren 570S, Luis felt like a truly wealthy man. Two hundred million in the bank, in one of the richest cities in the world. He cruised the streets of Monaco with the top down and his favorite Anuel AA tracks blasting. In the past forty eight hours, he'd gotten a pretty nice introduction into the truly finer things in life and he was basking in the moment. He felt lucky as he watched the sun setting off in the distance, creating a colorful masterpiece in the sky and reflecting off the Mediterranean waters. The lights throughout the city were beginning to flicker on, highlighting the more luxurious corners of Monte Carlo. It felt like a movie. And he was the star attraction.

The roads here were perfect for the suspension and speed the McLaren was capable of, so he gripped every winding corner and slammed the gas on the straightaways. He made a mental note to look at the price tag for one of these cars and adding it to his future collection.

After the short joy ride, he made his way to the casino to finally meet Jasmine again. Casino De Monte Carlo was the Mecca of Monaco. Built over 150 years ago, the casino was the primary source of income for the tiny nation and it wasn't hard to see out why. The most affluent rubbed shoulders there to escape from their busy lifestyles and it wasn't uncommon to run into some of the most famous movie stars and athletes enjoying their holidays there. No paparazzi are allowed in Monaco so it was a place they could not only feel somewhat normal, but a place they wouldn't be judged or envied as much as usual because everyone was there was rich. Including Luis. He was definitely rich by most standards, but he didn't know how to be rich. His idea of being rich was only what he'd seen in movies, social media and what he'd heard in his favorite rap lyrics. He hoped to give off the persona that although he was very wealthy now, he was still humble and down to earth. It'd only been about six weeks since hitting the lotto and about two since getting the check. He didn't feel as if he'd changed much in that short time, but his wife would argue otherwise.

Luis followed in line behind a few luxurious sports cars as he approached the valet of the casino. He took in his surroundings. *Here we go*. The valet attendant skipped a few cars and ran straight over to him. The young man approached the McLaren and upon noticing it was Luis, he took a step back as if he'd been expecting someone else. "Oh sorry sir, I thought you were—nevermind. Welcome to the Casino De Monte Carlo. How are you this fine evening?"

"I'm great, thank you," Luis responded.

The attendant opened the door and took his keys. Luis slipped him twenty euros and the man looked at it as if he'd been given a piece of lint. He reached back into his pocket and pulled out a hundred. "Sorry, I didn't realize it was only a twenty," he said apologetically as he handed it to him.

The attendant returned a big smile. "Thank you, Mister—"

"Diaz. Luis Diaz." He couldn't believe it. He'd actually introduced himself like James Bond, just as he had practiced in the mirror.

"It's a pleasure, Mr. Diaz. Enjoy your evening and good luck."

Luis adjusted his tie, ran his fingers through his eyebrows and made his way to the entrance. *It was showtime.*

Upon entering the casino, sheer elegance radiated from wall to wall and floor to ceiling. He absorbed every tiny detail and took it all in. He now walked the same marble floors that history's most famous people had walked. The ceilings were strewn with awe-inspiring art that reminded him of the Sistine Chapel. Gold features were intertwined throughout the walls with masterfully carved woodwork. Dozens of grand chandeliers provided just enough lighting to the casino that gave it a certain glow, making it feel as if he'd stepped back in time. As he walked through the casino, he observed the people in attendance. The men and women were wearing their finest attire and everyone of them carried themselves with such classy mannerisms that you wouldn't think anyone here ever had a problem. Was it a facade or was this the kind of joy that wealth could buy? As he walked past certain individuals, he put a number on them, assuming how much they were worth. *He's loaded. She looks famous. He's a trust fund baby. That one's definitely a hooker.* Then he felt a buzz in his pocket.

Come save me, Jasmine texted.

I'm here, where are you? he looked down and replied.

By the bar in the back.

Just as he looked up to find the bar, he bumped into someone, spilling the drink all over the man's jacket. "I'm so sorry! I was looking for someone and—" He stopped talking at the realization of who he had bumped into.

"Don't worry mate, it's just a little water," Lewis Hamilton replied. The current Formula One champion and arguably the best driver ever. He looked at Luis, who's face was stuck with his mouth wide open. Lewis laughed. "Enjoy your evening, sir," he said as he patted Luis' shoulder and walked away. Luis watched him leave, a little disappointed that he couldn't at least introduce himself or mention how big of a fan him and his son were.

Then off in the distance he saw Jasmine standing by the bar surrounded by a group of older gentlemen intrigued by either her conversation or her looks. Probably the latter. His driver had mentioned how everyone had wanted her and he could see why. She was dressed in a shimmering red dress that looked like it could've been painted on her body. It covered one arm and left the other bare and had a thigh-high front slit that didn't leave much to the imagination. He could overhear her speaking to the men in French and them laughing back in unison. She finally spotted him and waved him over excitedly.

Jasmine excused herself from the men and wrapped her arms around Luis and gave him a small peck on the lips. "I've missed you," she said, staring directly into his eyes.

"Me too. Thanks for the invite. Today's been

incredible, and it just got a whole lot better." He winked at her.

She pulled him over to the group of gentlemen, who's faces had soured. "Let me introduce you to some of my business colleagues," she put her hand out to introduce them. "Everyone, meet my boyfriend from America, Luis."

Boyfriend? He was taken by surprise and was flattered, but now he realized why she wanted to be saved. It did make him feel good though. He would love to play along.

"Hello gentlemen, pleasure to meet you all," Luis shook each one of their hands.

"Hello, Luis from America. What is it that you do?" One of them asked pretentiously. Not out of curiosity, but to size him up. To see if he was in the big leagues or the minors.

"I'm an early crypto investor and it's been a hell of a ride," Luis lied, but this was the story he was going to stick to and the one he had told Jasmine back in the Bahamas when they first met.

They guys all start laughed. He wasn't sure if they were laughing at him or if they thought he was joking.

"Crypto?!" One of them finally managed to get out after almost choking on his drink laughing. "Well I'm glad it's been good for you because I know I wouldn't trust my money on the internet like that."

"But isn't that what you do already? Manage your money online and play in a stock market that clearly doesn't represent what's happening in the world right now. Do you *really* know who controls your money?" Luis tried to reason with them.

"Just seems like a Ponzi scheme to me, but to each his own," the man replied as he took another sip of his drink dismissively.

"You'd be surprised, Frank," Jasmine jumped in. "Cryptocurrencies are the future. I've made quite a fortune on them because of my financial advisor over in Switzerland. He introduced me very early on and I've had nothing but massive gains ever since. And I'm talking *massive*. Maybe you all should reconsider. With all that money you guys have, what do you *really* have to lose?" They all laughed again in unison like rich pigs. Luis could see why she was so respected. The way she spoke and attracted their attention, made her a force to be reckoned with. Luis appreciated her backing him up.

"Well if I know you, Jasmine, it's that you are always ahead of the curve," he looked up and down her curvy body and Luis felt like punching the old pervert. "Maybe you can share your contact and I'll consider looking into it," Frank finished. Luis wasn't sure if he genuinely was interested or if he wanted to appeal to Jasmine. Either way, he was hoping to exit the conversation soon before he let something slip.

"I'll send it to your assistant. Anyways, nice chatting with you boys but we'll be on our way now," she grabbed Luis by the hand and walked away. "Rich assholes," she admitted to Luis. "Unfortunately, we need these rich assholes to do some good in the world. They're major investors on this green project I'm working on with Lewis Hamilton down in Africa."

"The F1 driver, Lewis?" He was in awe.

"Yes, he's a good friend of mine. We met many years ago in Macau and have done a lot of charitable work ever since."

"Wow, that's incredible! I actually bumped into him earlier and spilled water all over him but I was too star-struck to tell him how big a fan me and my son are."

"Well, he's right over there. C'mon, let me introduce you."

After meeting Hamilton, Luis was elated and also impressed at how nice the most famous driver in the world really was. Lewis even offered to record a video on his cell phone for his son. He imagined Mikey's reaction and considered sending it to him, but then realization hit him that he would have to text his wife in order to get to him. A small sense of guilt came over him and Jasmine seemed to notice. "How about we head back to my place for a night cap. I feel like I'm still at work here."

"Sounds perfect."

CHAPTER 19

As they walked out of the casino, the valet attendant from earlier ran towards them. "Jasmine! I thought that McLaren looked familiar," he looked at Luis with more respect this time around, then gave her a hug and a kiss on the cheek. "I'll have it over right away."

"Thanks, Leo," she said as he sprinted off.

"You know everybody, huh?" Luis asked curiously.

"It doesn't always have its perks."

When Leo brought the car back around, Jasmine placed her hand out, stopping Luis from walking to the driver side. "I'll drive," she insisted as she kicked off her red-bottom heels and tossed them behind the seat. His testosterone levels shot through the roof. Seconds later, his body was being pressed back into the seat as she sped through the winding streets of Monte Carlo. Her small hands gripped the wheel at the ten and two position in line with the paddle shifts. After rounding a corner, she flicked the left paddle to downshift and accelerated through a long straightaway where she must've hit at least 100 MPH in just a few seconds. His adrenaline soared as he watched her looking fiercely at the road. He was sure he'd never been so turned on in his life and couldn't wait to get back to the condo.

A split second after arriving at her place, she jumped on him and wrapped her legs around his waist. They kissed furiously, releasing pent-up steam they were both carrying from their long day. She was breathing heavily as he kissed her and bit her from her clavicle, up her neck a then her ear. He pressed her up against the wall, knocking over pictures but neither of them seemed to notice or care as she dug her fingers into the back of his head and demanded, "Give it to me already." He shifted her weight to one arm as he used the other to unzip his pants and pulled her dress further up. He gripped her ass with both hands as she hung on and they started going at it aggressively, bouncing from the wall to the bar and onto the couch where she got on top of him. She took control by pinning his arms back and stared deep into his eyes before looking up at the ceiling, moaning loudly with every thrust. A minute later they climaxed and she collapsed into his arms.

"Holy shit," he said in between breaths as he was trying to catch it back. That was the best sex he'd ever had and he was hoping she would feel the same. *Probably not.*

"Wow, that was incredible," she sighed, also trying to catch her breath. She jumped off him and disappeared into her bedroom. Luis just watched her the whole way, thinking about how lucky he had been. But as incredible as she was, he was ready and anxious to know more about her. How much was she really worth? Did she really make a fortune with crypto or did she just jump in the conversation to save him? Maybe she could connect him someday with her financial advisor so his money could grow instead of letting it sit idly in his new checking account.

A few minutes later, she reappeared with an ice bucket and a vintage bottle of Moet with two glasses. Luis got up to open the sliding door for her and they laid down in her cabana-style bed and watched the night sky once again, just as they'd done in the Bahamas. He reached over and popped open the bottle, poured the glasses and raised it for a toast. "Here's to living," they clinked glasses and took a sip. "Looking up at the stars with you brings me such peace of mind and tranquility. Cheesy as it may sound, it almost feels like I'm living in a dream."

"It's not cheesy. I used to look at things the same way you are right now. But that dream can become daunting if you don't learn to take time for yourself," she said as if she had become overwhelmed with stress. "I've been working nonstop for the last year and haven't had a chance to really enjoy myself. That is until we met. Your energy sparked something within me and I'll admit, I've been thinking about you almost obsessively." She chuckled in slight embarrassment. "The way you were with your friends and how they were with you. I could see that you enjoy making others happy, even at the expense of your own happiness sometimes. I don't come across people like you in my circles quite often. You're genuine and one-of-a-kind and I love that about you."

"Well thank you, but life isn't that pretty for me at the moment either. That's why I came here." He didn't want to give too many details and spoil the moment. "I also needed an escape from a few things back home and to be honest, I don't know if I'm making a mistake or not. I'm sure things won't be the same if I decide to return but one thing I do know is that as long as I'm here with you, I *will* be living in the moment. The past will have to stay put and I'll deal with the ramifications later."

"So you *are* human," she smiled at him. "You know, I've been considering taking some time off to just live a little as you say. What I'd do to just unplug, disconnect and have sex all day while cruising the Mediterranean."

"Well, what's stopping you then?"

"If you asked me two hours ago, I'd give you a long list of excuses. But right now? I can only think of one reason that would stop me." She put her glass down and leaned closer to Luis, making eye contact with him. "I'd only go if you came with me."

"Let me check my schedule," he picked up his phone to pull up his calendar. She waited quietly for a moment, curiously waiting for his response. After a few seconds he looked at her and laughed, "Yeah there's nothing on my calendar, what do you have in mind?"

She immediately reached for her phone and pulled up her own calendar. "Well tomorrow is qualifying day for the race and I have a daytime thing I need to attend. You should come, it's actually on board that one right there." She pointed at a massive yacht docked less than two hundred yards from where they were laying down. It was full of people mingling and dancing along to some house music. "The owner is a really good friend of mine and he has a whole fleet of yachts and catamarans throughout the world. I could see if he has any available in the area and maybe we could set off tomorrow night."

"And miss the race Sunday?"

"I'd rather be out of here before race day. Besides, the race will most likely be decided tomorrow at qualifying. There's not too many places to pass on this course so historically the quali winner also wins the race."

He was impressed she actually knew her Formula One facts and wasn't just a fan for the big event that it was. "Ok then, tomorrow it is."

A few hours later, Luis woke up from a short sleep after having stayed up all night watching the sunrise with Jasmine. He hadn't done that since him and Krystal were dating, which also marked the first time they'd confessed their love for each other. Now he was experiencing similar feelings. It obviously couldn't be love, it was too soon. But it was something. He felt a connection he hadn't felt in a very long time. Having only spent three days with her in total, he was starting to get the impression that Jasmine needed him. Not for money, but the opposite. To remind her how to take life a bit easier and slow down a bit, but what attracted Luis to her was her lavish lifestyle which was beyond anything he'd ever imagined. He admired her confidence and independence which gave her the freedom to do as she pleased. Something he desperately wanted now. He could learn a lot from a woman who seemed to have it all. The good and the bad.

But he sensed she was looking for an escape. The forced smiles around the casino, the need to please everyone in her presence, it can become too much for anyone. He sympathized with her and could imagine himself turning into a version of her someday. But at the moment, a woman of her stature needing someone like him, inflated his ego and he would do whatever he could in order spend as much time with her as possible. Right now, they were both in pursuit of something the other had, in order to balance the scales of their hectic lives. Something that sounded like absolute bliss.

Luis turned over in bed to see Jasmine through the open door leading into her bathroom. She was wearing a bathrobe and dancing in the mirror to some EDM while getting ready. He slowly crept up behind her and wrapped his arms around her waist, kissing her cheek and taking in her fresh vanilla scent. She closed her eyes and sang along to the song playing on her phone and danced on him.

"Someone's in a great mood," Luis said while looking at their reflection in the mirror.

"Yup. I love quali day in Monaco," she opened her eyes and looked at him through the mirror. "But more exciting is that I'm finally taking a holiday." She turned around and wrapped her arms around his neck and pulled him in for a kiss.

"With you."

He looked down in search of some toothpaste but noticed two powdery white lines evenly cut and spaced out on the countertop. His facial expression changed and she noticed. Not because he was against it or anything, but he was surprised that she was so open about doing cocaine like it was nothing. It'd also been the same reason he got kicked out of his house and it gave him flashbacks. "I'm sorry, I just got caught off guard. I don't have a problem with it," he tried to explain. The memory of an elderly man he once met while traveling in Costa Rica came across his head. In reference to drugs, alcohol and life in general, the old man advised him, *"it's okay to enjoy anything in life, but in moderation."* He still held that belief.

"Well good, because I lined them up for you. Between the jet lag and lack of sleep, you're gonna need it today. And don't worry, I only get the cleanest stuff." She grabbed a small straw and snorted a line and handed it to Luis. He didn't even hesitate as he pressed his left nostril and inhaled it through his right one. He felt his eyes water and a few seconds later, the rush of adrenaline that comes along with these substances hit him. It was go time.

CHAPTER 20

Luis watched the Formula One cars zoom past at excesses of 150 MPH just twenty yards away from his vantage point aboard the yacht. The loud engine roars drowned out everything around them until the cars disappeared into the next bend. Applause and cheers would follow depending on which driver had clocked in their qualifying time for the big race. The scene from the condo a day prior had been pretty amazing as they ran their practice laps, but today he was looking up at the city from the opposite end and it was quite breathtaking. There wasn't an empty balcony as far as his sight could reach. Every yacht lining the track was at capacity and seemingly in competition with their neighbors with an incredible lineup of the world's top DJ's spinning their latest music to VIP hosts and guests. Aboard the yacht he was fortunate to be on, the Martinez Brothers were were putting on a great set, feeding off of each other and inducing the crowd into a trance.

Luis sipped on what seemed like a bottomless glass of champagne, since every time before taking his last sip, a cocktail waitress would be there to top him off once again. He'd actually tried drinking one glass quickly to test their awareness and reaction time. And as soon as the glass separated from his lips, another beautiful waitress was standing by a foot away from him, smiling and offering a refill. "Damn, you're good!" he teased the latest one. She filled his glass, gave him a wink and continued on her way.

As he made his way around the yacht, he got the impression that most of the women aboard the yacht were either escorts or gold diggers. The women outnumbered the men at least three to one and there wasn't one aboard that couldn't be featured on the front cover of the next month's Vogue magazine. They were all stunning. But the men did outnumber them three to one in one category. Age. Not that it mattered to either party. The men walked around with a confidence that paralleled the measure of their wealth, something Luis had yet to acquire. But he was more than content with his current situation. Jasmine had what these girls wanted, and Luis had Jasmine, so all was right in his world. He wasn't looking for another sleazy hookup, he was looking to see how far he could explore this relationship.

After weaving through a few party goers, Luis found the restroom. He went to open the door just as Jasmine exited, rubbing her nose. "Getting fixed without me?!" Luis asked jokingly as she looked up and realized who it was. She reached up for a kiss and placed her tin in his hand.

"Meet me in the upper deck when you finish." She then grabbed his crotch and walked away. He stared at her the whole way out. *Damn, I'm so lucky.*

Inside the restroom, he looked in the mirror to check himself out. He was feeling the buzz from the champagne as the drugs from earlier were wearing off. "You're the fucking man, Luis." He told himself looking at the mirror trying to boost his confidence as he worked different poses. His reflection was the same Luis he had always been, except this guy was now wearing Prada shades along with a short sleeve Gucci floral shirt. He kept trying to appear as rich as he was, but knew it would take time and practice. What better place to do so than aboard a hundred million dollar yacht full of models while watching the Monaco Grand Prix? He bobbed his head and danced to the beat he could hear bumping through the walls and pounded his chest rhythmically. He unbuttoned the rest of the shirt like the other men at the party, who had much lesser muscular physiques than he did.

The tin Jasmine gave him was just like the one

he had gotten in trouble for having and it kept taking him back to that instance but he quickly brushed it off his mind, trying to snap back to the present. He opened it up and was once again staring at fine white powder. *Fuel for the rich.* His opinion of people who did coke was suddenly not so harsh. This was a way to keep up in a fast-paced lifestyle and he was starting to understand why. Jasmine had been going nonstop since before he even landed in France and coffee was not going to keep her battery charged. She also explained to him that dealers for the wealthy did not cut their product with fentanyl because they were already earning a premium from their customers. It's the stuff on the streets that people had to be wary of. Small time drug dealers trying to maximize profits.

Luis scraped a small portion out of the tin with the corner of his credit card, sniffed it up and licked the residue. He stared in the mirror again, lowered his sunglasses and winked at himself. Then he walked out the door and shrugged his shoulders to the music as he passed a group of models. They stared at him like prey as he continued on without excusing himself or giving them the slightest bit of attention. He found the stairs at the back of the yacht and was stopped by a security guard at the bottom of the steps.

"I'm with Jasmine," he said matter-of-factly and

kept walking past as the guard angled his body to let him through without any hinderance. She saw him and waved him over with a huge smile on her face. He reminded himself to smile because for a moment his mind was playing tricks on him, making him think this was *his* yacht. The sudden urge made him think he had become superior to everyone here. He shook his head to recollect his thoughts.

"Are you alright?" Jasmine asked with a small look of concern.

"Oh yeah, I'm good. Sorry, just a little headache. Probably from the jet lag." He regained his composure and flashed his usual smile. "How's it going? I'm Luis." He reached his hand out to a man sitting with a front and center view to the race, all of Monaco, and of course, all the beautiful women on board his yacht on the lower deck.

"Mo," the massive man replied. "Welcome aboard. Any friend of Jasmine's is a friend of mine." His gargantuan hands almost swallowed Luis' whole, just as he'd probably made a habit of swallowing things whole to build the impressive round figure he boasted. Mo, short for Mohammed, was from Emirati royalty but had been defected by the family because of his disloyalty and dishonor to their religious views. He loved to self-indulge in everything from food to drugs to women, and had once been investigated for international sex trafficking until the charges miraculously disappeared. Perks of the mega rich.

Jasmine still considered him a friend because they'd apparently known each other since before he was a troubled man and he always looked out for her as if she was a little sister. Jasmine turned to Luis, "So I was talking to Mo and he said he had a couple of catamarans available for us. One in Nice and one in Menorca."

"Yes, yes, take whichever. Take both, it doesn't matter to me. Anything for my little sister," Mo insisted, obviously not caring either way and much more interested in the three women boarding his yacht. He signaled to the security guard to lead them upstairs. Then he motioned his security to get rid of the women currently on the upper deck. As the guard shushed them away, the ladies snapped their heads and left in disappointment for not having made the cut for the evening.

"Okay, so you're thinking what I'm thinking?" Luis asked Jasmine.

"If we go to Nice, we can sail the south of France. Cannes, St Tropez, L'Ile De Porquerolles, some of my favorite places! The food, the wine and champagne are all spectacular! I would love to show you."

"Yeah but if we go to Menorca, it would be

more low-key. We can truly disconnect. I have a feeling that work would chase you to those other places."

She thought it over briefly. He was right. "You know me too well, Menorca it is. I'll arrange a flight for tonight."

Mo invited Luis to approach him. Then he waved him even closer as he was making no effort to move an inch from the couch. He heavily whispered, "You take care of her, or else." Mo pulled his glasses down flashing his bloodshot eyes so Luis could see his seriousness. Then he let out a thunderous laugh. "I'm just joking my friend. She's a big girl. Just return my boat in one piece! Or not, I don't care!"

Luis joined him in laughter and shook his hand again before insisting, "If you need help with those three that just came in, you just let me know." He slapped his colossal shoulder and walked away.

"I like that man!" Mo said to Jasmine as she thanked him and kissed him on his sweaty cheek.

They rejoined the party on the bottom deck and all of the men had their attention fixated on the race track, while the women all congregated by the bar likely plotting on who was going to make a move on who.

It was time for the final round of qualifying, which determined the order of the racing lineup for the next day. Different currencies exchanged hands between the men as they increasingly raised their voices over the sounds of the approaching cars.

"Hamilton!" one said.

"I got Max!" the man next to him yelled.

"I'll take the hometown kid, Leclerc! Let's go!!!" shouted another.

Luis asked Jasmine, "Who do you have?"

"Well of course my friend Lewis. You?"

"I'll take the Dutchman, Max."

They looked towards the giant screen that indicated there was less than a minute left for the drivers to get in their fastest laps. The crowds started going crazy as one by one their favorite drivers crossed the finish line. This was one of the most intense sporting events Luis had ever witnessed live and he wondered if his kid was watching back home. He started recording on his phone so he could show Mikey. The roars turned into a collective gasp as the screen showed Leclerc in the red Ferrari crashing into the wall. The qualifier was halted and luckily for Leclerc, he had the fastest lap prior to the crash, so he'd be at the front of the pack for the big race.

"Told you, mate!" Yelled the lone man who chose Leclerc to win. He doused himself in champagne, missing his mouth on purpose. "I'll give anyone ten to one odds he'll win tomorrow!"

He drunkenly stumbled around looking for a suitor until one took him up for it.

"A hundred grand! Leclerc doesn't win, you owe me a million," he clarified the bet, making sure enough people witnessed the drunken man accepting before shaking hands.

"Easy money," the man shook his hand and poured some more champagne, this time in his mouth.

Luis and Jasmine looked at each other before she tilted her head towards the exit. He agreed and they made their way to the ramp. Before stepping off the boat, Luis glanced up at the top deck one last time and noticed the three women from earlier adorning Mo. He made eye contact with Mo and Luis cracked a smile and gave him a hand salute as if to say *thank you and good bye, ya filthy animal.'* Mo returned the salute, knowing exactly what Luis was trying to relay. Guy code.

CHAPTER 21

The next morning, Luis woke up to Jasmine's arm wrapped over his abdomen and her head tucked under his arm pit. She was breathing lightly in sync with the slight rock of the catamaran they had spent the night on and likely would spend the next few days or weeks sailing. He marveled at her natural beauty and couldn't get over how lucky he was to have her at his side. She was full of surprises and he never knew what to expect from her. He'd never met someone who matched his level of spontaneity. Halfway through their flight from Nice to Menorca, she went to restroom and came out in a black see-through lingerie. Luckily for him, there was nobody else on the plane besides the pilots and a few minutes later, he became the newest member of the 'mile-high club.' Now as he stared at her half naked body, he wondered how long this adventure would continue, she seemed to be in for it as much as he was. Luis noticed the way she looked into his eyes every time he spoke and how carefree she acted around him, as if she was free from any real responsibilities. As if she had found life again. The feeling was mutual.

He slipped from under her arm and walked outside of their room to get a better look at the city they were docked at. They had a front row view of Ciutadella, located on the easternmost Balearic island of Menorca. The city was peacefully presenting itself as the sun rose on the opposite side of the island. Pink and purple hues painted the sky over the pastel colored buildings that lined the coast. Behind him, the canal was bordered with boats of all sizes, theirs being one of the more grandiose, because of course Mo wouldn't settle for anything lesser.

The city had yet to wake up except for the few fishermen and deckhands preparing to spend their day in the Mediterranean waters, hauling in the local catch of the day for the many restaurants on the island. Luis always admired these guys because they lived such a simple life without much complaint. He'd considered many times in his past, more often in the recent years, just quitting his career and living simply on a beach. There he would take on random jobs like fishing, bartending at a local restaurant or maybe even giving tours for visitors. Pretty much anything else that wouldn't require too much dependability as long as it kept a little cash in his pocket. Jobs mostly to pass the time. But then he hit the lottery. Now he didn't have to think about how to be happy living a poor man's life, instead he'd have to plot on how to make his money last so he wouldn't end up a poor man. It was all too common and widely known that these lottery winners go broke in a few years because they couldn't control themselves. Luis thrived on proving others wrong and that's what he was thinking to himself as he gazed out into the bright blue waters ahead.

He pulled out his phone to watch the videos he'd recorded for his son. He missed his kids tremendously but he wasn't prepared to explain to his wife what he was doing, although he was curious as to what she must've been thinking and if she had any idea as to where he might be at. He decided to finally turn on his other phone which he chose to keep, just in case. The phone buzzed over and over. Dozens of text message and voicemail alerts appeared on the phone.

Where the hell are you?

Did you take that money out of our account? I think we were hacked.

What kind of shitbag father…

That was all he read before hearing light footsteps approaching from behind. He put his phones back in his pocket, then heard a *click*. Luis turned around to see Jasmine wearing one of his long sleeve shirts and most likely nothing underneath. At least that's what he imagined. "I can't remember the last time I used one of these," she said as she reeled the disposable camera to prepare it for the next picture. "I swear, you take me back to some of the happiest days of my life." She puckered her lips and waited for Luis to meet her the rest of the way.

"I guess we're doing this then. No phones all day. Only this 20th century camera."

"Already beat you to it," she smirked as she handed the camera to Luis and walked to the bow of the boat. She looked off into the distance and Luis lined up the camera to get a good shot, but what he saw next made it the *perfect* shot. She unbuttoned her shirt and let it drop to the ground, revealing her nude, slim and perfectly tanned body as she threw her hands up in the air. *True freedom,* he thought, and snapped the picture. It was easy to see why she had a modeling career. She posed so effortlessly, almost as if there were no cameras and she was just being in the moment. The fact that she didn't care about who in the vicinity may have seen her naked, kept confirming to Luis that this is who she really was. A woman with the sort of confidence to be bold and brave. That's what he found most attractive about her.

"So where to, Mister?" asked Jasmine as she slipped the shirt back on.

"Well first, I'm gonna need some coffee. Let me look to see where we can get some good brew around here." He reached back into his pocket for his phone out of habit and after unlocking the screen, she quickly snatched it from his hands.

"Nuh uh, you'll get this back tomorrow," she waved the phone over her head. "Put your other one away too!" Then she danced down the stairs, back into the cabin. He just smiled and laughed to himself as he watched her leave. Jasmine also took him back to some of the happiest days of his life. A time where he too was free from responsibilities.

"I used to come here with my friends for holidays during my uni years," Jasmine said as she reminisced. "I was so young and naive to the world. Can you believe I wanted to be a marine biologist? I wanted to save the ocean and everything in it since I was just a little girl."

They sat atop a cliff by the water with nobody in sight, drinking a bottle of local Spanish wine from two plastic cups they picked up at a convenience store. Luis yearned for these moments where they sat uninterrupted, learning more about each other, peeling back layers, letting their guards down and furthering their connection.

"Oh yeah? So what happened to that? Did you realize it was an impossible task?"

"I realized it takes *money* to solve the world's problems," she responded as she took a sip of her cup and looked out at the sea. "We went on a trip to the Galapagos Islands to study some native species and ended up getting involved in an investigation as to why it had become such a hot spot for shark finning. They needed help figuring out who was behind the whole operation. It started as a very inspiring trip and by the time I left, I was so heart broken. It was my own people down there, the Chinese, funding these expeditions and paying off locals to help them capture these sharks. Just for their fins! We asked the locals why they were helping them out and if they knew what the ramifications were but they bluntly said that they needed the money."

"I'd heard about that on a documentary, they just cut their fins and dump the rest of the body in the water, huh?"

"With no chance to live. It's actually a slow and painful death for them. These people have no idea what it does to the ecosystem." Jasmine was distraught. "And all for a bowl of soup and status symbol."

"That is heart breaking," Luis replied, never having put much thought into any serious dilemmas around the world, but he could see how much it affected her. "So what did you decide to do afterwards?"

"I decided I had to find a way to either pay the locals more than what they were receiving or I was going to have to infiltrate the group that was paying them. Of course I was still a student, so money wasn't going to be the solution just yet. But being Chinese and an attractive young woman got me just what I needed and it wasn't difficult to get answers that ultimately led me to the supply chain. I altered a few batches of fins with some marine bacteria that would cause some serious stomach aches and illnesses for the shitty consumers and it wasn't long before they thought the sharks in the Galapagos were no longer worth their time or money."

"That's actually pretty genius. You made the difference you wanted to make, although a bit unconventional, but who knows how great of an impact that made on the ecosystem there."

"It was very satisfying to know I made a difference using my wit instead of the traditional diploma and impressive resume. I knew I could create a path to find wealthy individuals who cared about the environment as much as I did and I would use their donations to do the work they didn't have time for. And that's how my interest in modeling came about. It took me a few years to make a splash in the industry, but by the time I did, I was rubbing shoulders with all the high-rollers around the world. And there's nothing they love more than a model with brains." She smiled in a cute sort of ditzy manner and tilted her head. "Gotta play the cards you've been dealt."

Luis was finally getting to see who Jasmine was, as she revealed more and more of herself. "I am just so impressed by you. I've never met a woman with such an incredible drive and passion for wanting to do good for others. I mean, we all *want* to do good, but we're so good at finding excuses that we end up doing nothing. If I can't help your charity personally someday, I'd love to at least donate to a cause you're involved in."

"Maybe one day, but for now, I just want to live in the moment. You really don't realize how much I needed this. I needed time to reflect on my work and do something for me. For once." She grabbed the bottle of wine and poured the last little bit right into her mouth. Then she grabbed the camera and tossed it to Luis as she skipped and flailed her arms towards the edge of the cliff.

For a few seconds, Luis stared at her in a state of infatuation as she moved her hands in a motion that made her look as if she was possessed by the wind. She turned to blow a kiss at Luis as he was preparing the camera to snap a picture and a split second later, she jumped off the cliff.

He got up quickly with his heart pounding out of his chest and ran to the edge. All he could see was small waves crashing against the rocks below. He thought about jumping in after her but after looking down at the dark blue waters, there was no telling where the rocks could be. He then reached into his pocket for his phone, before realizing that he didn't have it on him. "Shit!" He muttered to himself as he looked down again to gauge how high of a jump it was. Twenty, maybe thirty feet? But just as he was getting ready to jump, she popped out from the surface and yelled excitedly.

"C'mon! Jump!" She waved him over.

"You're fucking crazy!" He yelled back and laughed at the realization that she was in no immediate danger.

"It's only ten meters! I've jumped here many times before! Don't be a—"

Luis didn't let her finish her insult. He was the one to always instigate this daredevil behavior and now he was being shown up. He loved it. His life was starting to become one thrill after the next as he let out a loud scream, "Wooooooh!" The jump from a cliff always felt much longer than what it looked like from afar. The fear of everything that could go wrong, shortly followed by the satisfaction of having survived was as gratifying as any. When he splashed into the water, he opened his eyes to see how close the rocks really were. He was inches from the bottom, furthering his amazement of Jasmine's fearlessness. When he came back up, she latched on to him and pressed her salty lips against his.

He stared deep into her eyes and said, "There's just something about you."

She winked at him and pretended to go in for another kiss. When he closed his eyes, she pushed him under water and swam back to the shore. He was hooked.

CHAPTER 22

"So what do you think about taking our relationship to the next level?" Luis asked after finishing their romantic dinner at Seaside Cafe Bar which was located inside a cave overlooking the water. "And maybe allowing *me* to pay for once." He laughed after noticing her putting her clutch back down. She'd been pretty slick setting up just about everything since they had met. The private jets, the transport and accommodations. Even the places they'd wined and dined for the last few days in Menorca. She'd either taken the check while he wasn't looking or slipped the server enough cash to cover the tab, and then some.

"I'm sorry, it's just habit. Normally, when I let men pay, they assume they've bought me and I owe them something. Besides, I invited you. Can't a woman be chivalrous as well?" She leaned forward and raised her eyebrow.

"Your chivalry is unmatched, my lady," he replied in a terrible British accent. "I would just like to return the favor for everything you've done for me."

"But you do. Every night. And twice this morning," she winked and blew him a kiss.

He leaned back in his seat and crossed his arms. "Ooooh. It makes sense now! I'm your *boy toy*, huh? Not bad for a 36 year old with a dad bod, I guess. I'm quite flattered!" They laughed out loud as the server approached him with the check. Luis waved him off, "Oh no, I'm the *boy toy* here, my friend. Hand that to my sugar mama, please." Jasmine laughed and covered her face in embarrassment as she handed the server her credit card.

"I don't know what I'm going to do with you, Luis," she said as she finally caught her breath from laughter and wiped her tears of joy.

The last few days had been just that. Sex, food, wine, talks, laughter, naps, repeat. After being phone-free for the first day, they'd continue to be on a mostly phone-free escapade the last four days in Menorca. While there, they rented a convertible Porche 911 and explored every corner of the island. From small family-owned vineyards to quaint restaurants in the hilltop villages, they'd embraced everything the small Balearic island had to offer. It was the perfect island to get away from it all. Not too touristy, but not too quiet.

"I told the captain we could set sail in the morning and head over to Mallorca for a day or two, before setting off to Ibiza to party a bit, ever been?" asked Jasmine.

"Oh yes, and I've been dying to go back. I was hoping you'd keep me around long enough to suggest that."

"I think I'll keep you around for a little while longer."

The next morning, Jasmine woke Luis up to some French-pressed coffee as she had gotten him accustomed to since they began sailing. He noticed she would only drink a few sips of coffee and didn't seem to have a fondness for it as much as he did. But he'd known since they met in the Bahamas that she had a different source of fuel and it was in that gold tin she always kept on her. At first, he felt a little uneasy about her doing it so often, but she didn't give the sort of 'cokehead' vibe that would normally be associated with that kind of behavior. Technically, coffee could be classified as a drug. Pretty much anything you abuse can be harmful, so what's a small bump here and there to keep you going throughout the day when you live a faster and more opulent lifestyle than the vast majority of the world? What he appreciated most was that she wasn't hiding it from him. She also wasn't pushing it on him. Not that she needed to anyways, Luis liked to indulge from time to time, and he was finding himself taking bumps from the same tin a few times a day. It gave him that boost he needed in order to take full advantage of the days spent abroad. Not to mention the sexual stamina that it enhanced to the level of his teenage years.

"Good morning, babe," Jasmine said as she set the coffee on the nightstand and slipped back under the covers next to him. *Babe?* That was a first for them, but he had to admit to himself, it did make him feel more upbeat. He'd just been trying to live in the moment but every time their relationship progressed a step, he thought back to what he had at home. His kids, his wife, who also called him *babe*. His friends and family that would surely disown him if they found out he ran off with another woman. "Are you ok?"

"Yeah, sorry, just got a lot on my mind," he replied.

"You know, you can talk to me. I'm not just here for fun and pleasure. I know it can't be easy being away from your kids. I didn't want to bring it up until you were ready but I can see it's weighing on you."

"Well, it's not only that," he paused. Luis hated lying. It took too much time and effort to keep a lie intact so he'd learn to be a pretty honest person, even if sometimes the truth hurt. But what did he have to lose in this situation? She'd either be upset and leave, or maybe she really would understand. "I also left my wife. I mean, I wasn't intending on it being permanently, but who knows? Our marriage was crumbling and I ran off before I even tried to fix it."

She didn't seem shocked by the news of the wife, "I remember you telling me in the Bahamas that you were married, did you forget?" She had a confused look on her face.

He actually had forgotten. The night he met her had been such a blur that he literally had no clue as to what they may or may not have discussed. Then he vaguely remembered bringing it up after hooking up in the yacht the first time but he was pretty messed up that night as well and had completely discarded the memory, instead choosing to remember the highlights of that night. So this whole time he thought he was keeping it a secret, she'd known all along, and had no problem with it. *Off to a good start*, he thought.

"No, I remember telling you, but things went downhill after I went back home from that trip," he tried to cover up. "I felt such a connection with you that last night on the yacht, and I knew it was wrong. I really hadn't planned on pursuing it, as much as I wanted to. I'm a married man after all, I was ready to go back to my family and put it all behind me, but then everything changed. We just started fighting all the time and a switch inside me flipped. I'd had enough. I left and didn't feel any remorse, it was weird. I didn't care anymore. I just wanted to live, but I felt trapped. And right now…", he wiped a tear from his eye, "…right now I feel like I'm finally living. And to be honest, I still don't feel guilty about leaving. Does that make me a shitty person?"

"Luis, you are a gem. You have the biggest heart and you are so kind and unselfish and I love that about you. I'm sure you're a wonderful father and nothing can stop you from being that. But in these times we're living in, love comes with an expiration date unfortunately. We're constantly in search of the next thing. Something flashier, younger. Someone who makes us feel better. When you've lived the life I've lived, you learn to accept that. You take the good and keep it around as long as it is *actually* good for you. I've fallen head over heels for so many men but it always fizzles. Never fails. But I don't have the time in my busy life to try and reconcile relationships nor the time to be sad or angry. Like you, I want to live. Be happy. Make wonderful memories. Fall in love a hundred times. This thing we have, you and me, this is what I live for. The part in a relationship where you fall in love, fuck all day and laugh about everything. Then when it fades, we part ways and do it all over again with someone else. Maybe we rekindle every few years."

That was a lot for him to digest. He understood her point of view but didn't necessarily agree with it. Partly because he was beginning to imagine a life with her and she didn't seem to share that vision. But he also managed to catch her saying she was falling in love and normally love did things to people that they didn't imagine were possible. Maybe *this* love would change her views, maybe it wouldn't. Could it be that she just never found the right one? Or maybe she was heartbroken so badly that she gave up on true love? One thing was for sure, in this minimal amount of time they'd spent together, he was developing true feelings for Jasmine. He was not going to hold back now. She was a special woman and he was going to treat her in a manner she'd never been treated before. At that moment, being back home didn't matter as much as being here and doing everything he ever wanted to do. Travel the world aimlessly with a partner who wanted to do the exact same.

"So let me get this straight, you're saying you don't believe in true love or *the one*?"

"I believe in love. I choose to love who I want and how I want. Men, women, anyone. When I don't want to love anymore, I just turn it off. Like a switch." She flicked her finger in the air as if turning off a light switch while showing a lack of empathy. "It may sound harsh but it's what works for me."

Maybe she was right, maybe it could work for some. But Luis had always been a hopeless romantic and as much as he wanted to prove her theory wrong, he decided to play her game. Then he'd reel her into his. This woman was desperate for love and attention when he'd first joined her in Monaco. As much of a free bird as she portrayed herself to be, there was a noticeable emptiness she exuded. An emptiness he wanted to fill.

"Well since I apparently have an expiration date, tell the captain we're skipping Mallorca and going straight to Ibiza then. Let's cut the romantic shit and do some real living." He got up and went to the bathroom and returned with her tin. He prepared two lines of cocaine on the nightstand and they both took a hit before quickly undressing and making love, more passionately and aggressively than ever before.

CHAPTER 23

The old town of Ibiza was coming into view. A majestic castle sat atop the portion of the island they were approaching. The rest of the coastline was covered with white and pastel colored buildings that looked like they were stacked on top of one another. At the very bottom, boats and yachts squeezed in tightly to their respective parking spots where it wasn't uncommon for the regular folks to cross paths with worldwide superstars and celebrities. Luis' adrenaline was beginning to kick in. He'd been there once before and was very familiar with the vibrant and alternative lifestyle that it was known for. It was pure hedonism for the masses that flocked the island during the summer months, to escape reality and indulge in everything from sex to drugs, with a backdrop of endless luxury and bass-thumping music. Luis was just backpacking Europe on his way through Ibiza his first time and on a limited budget. Although he had an unforgettable experience, it was going to be nowhere near in comparison to this time around. He was a multi-millionaire, joined by another multi-millionaire. The possibilities were endless.

"This place gives me chills. I've got quite the memories here," Luis said to Jasmine as he stared at the coastline. He'd made lifelong friends from Australia there and they kept tabs on each other all these years later through social media.

"I can bet you haven't done Ibiza like I do Ibiza," she challenged him.

"Oh, it's on!" he accepted ecstatically.

"You see, because of *my* connections, I've arranged a nice suite for us in Ushuaia and Mo just happened to loan me the keys to his car that should be waiting for us at the marina." She dangled a key in front of him to see if he'd recognized the emblem. It had a backwards E connected to a B.

"Is that a—" he asked with his mouth wide open. She handed him the key. "A Bugatti?!"

"Bugatti Veyron. Only one on the island."

"Holy shit, I think I love you!" he jokingly confessed as he hugged her and lifted her up off the ground before spinning her a few times. "You still sure you don't believe in true love?"

She shrugged and gave him a peck on the lips.

"How about a 'pick me up' before we dock?" Luis suggested.

"You read my mind."

"Let's take the long way around, make a left here," Jasmine told Luis as he downshifted gears in the Bugatti and slammed the gas. The 1000+ horsepowers of the machine created enough g-force to press them deep into their seats as he let out a loud yell from the rush of excitement. The late afternoon weather was perfection without a cloud in the sky. Jasmine raised her hands high in the air and looked up at her fingers twirling in the wind. Luis watched her and admired her for just a bit. She looked as happy as he had ever seen her and he still couldn't fathom how she didn't believe it was possible to find a partner to create lasting memories with. They were creating those right now. He imagined them doing this very thing from one country to the next. She could quit everything, just as he had. If there was ever a monetary number to leave everything behind and ride off into the sunset, like they'd talked about at work long ago, he'd surpassed it. By a lot. And who knew how much her wealth would add to it.

They finally pulled up to the hotel where the valet attendant made sure to clear everyone out of the way, as the multi-million dollar car approached with a menacing rumble. He waved him over to where only a select number of cars were allowed to park and guided them in. "Welcome to Ushuaia!

Luis and Jasmine, I assume?"

Luis stepped out of the car and shook the man's hand with a generous tip and gave him the key. "Take good care of her."

A moment later they were approached by a young Spanish lady in professional attire holding a leather notebook. "Hola! Mr. and Mrs. Diaz, my name is Natalia and I will be your concierge for the duration of your stay. Right this way." They looked at each other and laughed. Instead of correcting her, Luis wrapped his arm over Jasmine's shoulder and pulled her closer to him.

"Let's just go with it," he whispered to her and she smiled.

"As our very VIP guests, we made sure to place you in our nicest suite available. Here you'll have a marvelous view of the beach and if you look this way, you can also see the music stage. Martin Garrix just took the stage, and tomorrow night we will have Dmitri Vegas and Like Mike."

"Hell yea!" Luis exclaimed like a little kid. He was a big fan of both.

They walked into the suite, which left Luis speechless. The room screamed 'rock-star lifestyle' with massive panoramic windows from one end to the other overlooking the sea. It was decorated in purple velvet and black furniture throughout the multiple rooms. Mirrors hung everywhere, including the ceilings. *Nice touch*, he thought to himself just as every guy surely did when they saw those mirrors. To the right was a fully stocked bar and a fridge that glittered in gold with all of the champagne it was keeping at the perfect temperature. The suite also included a private terrace with sun beds and a Jacuzzi overlooking the coastline and the sea. Looking to the left from the terrace, you could see Martin Garrix on stage with all sorts of lights and pyrotechnics dancing in sync to the music. The crowd was packed with people from every corner of the world. He remembered being down there in the same crowd one summer, watching Swedish House Mafia and feeling his whole life changing. He was having that same feeling again. But this time, he was looking from high above the crowd, in a suite aptly named 'I'm On Top Of The World.'

"This place has three jacuzzis, it is perfection!" Jasmine said excitedly.

"I'm looking at that champagne fridge over there. Would you like a glass or a whole bottle?" Luis asked sarcastically.

"I'll take a glass for now," she laughed.

"Lightweight."

"If there's *anything* you need while you stay with us, just shoot me a text and we'll have it right over. Enjoy your stay with us at Ushuaia," Natalia smiled at Luis, handed him a card and dismissed herself.

After pouring Jasmine a glass and helping himself to the rest of the bottle, they headed over to the balcony overlooking the sea and the stage. "You've outdone yourself already. I give up, you win," Luis conceded. "This is incredible. No way you can top this."

"I've actually got a treat for you tomorrow," she reached up and kissed him again, with her lips wet, tasting of champagne. He didn't want to ask, he loved being surprised.

"Guess I'll have to find a way to make it up to you then. For this, for everything."

"A girl likes to be surprised from time to time, too, you know," she walked away and looked back at him before heading back inside. She grabbed her phone, typed a few things, smiled and threw herself back on the oversized plush bed.

He walked over to join her. "So this is what you do, huh? I'm becoming quite fond of your lifestyle."

"I take pride in it. I've worked and sacrificed many things to be able to do anything I want. That's something a lot of people don't understand."

"Oh I understand fully, and admire it more than you know. You're like my spirit animal. A very *sexy* one," he made a growling face and she meowed back.

"I know you do. I see a lot of similarities in you and that's why we match so well. Once you've surpassed a certain amount of wealth, money just doesn't hold the same value. Time and experiences do. Do you think we would've ever met if it wasn't for the money we have?"

Luis shook his head, realizing she was right. But also realizing how much different his life would've been had he not hit the lottery.

"That's what I mean. I've just developed myself into a person who'd spend anything on an experience that brings me joy and happiness. I make my time count. We're only here for a short ride, why waste it?" She was speaking his language. And not just speaking it, she was putting it into existence. Jasmine rolled over and sat on top of him and kissed him intensely. Then she hopped off and began dancing on the bed to the music coming from outside. He just smiled and marveled at her as he took another swig of the champagne bottle.

Luis knew he'd have to do something big to impress a woman who was so good at impressing herself. A woman who not only had everything, but could do anything. He knew it'd be near impossible to be this lucky again and meet another like-minded soul. And not because there weren't any others out there, but for them to be interested in him the way that she was, just seemed unfeasible. He struck gold again and he wanted to keep this treasure to himself this time around. He was convinced he needed to go big, and what is every girl's best friend? *Diamonds*. Lots of them.

With the help of the concierge, he'd managed to contact a world renowned jeweler who specialized in customizing some of the most extravagant jewelry pieces for the elite. Although it would take him a few weeks to make what he requested, he assured Luis that he'd be able to get it to him promptly, no matter where in the world he was located. It was the biggest purchase he'd made since hitting the lottery, with the figure floating somewhere between three and four million. The exact price would be determined upon completion, but the price tag was meaningless to him. She was everything to him.

CHAPTER 24

The next day they woke up to the room shaking from the bass outside. It was 1 PM, and the resident DJ was beginning his routine of melodic trance music in order to revive the crowd that had been partying until just a few hours ago. A short nap, a few substances and you better be ready to do it all over again. If not, the place just isn't for you because in Ibiza, the party never stops. To keep with the times and tradition, Luis brushed his teeth and prepared four lines for himself and Jasmine. He laid in bed next to her and placed the small mirror between them and handed her the rolled euro note. "Breakfast in bed," he joked. She took two hits per nostril and he looked at her in shock.

"Gonna need it today, we're in Ibiza baby," she said as she squeezed her nose and squinted her eyes. She shook her head and took a deep breath. "Your turn."

She popped up and went to the bathroom to fix him a line, except this one was shaped as a heart.

"For you, my love," she said in her best damsel voice and placed it next to him. He took the euro note and split the heart between each one of his nostrils. And just like that, they were up and ready to seize the day. A mere four hours after they had gotten back to their suite after partying the night away at Privilege.

It was the biggest nightclub in the world and quite a sight to see. The DJ on the main dance floor stood atop her island shaped booth that gave the illusion she floating in water as thousands of people were put under her spell. The power she had was all in her fingertips. She could alter the mood of every person in the room by the turn of a knob, whether she wanted them to jump, dance or feel tremendous amounts of love. She had the right track for it all.

As Luis and Jasmine reveled amongst the crowd, there was a moment in which they locked eyes and kissed for what was at least a minute or more without a care of who was around. She jumped up on him and he held her up as if she were weightless. She then whispered something to him but he couldn't quite make out what it was because of the deafening music but he had a feeling that she whispered, "I love you." He tried to get her to say it again but she shied away and kissed him instead. Was it the ecstasy they had taken that made her feel this way? Or could it be that she was having a change of heart? He preferred the latter. She jumped off him and started dancing rhythmically to the beat with her eyes closed as if she were all alone in the club. The elevated amounts of serotonin in his brain made him imagine all sorts of things. One being the fact that he was falling in love with this woman and he wanted to yell it at the top of his lungs. Sure it wasn't *true* love, but it was love. He thought he was crazy, they'd only spent a few weeks together. They still didn't know too much about each other, but he was certain, that he knew enough. *We only live once right? Don't waste your time here Luis*, he kept thinking to himself.

"I love you, too!" he yelled in her direction. She kept dancing but put her hand up to her ear as if she couldn't hear him. He yelled again, "I fucking love you!" No way she hadn't heard him that time. Everyone around looked at them and stared in awe. She put on a sultry smile and pointed at him to come over.

"I know," she mouthed and then told him to his ear, but much louder this time, "I fucking love you, too." The crowd closed in on them, forming a circle and jumped up and down with them in celebration. After that, the night had been a blur, in a similar way as it had been in the Bahamas. He remembered them tagging along with some of those people they had met on the dance floor and hopping from club to club until a taxi brought them back to the entrance of the Ushuaia hotel well after the sun had risen.

Currently, he had only kept one thing from her and that was the fact that he'd become rich by hitting the lottery, unless he'd unknowingly confessed while inebriated as had been a recurring theme. He wasn't sure why but admitting that to such a successful person seemed a bit embarrassing, because he hadn't actually worked or made sacrifices to earn the money. He'd just played a two dollar game and hit a one in fourteen million chance. He got lucky, but he always felt like he got lucky. Now his luck had gotten her and he was itching to let her know so he could stop carrying that secret. He figured she could help him move his funds overseas with her connections, that way it could not only stay safe, but it could begin to grow via investments.

"How about we take a spin in the Bugatti and explore the island a bit. No way in hell I'm letting that thing sit in valet the whole time we have it," Luis picked up the key and held it close to his heart.

"I know of a nice place on the other side of the island in Sant Antoni. A place I haven't been to since my uni days. I hear it's still open," Jasmine replied enthusiastically.

After taking the long way around and exploring the many other sights Ibiza had to offer, they arrived at Cafe Del Mar. A restaurant that had apparently been around since 1980 and frequented by tourists and famous people alike. It wasn't a grand restaurant, but that was part of its allure. Most of the seating was outdoors, covered by massive white sunshades that ran from one end to the other. It was conveniently located facing west on the water and made for an incredible place to catch a sunset before indulging in sinful activities later in the evening. The hostess showed them to their table as they took in the views and atmosphere.

"So last night was fun, huh?" Luis broke the ice, wondering if she'd remembered their whole teenage love affair moment. They hadn't become awkward since waking up, like one would normally expect after saying something they didn't mean or something they'd regret later. Instead, they kept up their routine as usual. Sex, drugs, then explore.

"Yeah that felt like a movie, didn't it?" She sipped her water as she chuckled and blushed in embarrassment. It'd been the first time he'd seen her like that and he enjoyed it. He felt like he was reeling her in. "I know we were under some heavy influence of ecstasy, but I don't take back anything I ever say. And I know what I said."

"What'd you say then? I'm having a hard time remembering," he joked back hoping to hear those three words again.

"I said, I love you."

"Oh yeah, that's what it was!" He was elated to hear it again and also at the fact that he'd been able to change her views on love.

"But remember what I told you before. This could end next week, next month or in a couple of years, don't say I didn't warn you."

"We'll see about that," Luis replied defiantly.

The server took their order and brought them a bottle of Prosecco as they recapped the last few weeks together and spoke about where they could go next. Luis spoke of going to Italy and eating their way through all of the regions of the country, from Lake Como all the way down to Sicily. Something he'd be doing currently with his family if he hadn't been given the boot by his wife. Jasmine said she'd love to take him to Singapore and show him why it's one of her favorite places in the world before jetting off to Bali for some more rest and relaxation.

"So Jas…I've got something I've been wanting

to tell you. I can probably use some of your help as well," Luis finally decided to tell her his secret. She listened attentively. "You know how I told you in the Bahamas that I made my fortune by investing in crypto pretty early on, right?"

"Yes, I remember," she responded curiously.

"Well, to be honest, that was a backstory me and the guys had created for the trip. I guess I just sort of ran with it and never told you how I really got my money."

"Well why would you think I cared? It's your money."

"I didn't think you would and I guess it didn't really ever matter until now. The reason being that whether or not you and me end up together for the foreseeable future, I need help moving my assets overseas. I can't have my wife getting access to my cut of the winnings. I left her half, I think that's fair enough."

"Winnings?" she asked.

"Yeah, the lottery. I won 684 million dollars and took a lump sum payment of around four hundred million."

Her jaw dropped. "Oh my. That's amazing! You're quite the lucky man!"

"Well it hasn't been all luck since then, but it did lead me here. And after thinking about it these last few weeks, I think I'm ready to leave that life behind. I really admire your free-spirited views and to have all of this money and needing permission or approval to do what I want to do—" he paused. "That is not how I want to live. I wanna fall in love a hundred times like you do. I want to see the world on my own terms and even use some of that money to help people and maybe even make an impact environmentally. There's just so much I wanna do and I can't do it if I go back home. Every time I think of going back there to reconcile with my wife, it just doesn't sound appealing anymore."

"I sympathize with you, Luis. Because I've been in your shoes before, until I decided I was going to be the one to dictate how my life was going to be. I left everything in the past and charted my own path, one that also led me here." She pulled down her sunglasses and looked at him in the eyes. "And believe me when I tell you, this is exactly where I want to be."

He could see the sincerity in her eyes and he'd already decided on how he was going to chart his own path just as she did. He hadn't just been enamored by her, he was inspired.

"So, I heard you mention back in Monaco that you had a financial advisor that handles your money. Any chance he could help me transfer about two hundred million overseas and manage it?"

"I don't see why not. He's worked miracles for me before. He's actually based in Geneva, but he can meet us anywhere if I arranged for him to do so."

"I wouldn't mind a trip to Geneva. Matter of fact, I'd love to go there." He was very enthusiastic about it because Switzerland was a place he'd always dreamed of going to. It was another trip he'd planned to take the kids on so they could eat endless amounts of chocolate and fondue. The thought of it saddened him though, but he held on to the hope that he would have the opportunity to take them there someday.

Luis had also seen what the country could offer to its more prestigious visitors and the idea of that lifted him back up. He pictured himself walking around the shopping district in Geneva and buying custom watches from Hublot, Audemars, Rolex and all those other brands he'd heard about in rap songs. Maybe he'd even buy a condo in the city to make it his home base in Europe as he made business deals across the globe. "Book the jet for tomorrow, Jas. And *please* let me pay this time."

"Okay, I'll text him and see how soon he can meet us." She typed a few messages on her phone and placed it back on the table face down while Luis poured some more Prosecco.

"Cheers to the next leg of our adventure," he raised his glass towards Jasmine.

"Cheers, my love," she clinked her glass with his and they each took a sip as they stared out over the Mediterranean waters. This was the good life.

CHAPTER 25

Back at the hotel, Luis felt so relieved having told Jasmine the last secret he held. Her reaction was better than he'd expected, as usual, and everything he felt so insecure about just faded away. She couldn't have been more excited for him and even laughed at him for thinking he was a loser because he'd won the money instead of earning it. She admitted she would've loved to have won the lottery instead of dealing with all the shit she'd had to deal with for the last decade in order to get to where she was now. He was very appreciative of her because of how she made him feel. Not superior, not lesser, but a true equal. They were both in this together. Both contributing to the decisions they made, never hassling over anything or passing any judgement. The way it was supposed to be.

"I'm pretty pumped to see Dmitri Vegas and Like Mike tonight, you heard of them?" Luis asked while shaving in the bathroom and dancing to the music coming from outside.

"Actually, I may or may not have had a thing with one of them before," she admitted as she snorted a line of coke from the bathroom counter next to him.

"No way! Like Mike?" He stepped back and looked at her amused and in disbelief.

"Nope. The quiet one, Dmitri," she covered her mouth as if she'd let something bad slip.

"Wow! Look at you!" he replied. "Any other famous people I should know about?"

She nodded her head. He wasn't even jealous. On the contrary, he was quite impressed. He was hooking up with a woman who not only associated with some very famous people but had also apparently been in bed with a few of them. Sex was such a private thing back in the states, but almost everywhere else he'd traveled to, people spoke about it so openly and freely. He knew he'd have to adapt if this was going to be his new life.

"Maybe one day I'll tell you some more stories," she said as she danced in her underwear behind him.

"Can't wait to hear them…I guess," he laughed and continued to get ready for the party.

As the evening progressed, they continued to sync on all levels as if they'd been dating for years. He'd pour the perfect cocktail for the appropriate time, she'd order the finest selection of foods through room service. Every few hours like clockwork, they'd alternate on who was preparing the next fix. They laughed, joked and day-dreamt together after having sex time and time again in every corner of the suite.

Luis knew this exact lifestyle wouldn't be a sustainable one, but they were on vacation, and while he was Ibiza, he was going to indulge in *anything* that made him feel good. He tried to imagine what the future would be like, after the partying and traveling. But it just gave him a headache and anxiety, so he decided to stop thinking about it and returned to the present, as Jasmine approached him with her hair pulled up, wearing a dazzling golden bikini top with a short black bikini cover. She walked towards him with her best model strut, placing one red-bottomed stiletto in front of the next and swinging her hips side to side. Then she spun and fell back into Luis' arms without spilling a drop of champagne from the glass she held on the opposite hand. He leaned over and kissed her.

"Ready?" she asked as she gazed up into his eyes.

"Always," he replied confidently as she placed a pill on her tongue and stuck it out for Luis to make a move, which he immediately did.

It was their last night in Ibiza and the atmosphere at the poolside stage in Ushuaia was electric. The sun had just set and the laser and light show was more vivid than ever. Luis and Jasmine made their way to the middle of the crowd centered on the stage, grabbing each other's hands tightly, as if letting go would separate them for an eternity. Dmitri Vegas and Like Mike were deep into their music set and had complete control over the crowd. They were all so lost in the music, they seemed to have forgotten phones existed as you couldn't find anyone recording the performance as had been customary these days. Everyone pumped their hands in the air and shuffled to the beat as the effects of the drugs and alcohol took hold over their bodies. Love was in the air once again as Luis started peaking. He wrapped his arms around Jasmine and kissed the side of her head as they watched the show intensify. *I love this*, he thought to himself. *This is the fucking life.*

After a few songs, he noticed Jasmine's phone light up and she stopped dancing. She glanced at the incoming message and then looked around the crowd. A few seconds later, she leaned up and told him, "I'll be right back. Stay here, babe." He nodded back reluctantly, not wanting to let her go. He hoped it wasn't another guy from her past or maybe a business call that would ruin their last night in paradise. For a second, he thought maybe the DJ had spotted her in the crowd and asked one of his guys to come and get her. The overwhelming love he was feeling just a minute ago turned into an inner monologue of insecurity and jealousy. *Why didn't I follow her? What if she's not safe? What if she leaves me?*

He decided not to wait for her and weaved his way through the crowd in the direction she had taken off, but with the hundreds of people jam packed from one side of the venue to the other, there was no way he'd be able to find her quickly.

"Excuse me...sorry...*con permiso*...thank you," he said as he gently pushed his way through people who had their eyes locked straight at the stage with no awareness as to what may be happening in their immediate surroundings. He got stuck behind a woman with huge natural curls staring down at her phone and tapped her shoulder to try to get by. She turned around and was overcome by a sense of relief.

"Oh my god, finally!" she excitedly wrapped her arms around Luis.

"Maya? What are you doing here?" he was in shock to have seen her here in Ibiza after their brief connection aboard his yacht party in Bahamas. She looked finer than ever and for a moment he contemplated leaving it all behind and setting off with her instead, but he remembered her saying 'she wasn't one of those girls' so he was better off not ruining the good thing he had going. But still, what the hell was she doing in Ibiza?

"I guess Jasmine didn't tell you," she smiled.

"You two are friends?" he asked as if he hadn't known from creeping on her Instagram a few weeks back.

"I've known Jasmine for ages! I was in town for a shoot and she invited me to come hang with you guys," she replied. "I'm so happy to see you again!"

"Yeah, me too. I heard you left kinda suddenly from the yacht party, did something happen?"

"Oh no, I just had to attend to a matter my stupid agent blew out of proportion," she said dismissively.

"I hate when that happens," he joked back. "Hey, I know it's random, but did you ever mention to Jasmine that I won the—" he was interrupted by Jasmine who had made her way back to them.

"You found each other!" She hugged Maya tightly.

"Yeah, I just bumped in to her! I remembered her from my party. Had no clue you two were friends."

"Actually, we're a bit more than friends,"

Jasmine replied promiscuously as she placed a pill on her tongue again. But this time it was for Maya as their mouths slowly came together until their lips were locked.

Luis couldn't believe what he was seeing. He found himself putting both hands on his head with his mouth agape in disbelief before quickly realizing he needed to play it cool and not act so shocked and desperate. A few seconds later, Jasmine placed another pill on the tip of Maya's tongue and looked at Luis, motioning him towards her. Maya bit her lip and stared at him, inviting him in, so he reached for the back of her neck and tangled his fingers in her curls as their lips pressed together.

What. The. Fuck. I am the luckiest man alive.

Jasmine grabbed them both by the hands and made her way towards the room. "Should we continue this party upstairs?" Nobody opposed.

They laughed and joked all the way back to the room, kissing and feeling up on each other the whole way up. The MDMA in their bloodstream facilitated those actions. Upon entering the room, they opened all the windows and curtains so the lights and sounds from outside could make their way in. As the girls danced like nobody was watching, Luis went to the bathroom mirror to check on himself.

"Don't fuck this up! You can do this! You're the man!" He slapped himself a few times in the face, pumping himself up to what was sure to be the most memorable night of his life. He splashed a little water on his face before going back out. The suite was dark except for the lights penetrating the windows and the champagne fridge glowing by the bar. He went in and grabbed a bottle at random and popped it open, not choosing to bring any glasses along. It was his new favorite way of drinking champagne.

Luis looked around for the ladies but couldn't hear anything over the music that was blaring from outside, so he continued to walk around the suite. Then he saw a piece of clothing being tossed in the air by the patio. He proceeded in that direction. "Anyone care for some champ—" He paused when he crossed the threshold to the patio as he saw Jasmine sitting on top of Maya removing her bra and tossing it to the side.

"You can sit over there and watch, mister. " Jasmine directed Luis to a chair near the bed while Maya reached up for Jasmine aggressively for having taken her attention off of her, even if only for a second. He sat obediently.

Still in a state of euphoria, Luis had a hard time containing himself. He wanted to join but not ruin the mood. He thought about undressing and pleasuring himself, but that could seem weird. He considered using more drugs, but he was sure he'd had enough in his system. He then talked himself into staying put and enjoying the show while he sipped on his bottle casually. After a few minutes, Jasmine got off of Maya and walked over to Luis. "Your turn," she motioned him to Maya for the second time that night. He briefly wondered if it was a trap until Jasmine reassured him, "This was the treat I promised you, go on." He pulled his shirt off and threw it to the side and walked towards Maya who was laying in bed naked signaling him towards her. *Game time.*

CHAPTER 26

Luis woke up the next morning in bed lying on his back with Jasmine sleeping under one arm and Maya under the other. It wasn't a dream. This was his new reality. Nothing was far fetched anymore. If he wanted it, he could have it. And with Jasmine at his side, who knew what else life would bring his way because so far it'd been nothing but pleasurable moments. The sunlight slowly crept into the dark room that was littered with bottles, undergarments, bed sheets and pillows strewn across the floor. Jasmine opened her eyes and saw Luis staring down at her. "I am worn out," she chuckled and slid her hand across her face. "I hope you didn't mind me inviting her last night. I mean look at her. Lesbian or not, who could resist such a beautiful human being?" Jasmine reached over Luis and caressed Maya's face as she slowly opened her eyes and smiled back at the compliment.

"Mmm," Maya closed her eyes again and moaned as she felt Jasmine's gentle touch on her cheek.

Luis kept quiet and observed Maya's peacefulness, leading him to believe that he had done enough to perhaps warrant a second rendezvous in the future. Jasmine rolled out of bed and looked across the floor for her underwear before deciding to give up and grabbing a robe from the closet instead.

"Good morning," Luis turned to Maya as he heard the shower start to run in the bathroom.

"It is," she replied and nudged herself closer to him. He smelled some sort of coconut product in her hair which he couldn't get enough of and took another whiff.

"Hey, I tried asking you last night but it was a bit loud out there. Did you ever happen to mention to Jasmine what we discussed on the yacht? About me hitting the lottery?"

"I didn't even know you were a thing until she texted me last night. You haven't told her?" she asked.

"Well I did, but just recently. I dunno. I just get in my head sometimes."

He trusted Jasmine but from the conversation Maya and him had the first time they met, he felt at ease confiding in her as well. She seemed pure and innocent. Less influenced by money and opulence. Maybe in a different scenario, he'd have chosen

Maya over Jasmine but what he had with Jasmine was much more than he could have ever imagined. Regardless, he still ended up getting Maya as an added bonus. It was hard to complain.

She placed her soft hand on his cheek and locked eyes with him. "You have nothing to worry about, Luis." She put her hand on his heart and then pointed at his temple. "Just listen to your heart and your mind and everything will be just fine." She kissed him on the forehead, rolled out of bed and walked to the bathroom. He stared at her the whole way until she was out of sight.

Luis stared up at the roof and looked back at the reflection in the mirror he'd forgotten was there. There he was, laying all alone in bed after experiencing just about every man's fantasy. He was impressed with the man in the mirror because he held his own with the two more experienced ladies. But a sense of loneliness washed over him when he continued to stare at himself. Normally his kids would be jumping in bed with him and his wife around this time. He pictured them arguing with each other as to who got to lay down on what side and who's turn it was to pick the morning cartoons. A smile came to his face as he closed his eyes and he wondered what they were doing right now. One thing he couldn't take away from Krystal was how good of a mother she was and he knew she'd be doing everything possible to make sure the kids were happy throughout the time they were separated. But the real question was whether this would be a separation or a split. He'd done everything to merit divorce papers from her. From being unfaithful, to taking half of their prize money, bringing drugs into their home and exposing the kids to it. It would take an incredibly forgiving person to accept someone again after all of that.

Luis decided he wouldn't close that door completely but he wasn't ready to peek through it again for some time to come. At the moment, he was infatuated with Jasmine, even more so after she brought Maya along. What were the odds this could happen to someone like him? Surely, it was drastically lower than hitting the lottery, but still pretty high. He was convinced it was the tremendous amount of luck that had followed him since birth. That's why he was always so optimistic. Everything always worked out for him in the end.

He decided to finally roll out of bed and walked to the bathroom where he heard the ladies chatting and giggling. They were standing there side by side above each of their own vanities as they applied their makeup. Jasmine looked over at him and said, "Jet will be ready in about two hours.

They'll fly us straight to Geneva."

"Us as in *us* three?" He secretly hoped Maya stuck around for a while longer, if not indefinitely.

"I wish I could but I've got to stay behind for a photo shoot tonight," she pouted in his direction through the mirror. "But I'm sure we'll do this again sometime soon." She winked at Jasmine.

"We can never go more than a month without seeing each other," Jasmine blew a kiss back.

That put a smile on Luis' face. Not only would he be seeing Maya again, but it could be a monthly occurrence. He chose not to express his excitement aloud, just in case.

"Don't worry, Luis. I'm not jealous," Jasmine turned around and looked at Luis, knowing very well what was in his mind. She already knew how to read him. *Not good*, he thought.

A few hours later, the three of them said their goodbyes and Luis and Jasmine were off to the airport, cruising in the Bugatti one the last time. As Luis drove, he kept quiet, deep in thought. The last few weeks had been such a whirlwind. He'd been going full speed since he landed in Europe and ironically he was driving one of the world's fastest cars. Jasmine noticed his quiet demeanor and opted not to say anything, but she reached out for his hand, which he grabbed and squeezed tightly. The squeeze represented so much without the need to say any words. Nonverbally it translated to, *I chose you. I trust you. No looking back. It's just us now.* She seemed to understand him when she squeezed back and looked into his eyes, gently nodding her head in agreement as if to say, *I'm with you.* That was the assurance he was searching for. He gripped the steering wheel tightly and pressed down hard on the gas. Full speed ahead.

CHAPTER 27

As the private jet made its descent into Geneva, Luis marveled out at the snowcapped Swiss Alps after having napped for most of the flight. This part of the flight was always his favorite. Looking out the window and seeing the destination and all of its surroundings come into view and wondering how people across the world shared so many commonalities and differences at the same time. But now, he was seeing the world through a different lens. The wealth was changing him and he was aware of it. Instead of being excited about getting lost in the less touristy parts of town, he craved the upscale experiences where he would be catered to rather than dealing with the inconveniences annoying tourists and angered locals brought along.

He looked down at Jasmine who was sound asleep with her head on his shoulder. It reminded him of when his wife would do the same as they traveled the world together. Both equally exhausted from their trips but still planning ahead to their next one. But never in a million years did he imagine having a different woman at his side. Krystal had been everything to him, and still was, but he couldn't go back and change the series of unfortunate events that led him to run astray. After Jasmine made it clear that this wouldn't be a forever thing, he initially took that as a challenge to convince her otherwise, but as time lapsed, he'd begun to wonder if maybe that was a sign for him to return home once their whirlwind romance expired. He could work on winning his wife back. He'd have to confess everything, otherwise it would eat him alive for the rest of his years. Then he'd have to vow to never speak or even look at another woman that walked past. Something he wouldn't have a problem doing *if* she were to take him back. One thing was becoming clear to him, he missed her.

His deep thoughts were interrupted by the pilot announcing that they'd touch down in about half an hour. Jasmine looked up at Luis and grabbed his arm tight as he brought her in closer. He knew he was making a mistake being with her, but over and over again, it felt like it was a mistake that was worth committing. He'd learn from this someday and blossom into a better man. The fact that he still had total control over everything he'd been doing thus far, assured him of that.

"I love it here. Sometimes I'll come here just to escape and rent a cabin with a hot tub and drink loads of wine," Jasmine said in a very calming tone as if she was daydreaming the scene. It sounded inviting to Luis because he had previously researched an itinerary that would take his family from the busy city of Zurich, through the lakes of Interlaken and all the way down to the countryside of Lauterbrunnen. Maybe he'd bring up the idea for them to go there next after enduring a drug-fueled couple of weeks that had them clinging onto each other for strength. He heard a phone buzz repeatedly and tapped his pocket. Not his phone.

"Is that yours?" he asked.

She reached in her bag to grab the phone and unlocked it. He could see the stress wash over her face as she placed the phone down on the tray and tilted her head back in revulsion. "Shit hit the fan at work in Nice and I have to go back," she uttered in disappointment.

"Let's just have the pilot take us now then. The transfer can wait," he said to try to ease her obvious discontent.

"No, no, no. *They* can wait. I sure pay them enough to solve these kinds of problems and they'll have to do without me until tomorrow. I'll fly out after we finish with your appointment. Besides, I need the day to recover from all this partying, you've got me running around like I'm in my twenties again," she laughed. Her mood brightened after the brief set back.

"Don't get me started on who's responsible for all the peer pressuring these last few weeks!" He poked at the tip of her nose and tilted her head, before kissing her again. "Listen, if you need to attend to business alone, I can stick around here for a while. I'll understand."

"You sure you don't want to see me tell a bunch of old perverts how I need their money to save the planet their great grandchildren will be living in?" she said sarcastically as if she'd done the same thing an infinite amount of times. That was her gift. The allure she possessed made men do things they wouldn't otherwise agree to. Especially cutting nine figure checks in order to impress her for a cause they'd never in their lives cared for until she entered the room. "You know what, it'd probably be better. I wouldn't want to bore you. We can take a few days apart and then meet up again next week?"

"Oh no, is this the part where you're dumping me?!" He joked and put his hand on his heart as if she'd torn it into a thousand pieces. They laughed hysterically before catching their breath again.

"My goodness, Luis," she paused and shook

her head. "I haven't got enough of you yet actually. As a matter of fact, next week the dragon boat races are being held in my hometown of Macau. I grew up going to them every year with my family but since my parents are no longer around, my brother and I still try to keep the tradition alive. Maybe you'll accompany me this year?"

Luis felt honored. Being let in to a family tradition, in China? And meeting her brother? He wasn't sure what her intentions would be but going to experience dragon boat races in the Las Vegas of Asia didn't sound like an opportunity he'd pass up. If things didn't go well or if the romance fizzled, he would start formulating a plan to make it back home.

"I accept. I'd love to go to China with you and watch *dragons* race," he said with a straight face as she burst into laughter and tears once again.

The VIP treatment that Jasmine set up again was top notch. Decked out sprinter vans were the new limousines as they were much more comfortable, and the extra room allowed for some pretty extravagant customizations. They sat back and indulged in a bottle of Sauvignon Blanc made from Swiss *chasselas*, or grapes, and assorted cheeses and chocolates from local shops, while the driver took the scenic route around Geneva at Luis' request. The old architecture in European cities always made Luis think back to the countless generations who roamed the same streets. Every generation dealing with a different set of social standards and problems. Sometimes he wondered how his generation fared in comparison to past and future ones. The world seemed to have become more materialistic as he aged but it was something he never related to, until now. It's one thing having money and affording nice things, it's another not having the money and still buying nice things to try and keep up with the Joneses.

Having nearly two hundred million dollars to his name and having spent very little of it, confirmed what he was always so sure of. He could properly manage his money in order to make it last a lifetime without blowing it all like your typical lottery winner that went bankrupt a few years after hitting. Now with a few investments, he was sure he'd see six figure returns monthly, if not weekly. Especially if he entered the crypto space. He thought about how unfair all of it really seemed to the lower-income class, who would never get the opportunity to invest in anything because they couldn't afford to buy stocks in companies. The system was rigged for the rich and now he was able to see why. Plain and simple, the fact remained that it takes money to make money, and he had a whole lot of it.

After settling in to their new villa overlooking Lake Geneva, they continued to sample different wines from the region as the cool, crisp air funneled its way from the mountains to the lake and onto their rooftop patio. Their breaths were deeper. Their state, calmer. They were masters at blending in to their surroundings, no matter what the scene. There was no need for drugs in a place like this. Just some wine, good company and sit back and enjoy the moment.

"So about tomorrow," Luis broke the silence they had enjoyed while the sun began to hide itself behind the mountain range. "I'm transferring a pretty large amount of money. Is all this stuff legal?"

"Of course it is. Unless you commit some pretty serious crimes with your money, your privacy will be impenetrable by choosing to go with a Swiss account. Nobody will be able to come collect your half of the lottery earnings. Not even your wife. And not just that but they have laws to where if anything ever happens to your money, you will be fully compensated. It's why the wealthiest park their money here."

"And your financial advisor? I'm assuming you trust him managing your money while you're out and about?" he asked to try and erase some lingering doubts he was having.

"He's a close family friend that has been doing this his whole life. He's got an MBA from Oxford and was wise enough to get ahead of the crypto boom and I've certainly reaped the benefits from it. I can have him show you some more detailed parts of my account so you can see for yourself," she insisted.

"Oh no, that's not necessary. I trust you. I'm just asking questions to cover the bases," he smiled at her and sipped from his glass. "So you're *rich*, rich, huh?" He laughed.

She shrugged and slipped a cheeky smile before finishing her glass of wine. "I can always have more," she joked light heartedly as she reached her glass out for Luis to top off.

CHAPTER 28

The next morning, Luis woke up in an upbeat mood even though he was about to make a decision that could have major implications on his future. He'd seen and read about the rich and shady individuals opening Swiss accounts, and here he was, playing the main character in his own thriller. He really was clueless as to what the near future would hold but that's what excited him most in life. The element of surprise and not knowing what was next, because in reality, who really did? You can try and plan everything out but that doesn't guarantee you will see it through. He wasn't a planner because he believed that people who planned extensively lacked the ability to readjust when a wrench was thrown their way. Which is exactly how life worked. You deal with matters as they come but you must always place yourself in a position to be ready for anything.

By securing his money overseas, he was taking control of his future. The ideal scenario in his mind would be to travel the world for the rest of the year with Jasmine, who had proven to have connections everywhere. Connections he was hoping to take advantage of. She'd treated him like a king since the very beginning and her selflessness made for an incredibly easy relationship. He hoped that after a bit of travel, he'd be able to go home and see the kids, whom he missed terribly. Then based on how his wife reacted, he would either continue on his path of 'soul searching' or begin his never-ending conquest of asking for forgiveness. The latter sounded like the tougher task but deep down it's the one he wished for.

Luis finally rose from the bed and saw Jasmine outside in the patio pacing back and forth on her phone. He felt her getting out of bed about an hour earlier, assuming she had to attend to her business matters. He could hear her yelling in a language he wasn't familiar with as she appeared frustrated and annoyed and made faces of desperation every time she paused to hear a response. After hanging up, she looked inside to see Luis standing there. Her facial expression went from *shoot me* to *save me*. "Sometimes I feel like I could just quit," she said, overwhelmed by the early morning stress.

"Then why don't you?" He teased her again and wrapped his arms around her waist, gently kissing her on the forehead.

"I'm addicted. As much as I hate it sometimes, I really do love it. It gives me a purpose, and what's a life without purpose?"

"You never thought of having kids?" he asked.

"I can barely take care of myself sometimes," she admitted, but quickly backtracked. "I mean, with all the traveling for work and such. I'd have to completely give up one life for the other and I don't think I want to do that. Doesn't appeal to me."

"Makes sense."

"We gotta get going soon. Your suit is hanging in the closet and I left you a little something in the bathroom," she smiled and kissed him again.

Initially, he thought she'd left him a line of coke on the sink as had been their tradition. He thought to himself there was no way he was about to consume drugs before going in to this meeting, *what was she thinking?* But when he got to the bathroom, he noticed a small dark wooden box by the sink. The top read 'Patek Philippe Geneve'. He opened the box to discover a gold rimmed watch with a black dial and a black leather band. Written on the inside of the box was a phrase that had become their 'go to.' *Love a hundred times*. He knew how expensive these watches were, so to say that he was surprised, was a mild understatement. He studied it carefully before Jasmine came in and took it out of the box and asked him to raise his hand. She wrapped it around his wrist and buckled it before stepping back to check him out.

"Look at that strapping fellow right there!" she complimented Luis, who was now posing with his watch, feeling his ego rise. He couldn't take his eyes off of it.

"You really didn't have to," he told Jasmine.

"When in Switzerland…" she responded. "Besides, I couldn't let you walk into a Swiss bank without looking the part."

"Good call. Thank you." He was ever grateful for her. "I mean it."

The driver from the day prior picked them up at 9:30 AM sharp for their 10 o'clock appointment. He imagined going into a grand bank that looked like it was built in the 19th century, but when they arrived at the location, it was a typical high rise glass building near the lake in the middle of Geneva's financial district. It was the first time Luis had seen Jasmine wearing anything other than a bikini or a dress, as she strutted along the sidewalk in her Alexander McQueen business suit, donning some large Gucci sunglasses. She was a fierce woman and walked with a confidence as if she owned the whole block. Luis kept up with her pace and tried to match her swagger. They entered the building and took the elevator up to the 6th floor.

"Banks are a bit less traditional here, I'm sure you noticed," she pointed out to Luis who nodded back. They exited the elevator and walked through a busy office where employees were finely manicured and groomed, dressed in their finest suits and Italian leather shoes. The room gave Luis sort of a Wall Street movie vibe but with much more class and sophistication. Jasmine led him to the back to an office door that read, *Leon Keller, MBA.* She knocked two times and walked in without waiting for a response from inside. Behind the desk sat a light-skinned black man with a shaved head and muscular build. Leon Keller, he presumed, a surprisingly much younger man than Luis had anticipated, although in this day and age, young men were advancing quite rapidly in these fields. Old men got left behind as social media and cryptocurrencies took off while they were reluctant to adapt.

Leon adjusted his tie and stood up to greet Jasmine with a hug and a kiss on the cheek. "Jas! You look gorgeous as ever, how are you?"

"I'm well, how's the family?"

"We're expecting another baby in a few weeks! Emma's belly is freaking huge! I'll send her your regards, I'm sure she'd love to have you over again after she gives birth."

"Oh my! Congrats! That would be splendid," she replied before quickly switching the subject. "Well this is my *very* good friend Luis. He's from America."

Luis reached for his hand but Leon came up closer and hugged him. "Sorry, any friend of Jasmine's is a friend of mine, and I'm a hugger. It's a pleasure to meet you, Luis from America. I'm Leon, from France by way of Nigeria."

"The pleasure is all mine," Luis insisted.

Leon sat back down behind the desk and started typing into his computer, which was all being reflected on a large monitor on the wall. Luis and Jasmine took a seat. Before he opened any sensitive information, he looked over at Luis seeking approval to do so in front of Jasmine and Luis waved him ahead to continue.

"Okay so with all of the details you sent me a couple days ago, I was able to contact your financial institution back in America and do the necessary leg work to start an account here. It wasn't easy, but I make things happen. That's why they pay me the *big bucks* as you say in America. I see here you have approximately two hundred million USD. What'd you do, hit the lottery or something?" he joked.

"Actually yeah," Luis admitted as Leon fell back in his chair.

"No way, really?!"

Luis nodded his head.

"Wow, this is a first. Congratulations! Anyways, my guess is that you're not looking for anything too risky because the last thing you want to do is see your money taking million dollar swings on a weekly basis." Luis nodded in agreement and Leon continued. "This is what I can do for you. I offer several financial plans, but for you my friend, I'm recommending the Leon Special. Same plan as what my beloved friend Jas is under. With your amount of wealth, we have to cover all the necessary bases first. Estate planning, trusts, wills, living wills, all of that. Power of attorneys. We can do that now or later on if you'd like. You can sit here and tell me about your financial goals but it's evident what you're looking for. You don't want your money to disappear. Instead you'd like more money to appear, make your money work for you. Well, I'm your magician. I make money grow on trees, wallets, computers, phones, clouds. The ones in the sky and the one you keep your dirty photos in, you follow?" He paused his pitch and waited for another nod from Luis.

"Okay then, here in Switzerland, 35% of your accrued interest year over year will be taxed. But we're going to evade all of that. How? Charities. You seem like a good man, so you'll donate to several charities I control as well as any other charities you'd like so we can get you maximum incentives. Now real estate. I'd suggest buying a condo or a cabin here in Switzerland. You can rent it out or just let it sit for when you decide to come back, but it will help me help you by owning some property here. Then comes the fun stuff. Where am I going to invest your money? Crypto. We all know that's the rage nowadays but I do know myself, it can be extremely risky, so we won't put all of your eggs in that basket full of holes. Instead, I will set up a diversified portfolio for you that will include crypto, tax managed funds, blue chip stocks, my own personal index fund that I manage daily and some bonds, just in case. I like them for volatility prevention. Last thing I'll do for you is provide various income protection vehicles so you always have money coming in. You'll have income protection for life. You take the Leon Special and you will have hit the lottery twice." Leon looked at Jasmine. "Or three times. Questions?"

Luis was mind blown. He could see why Jasmine confided in this guy with her money. Leon knew everything he was thinking and he had the appropriate plan of action to execute. Still, it just sounded too perfect and almost too easy. He tried to think of other questions to ask, but he couldn't think of any. Leon was *that* good. Luis became overwhelmed by his lack of preparation for such a major decision in his life. His face began to flush as he started to feel stressed, anxious and even embarrassed.

"Here's some water," Leon pulled a bottle from the fridge beneath his desk. He was even prepared for that.

Jasmine opened the water and gave it to him and tried to soothe him by rubbing his back.

"I'm sorry, I don't know what came over me," Luis said as he took a gulp of water and wiped his forehead which started to bead in sweat.

"If this is too much, we can do it another time," Jasmine said to him.

"No, no. It's ok, I just need a sec," Luis replied, trying to regain his composure.

Jasmine turned to Leon. "Maybe you can show him how you've managed my account so he can see exactly what it is you do."

Leon responded with a look as if to ask, *are you sure?* which received a nod back from Jasmine. He typed a few things and clicked a few others on the screen and Jasmine's account was now displayed on the monitor. Her total assets reflected on the screen surpassed three hundred million dollars with all sorts of charts, graphics and percentage numbers displaying how her assets were allocated and how much she'd been making year over year due to the 'Leon Special'. He spent a few minutes breaking down her annual rates of return, the comparison of her crypto vs common stock portfolios along with some real estate investments she had throughout Europe and China. Luis was not only amazed at how Leon managed her money, but at how this woman was able to build all of this wealth herself while still being such an incredible person. For the first time since they'd been together, he actually did feel as a lesser person than her, because although he'd been working pretty hard his whole life, he knew he wouldn't ever be able to reach the level of success Jasmine had reached. And earned. But he didn't envy her, he was inspired. If he backed out now, what would she think of him? He knew what *he* would think of himself. *Gutless. Coward.* She clearly took risks in life to get where she was at and he was ready to do the same. He wouldn't be intimidated.

"I've seen enough. Let's do it." He sat straight up in his chair again and found the confidence that had been drained from his body a few minutes prior.

"That's what I'm talking about!" Leon responded joyfully.

"You won't regret it, I promise," Jasmine reassured him.

"Okay," Leon shuffled some papers together

and pulled up a new screen on the computer. "We've got a lot of paperwork and details to go through, so Jasmine if you'd like, come back in about an hour and we should have everything wrapped up here."

"Great, that gives me time to deal with this situation back at work. I'll be at the cafe around the corner." She got up, gave Luis a peck on the cheek and walked out the door.

"Okay, we'll meet you there then," Leon said.

"Wow. How lucky are you?! First the lottery, then Jasmine? I know a lot of men that would kill to be in your position, and not for the money," Leon said as he clicked out of the current screen and opened up a new one.

"She truly is a great woman."

Leon grabbed a pen from his drawer and neatly placed a stack of papers in front of Luis. "Okay, so this is what I need from you…"

An hour later, the guys walked over to the cafe to join Jasmine, who was sitting at a small table outside sipping on a glass of white wine and attending to her phone. She must've sensed them coming because she looked up just as they approached her and greeted them with a smile, placing her phone back down on the table. Leon brought Luis in closer and patted him on the chest and said, "I got your man all hooked up! Now you two little love birds can go on your way and celebrate the best way you know how." He pointed at his nose and winked at Jasmine and Luis insinuating that drug use was in order. They laughed as Jasmine and Luis quickly shot that idea down since they were still recovering from Ibiza.

Jasmine pinned fifty euros under the menu and got up. "Not today, Leon. I actually have a flight to catch now, so we'll be on our way. Thank you so much again. I owe you." She gave him a hug and he kissed her cheek. "And please give your wife a big hug from me. I promise to come by after the baby arrives."

"Anything for you, Jas," he replied. "Well Luis, it's been a pleasure. I hope we can meet again soon for some drinks or what not. Here's my business card. For you, I'm available twenty-four hours a day, eight days a week." He handed Luis his card and gave him a firm hand shake followed by a hug. "If the money is not in there within forty-eight hours, give me a buzz, but I think the ten million I put in there as a retainer should hold you off until then. Unless you need more..." he stood back putting his hands up assuring he could get it done.

Luis laughed again. "That's more than plenty, thank you. From the bottom of my heart. I'll keep in touch."

"All right my man. You take good care of her now," Leon pointed at Luis and they parted ways.

"What a great guy," Luis said to Jasmine.

"He's the best. You'll see why very soon."

CHAPTER 29

A few days passed, and Luis was sipping his usual morning coffee, rocking back and forth in a chair outside of the cabin he rented in Lauterbrunnen. It was a tiny village tucked deep in the valley between two mountain ranges. The place had spectacular views during the summer, from vivid greenery to long thin waterfalls visible from just about anywhere in town. The rocky mountains that formed walls along the city, enhanced the picturesque views he'd gawked at while researching this place a few months ago. Except now he would enjoy it alone, unless he counted the aging property manager who stopped by a few times a day dropping off everything from select local beer and wines to different variations of cheese, also sourced locally.

The old man, Hans, was an interesting fellow and Luis quickly became intrigued by him as they sat a few nights star-gazing and consuming vast amounts of beer and schnaps, chatting about life and comparing Swiss, Puerto Rican and American traditions. Luis decided to keep his recent history to himself and shared family photos with the man, promising to bring them someday in the future and perhaps even purchasing one of his cabins. Hans was a widower and his adult children held high business positions in London so he lived on his own, but he insisted he never felt alone because he knew the whole village and *they* were his family. Not to mention the frequent guests that would rent out his five cabins throughout the year. Hans was full of life even if his body and face said otherwise.

While enjoying his scenery, Luis snapped a selfie on his phone with the famous Swiss cows lurking in the background and sent it to Jasmine. They sent each other photos and texts the whole time they'd been separated and after being together a few weeks now, he'd actually begun to miss her and wondered if she felt the same. It was nice to unwind and relax a bit but he was ready to move on to the next place, which apparently was going to be Macau, China.

His phone vibrated in his hand and he looked to see what her response was, except it wasn't her. The jeweler sent a picture of the necklace he'd requested to be made for Jasmine.

Take a look at this. It was made for a very wealthy client of mine but he had a change of heart. It is one of my proudest pieces. It features 24 oval pigeon blood

Burmese rubies (extremely rare) and is surrounded by white marquise diamonds. Was selling for 3.5, it's yours for 3.2.

The necklace was unlike anything Luis had ever imagined. The rubies were set in the middle of each flower with bright white diamonds forming the petals. It was the most extravagant piece of jewelry he'd ever laid eyes on, but now he had a decision to make.

After a few minutes of contemplation, he decided to go through with it. Jasmine had been so unselfish during their time together, and now with her financial advisor in his corner, he was sure that price tag would be recouped in a matter of months. He double-checked his account balance on his new banking app, seeing all of his money that had finally cleared the day prior.

Luis texted back, *I'll take it. I'm in Lauterbrunnen, Switzerland. Need it by tomorrow.*

The jeweler replied, *You'll have it by tonight. I'll email you the details.*

He couldn't contain his excitement and was anxious to surprise Jasmine with the gift. Especially after feeling empty-handed after she'd gifted him the Patek Philippe watch.

As he was filling out his details in the email, his phone buzzed in his hand with a familiar phone number that he couldn't quite guess since he hadn't transferred his contacts to his new phone. He opened the text.

Hey brother it's Victor. I need to talk to you, ASAP!

Shit, he thought to himself, *how'd he get this phone number?* Luis knew it was a matter of time before somebody found a way to contact him but not this soon. He didn't feel like explaining to anyone what he was doing or hearing anyone preach to him about how wrong he was for leaving his family behind, etcetera. Initially he considered it would be a bad idea to respond but he had zero clue as to what was happening back home and whether his family was doing fine or not. So he decided it would be best to call Victor, but if things escalated, he would just hang up and block his number.

Victor answered on the first ring, "Luis?"

"Yeah bro, what's going on?"

"Shit man, I was hoping I had the right number. The guy who helped me with your transfer called me and told me you transferred all of your money to Switzerland?!"

That's how he got my number.

"Yeah man, I did."

"Okay good, I was making sure you hadn't got kidnapped or scammed or something. I'm so glad you're okay. You *are* good, right?"

"Living life, you know me."

"Nice man, happy to hear. Well look, I did want to make sure that it was you behind the transfer but you should've consulted with me first. That shit out there can be sketch if you don't do the proper research, but I know you're smart enough to know that," he paused. "And I hate to get involved but don't you think it's time to get back to your family?"

Luis stayed quiet.

"Krystal came to our house hysterical. I think she knows I helped you but she didn't say anything in front of my wife. Probably for the sake of our own marriage. I started feeling really bad man so I've been checking in on her and the kids every couple days just to make sure they're alright —"

"You're checking in on *my* wife and *my* kids?" Luis interrupted him in a firm tone.

"Yeah we're like family, why wouldn't I?" Victor was confused.

"You stay the fuck away from my family. That's my mess to fix, not yours. Understood?!" Luis yelled at the phone and hung up before Victor could respond.

Luis' temper was boiling for the first time in a long time. He grabbed his coffee mug and launched it at the cabin's wooden walls, breaking it into a hundred pieces. The thought of another man caring for his family irked him in a way he'd never considered happening. He hadn't imagined that scenario, it was always supposed to be just him. And it wasn't just another man, but one of his best friends? He hoped for Victor's own sake that it'd only been cordial visits.

Hans rounded the corner of the cabin slowly until he saw Luis and asked, "Everything alright, Luis?"

"Yes. Sorry, dropped my mug but I'll clean it up and replace it." Luis felt guilty lying to the old man and hoped Hans hadn't seen or heard what actually happened. "Hey Hans, while I have you, I've got a very important package being delivered here tonight. Could you give me the address to the house?"

"It'd be easier for them to meet us at the bar in town. We can knock back a few while we wait. People always get lost around here since all the cabins look the same," Hans suggested.

"Okay, even better! Meet you there at six?" Luis asked and Hans responded with a thumbs up before continuing on his way.

He looked back down at his phone in contemplation. He missed his kids. The thought of Victor seeing his wife hysterical made him feel like shit because *he* had caused that. It was all his fault and the remorse was starting to set in. He went back inside for his other phone and decided to try and check in on her, hoping for the best but preparing for the worst. Maybe he would save the necklace for her instead.

Luis turned on his phone and just like the last time, it buzzed continuously until all of the messages had finally come through. A text would not suffice in this situation, so he decided to call Krystal. She picked up after a few rings.

"Hello?"

"It's me..." Luis said, not knowing how to begin.

"I know it's you. Where are you? It's been weeks since you left us, did you forget about your kids?!"

"I didn't. I miss them terribly. I was hoping to talk to them."

"You're not speaking to them until you get your ass back home and explain to them what a low life you have become."

"Look, I'm sorry but after what happened, I had to get away. I was so ashamed of myself. And then when you told me to leave and go figure out who I wanted to be, I thought you were done with me."

"I was furious! What'd you want me to say?! *Oh baby, all is forgiven, please promise you won't spill cocaine on our kids again.* I also don't recall telling you to take two hundred million from our account and disappear to who knows where for weeks!"

"I said I'm sorry. The money is safe. But I want to make it up to you when I get back. Please consider it and hear me out…" he paused as he heard her sobbing. It wretched his stomach.

"I don't know who you are anymore. The man I married would've never done this to his family. Fuck off Luis, have a good life." She hung up. He was heartbroken. It was karma, he should've known this was going to happen. He wasn't sure what came over him thinking that she'd be so easy to forgive and forget. She didn't even give him a chance to talk to his own children. That upset him. At the end of the day, she could get rid of him, but she could never keep the kids from him. He wasn't going to allow it.

He looked back down at his phone and considered calling back but his other phone vibrated. New text message from Jasmine. He took a long deep breath.

I've finally wrapped up down here! Going to catch a flight to Macau tonight, should I arrange y o u r transport for tomorrow morning?

His feelings were mixed. He'd just had his heart broken, followed quickly by a text from his mistress. It was a stark reminder that what he'd done had merited that response from Krystal. There wasn't much else he could do at the moment so he chose to accept the good that life was giving him. He quickly felt relieved and excited by the fact that he'd see Jasmine soon. She would help him get back in a better state of mind. A loving one. He'd just push his problems aside for a bit longer and deal with his situation at home at a later time. In the meantime, he was ready to go celebrate his great transfer of wealth at the gambling capital of the world, Macau.

Please do. Can't wait to see you again. I've got a little surprise for you. Luis texted back with a wink emoji.

She responded with a selfie of herself blowing a kiss. He kissed the phone and went inside to pack.

Later that evening, Luis swung by the bar to receive his package and bid farewell to the old man as he was going to make his way to Zurich immediately after, in order to catch his flight in the morning. Hans was seated at the bar chatting with the equally aged bartender when he noticed Luis walk in and waved him over.

"Here you go mate, pint's on me," Hans said as the bartender placed a cold draft beer in front of Luis.

"Thank you." He took a sip of the cool crisp lager and reached into his pocket for the cabin keys. He placed them on the bar and slid them to

Hans. "I'm headed off in a few, I'm ever grateful for your hospitality. This place is everything I imagined plus more."

"I hate to see you leave so soon, but be sure to bring your family next time so I can meet them," Hans replied. Luis' face was masked with a bit of sadness after he mentioned his family, but Hans stepped in again. "Hey, it's ok young man. I know you're in a pickle and I don't need to know what it is, but whatever you're going through, it's going to be alright. You're a good chap. We all go through things in life, but we either persevere or we're doomed. Here's to perseverance," he toasted. He raised his glass and clinked it with Luis'.

"To perseverance," said Luis.

"I think I see a fancy car outside, could that be the package?" Hans said as he leaned over in his barstool.

Luis looked down at his phone which had just received a text.

"My package and my ride. Thanks again for everything old man. I hope to see you again." He shook Hans' hand and walked towards the exit. "Oh and I left you a small envelope on the table to cover for the coffee mug. Be sure to make good use of it."

The small envelope was in fact a large one, containing fifty thousand euros. Those were the kinds of deeds Luis initially set out to do when he hit the lottery. Give good people random gifts of cash. Hans deserved it more than anybody he'd recently met and it made Luis feel great about himself. Plus his instincts told him he could use a bit of good karma for the near future.

CHAPTER 30

The flight from Switzerland to Macau was much longer than Luis had expected, but the beauty of flying private was that it all felt like a luxurious stay in a tiny hotel room. In the half day he'd spent flying, he was fed as if he had his own five-star restaurant on the jet. He also drank from an exclusive wine and champagne selection, binged on a Netflix series and slept enough in the oversized, plush reclining seats to be able to wake up refreshed and ready to seize the day in Macau. This was the life. There was no going back.

Soon after landing, Jasmine texted him that she'd be waiting by the VIP area in a black Rolls Royce that wouldn't be too hard to spot. As he made his way through security and customs, he'd skipped through lines that the other travelers were having to wait hours in. Again, perks of flying private. He wore sunglasses so he wouldn't have to look at their disgust with him. As he finally exited the airport, he spotted Jasmine by the Rolls Royce, and for a second, he contemplated which one looked better. He decided it was her, as she wrapped her arms behind his neck and pulled him in for a kiss as if they hadn't seen each other in ages.

"How I've missed you," she said dramatically while he dropped his luggage for the driver to pick up. He placed it in the trunk and opened the door for them.

This was a drastic change of pace from where he'd just been. From a humble life in Lauterbrunnen to the glitz and glamour of Macau. He had to admit, he was beginning to favor the upscale locations as he was now becoming more and more comfortable with the affluent lifestyle. Private jets, fancy cars, luxury hotels, world famous model and entrepreneur. It was just another day in the life of Luis Diaz.

"Are you hungry, babe? I want to take you to one of my favorite places growing up," Jasmine said.

"Lead the way, my love. Can't wait to see it!" he gushed as he replied. He felt special for her to want to take him to a place that held a sentimental value to her. Then he thought about maybe one day taking her on a road trip across Puerto Rico along the coastline, eating food and dancing the night away just as he had growing up.

After arriving to the tiny quaint restaurant outside of the main strip of Macau, Jasmine introduced Luis to a few local dishes that she grew up loving. "These are the moments that help keep me grounded. Sometimes it's important to remember where we came from to see how far we've made it. Wait until you try the *serradura*, it is my ultimate favorite dessert."

Just as she said that, the frail older lady who had been serving them brought out a small see-through dish with multiple cream and brown layers. Jasmine put the spoon in the dessert and grabbed the perfect scoop, before feeding it to Luis.

"Holy shit that's good. It's like a *tres leches* but better." He grabbed the spoon from her and dug in some more. "Order another one, this one's mine," he joked as he she tried reaching for it while he shooed her hands away.

"So what's the plan for tonight?" he asked her with his mouth still full.

"We're going to meet some of my friends at the casino we're staying at. My half-brother also flies in from Australia tonight, so if he's not too jet lagged, he may come out and meet us for a few. He's a lot of fun, you'll love him."

"Great, I'm excited to meet them. Do we have any, *you know*..." he pointed at his nose.

"I've got you covered," she winked back, "but

don't forget we have the dragon boat races tomorrow, 10 AM sharp."

"I'm really looking forward to it, although they're not real dragons like I had imagined."

They left a generous tip on the table and made their way back to the car, where the stoic driver awaited with the door open. Luis thanked him and he just nodded back. *Man of a few words*, he thought. As they neared the famous strip, Luis rolled down the window and stared outside in awe at the shimmering hotels and casinos that towered into the sky. He'd read that Macau created ten times more revenue than Las Vegas and he was ready to see why. Big money would be risked tonight, now that his new account offered more flexibility with his funds. Hopefully Leon would understand and not tell him he's making bad financial decisions.

When they arrived at the Venetian Macau, the place reminded him of the Bellagio in Las Vegas, but more majestic. The driver pulled right up to the front entrance and opened the door. As it opened, all of the lights and sounds of the casino rushed Luis' senses. He was exhilarated. Ready to show Macau what Luis Diaz was all about. Taking a page out of wealthy individuals, he decided he would not always try to engage with the help. Instead, he would give affirming gestures and tip well enough to make sure they knew who he was and that they attended to his every need without question. The bellhop quickly approached them and grabbed his luggage. Jasmine told him the room number, Luis handed him a hundred euros and the young man scurried off.

"You have to be the coolest woman on the planet. I mean you just walk in here like it's no big deal. Look at you!" Luis laughed and made her smile as she brushed her shoulders. *One time for the haters.*

As they entered the casino, everything became brighter. Louder. More glamorous. Decor-wise, it was very similar to the casinos he'd been to in Vegas and other places but here the audience was more diverse. More international. Every few steps they walked, he'd listen in on a different language being spoken. French, Italian, English, Japanese, and the many dialects of the Chinese. But the one thing they all had in common was that they all looked like *big money,* and he was one of them, so he felt right in place.

After arriving into their rooms, Luis walked over to the large wall to wall windows and took in the panoramic views of Macau. It started to become his own tradition where he stared outside of whatever new location he was in. He would take in a few deep breaths to center himself and reflect on everything that had led him to that moment. Too many good things happened for him to be in the position he was in. He kept winning. But he also felt like he had earned it. By being a good person his whole life. That golden rule he applied so adamantly. He definitely wasn't proud of his situation back home but he felt he'd done enough good by at least leaving his family the other half of the money, just in case things didn't work out in the future with his wife. Two hundred million would eventually buy them happiness.

As Jasmine got ready, Luis poured her a glass of champagne while drinking the rest from the bottle. "Here you go, my lady."

"Thank you, mister." She took the glass ever so elegantly and then pointed over to the side. "And for you..."

Two perfect white lines were prepared on the vanity with a Chinese yuan note neatly rolled next to it. He grabbed the note and took both hits before jumping back and shaking every limb as if it would help spread the drugs into every part of his body. Then he started to beatbox some techno music as he grabbed her and twirled her into a dance. "I'm so lucky. You're so beautiful and I cannot get enough of you," he gazed into her eyes.

"Well if you want some more if this, hurry up and get ready," she snarked back.

"Okay okay. I was just having a moment," he said as she returned to the mirror and continued applying her makeup.

"I know. I'm just teasing you...*papi*," she said with a perfect Spanish accent and blew him a kiss through the mirror. That word did it for him. A Chinese model with a slight accent calling him *papi,* inflated his ego beyond his imagination.

Luis got ready quickly and went to retrieve his duffel bag. Inside was the multi-million dollar necklace he had purchased for her. He knew it was an outrageous gift and briefly considered holding onto it for Krystal someday but instead thought, *what was three million dollars to a baller?* Just a number. A small one compared to what he had and what he would amass over the years to come. In four days alone, he'd seen his account grow by over a hundred fifty grand from investments. *That boy Leon is good!*

He took the necklace out of its box and admired the delicate features it possessed. It had a pretty decent weight to it as well, as he balanced it in his hands to try and measure it. He adjusted his tie, checked himself out in the mirror on the dresser and walked back towards Jasmine.

Luis caught her by surprise as she flinched and put her phone down on the vanity and smiled at him. "Wow, you look as handsome as ever."

."What can I say?" He raised his eyebrows a couple of times. "You look absolutely marvelous." Luis approached her from behind and kissed her neck and stared at their reflection in the mirror as she tilted her head back towards him, closing her eyes and enjoying his lips on her skin. She wore a body hugging, fire-red dress with her neck and shoulders exposed. "But you're missing one thing." He reached around and slowly put the necklace on her. "Perfection."

Her mouth dropped to the floor as she placed her hand on her chest and leaned forward towards the mirror to get a closer look. She was in shock. Leaning back to take a full look, then forward again to see the details, then back again with her mouth still opened before turning to hug Luis with a strength he didn't imagine she'd be capable of.

"I love it! Oh my god, this is the most gorgeous thing I have ever laid eyes on. How—"

Luis cut her off. "This is me showing my appreciation for everything you've done for me. You've showed me a different side of life and you've taught me that love should be a power we use more. When the time comes and we go our separate ways, I want you to have this to remind you of all the good times we've had and the love we shared. A piece of my heart is in that necklace."

Jasmine's eyes began to well up as she stared

deep into his. "I love you, Luis. You're different." She kissed him and turned to the mirror again, making a *wow* face and hopping in place in excitement. "Okay, well now I'm gonna need a few minutes to fix my makeup," she laughed as she wiped the tears from her eyes, running her mascara.

Before heading downstairs to the casino, they got one more quick fix in and she slipped a small vial in his coat pocket, containing what he assumed was cocaine. "For personal use, so people don't get suspicious every time we run off together."

"Good thinking," he replied and patted his chest where the vial sat.

CHAPTER 31

The night got off to a great start as Jasmine introduced Luis to her friends as her new boyfriend. All three of the ladies were drop dead gorgeous and of the same age, accompanied by their beaus who all spoke with a hint of arrogance. The usual 'what do you do for work' questions were asked and this time Luis decided to go with angel investor for green tech start-ups, an industry he and experts alike, predicted would boom in the near future back in the United States. He knew enough talking points to hold his own but also knew that if he was the one asking the questions, these guys would happily oblige to talk about themselves until dawn. Finally, he was learning to play the game.

After they all spent some time catching up, Luis decided to interject himself into their never ending conversation about work and how miserable business had been during the last year due to Covid. "Okay, so who's here to talk about work and who's here to party?" The group paused as he looked around, waiting for a reaction. "Raise your hand if you're ready to say fuck work and turn up. We're in Macau baby!"

They all stared at him, before one of the guys, Anthony, raised both of his hands high in the air in approval. "Finally someone says something. Thank you, Luis! I knew right away I would love this guy! All these people ever wanna do is get together and talk work. Blah blah blah."

The girls laughed and looked at each other before clinking their glasses together and finishing off the rest of their drinks. "C'mon girls, let's show Luis and these boys here how it's done in Macau," Jasmine said as she led them out to the casino floor.

Anthony came up behind Luis and grabbed him by the shoulders, "My man! Let's hit these blackjack tables. You play much? Ehh not like it matters, we have money to blow, right?"

Luis nodded. "You damn right!"

The guys chose a table and sat as their ladies stood behind them. They rooted them on as each one of them asked the pit boss for 500,000 in chips, although Luis wasn't sure what the currency or conversion rate was. He hadn't thought about asking before and he wasn't going to now. He had more than plenty to cover, especially if it was Chinese currency, like he'd assumed it would be. Once they all had the chips in front of them, the men placed their bets and a battle of who had the biggest *cojones* ensued. The first guy placed a hundred grand in chips in front of him. Anthony looked at him as if to say, *that's it?* and pushed half of his stack in. Two hundred fifty grand. He then leaned back in his chair as his lady handed him a cocktail, rewarding him for his bravado. Luis noticed Anthony was a one-upper kind of guy from the very beginning but this was Luis' show. He knew Jasmine was the leader in her pack so he was going to lead these two pups, as he pushed all of his chips in the pot. Five hundred grand worth of something. He still didn't know, but he didn't care. Anthony who was keeping an eye on him through his peripheral while sipping his drink, saw the bold move and grabbed Luis by the shoulder once again.

"I love this man! Jas, where'd you find this lad?!" Anthony exclaimed as Luis smiled, but he stayed focused on the table as the dealer was getting ready to deal the cards.

The dealer gave the first man an 8 of hearts.

Anthony was dealt a 10 of spades, and he made a celebratory fist.

Luis got a King of diamonds.

The dealer dealt himself a card face down.

Then the other man got a 3 of clubs. He had 11.

Anthony got a Queen of clubs. He had 20.

Luis got another King of hearts. Two Kings, 20.

Dealer dealt himself a 10 of clubs.

The first man asked for a hit. Jack of diamonds. 21. Winner.

Anthony stayed at 20.

Luis thought back to the Bahamas where he'd also been dealt two Kings and hit big. "Split," he said once again and everyone looked at him like he was crazy, except Jasmine. She'd been there in the Bahamas and it was the first time she'd noticed him. She cracked a smile as Luis looked back at her. It was nice to think back to when they first met and the journey they'd been through.

"You've got some balls, mate!" Anthony interrupted his thought and was slowly witnessing Luis steal his shine.

The dealer flipped a Queen of hearts on one King and a Jack of spades on the other. He'd hit 20. Twice. All he needed was for the dealer to end up with anything under 20 or bust and he'd triple his initial bet.

He dealt himself a 3 of hearts. The small crowd that moved in on them all watched and waited anxiously to see the next card.

The dealer pulled from the top of the deck and slid it dramatically across the table. When he flipped it over it showed a 9 of clubs. 22. *Bust!*

The guys all jumped up from their seats and

celebrated, high-fiving anyone within a ten foot radius. "Fuck yeah, mate! That was intense! We need more drinks if we're gonna keep doing that!" Anthony exclaimed, trying to take control of the group once again. "Hey boss, hold those chips for us, we'll be back."

Jasmine grabbed Luis, "I'm going to the ladies room to you know…" she tapped her nose.

Luis took her by the hand and headed towards the restrooms with her. "Your friends are great."

"Oh yeah, you've seen nothing yet. Anthony can be pretty intense but he's a big teddy bear. I'll meet you back out here in a minute." She propped herself up on her tippy toes and kissed him.

They went to their respective restrooms and after Luis relieved himself, he reached in his coat pocket for the vial Jasmine had prepared for him. *How nice of her.* He tapped a small bit into his hand and took the hit. His eyes watered slightly but he decided to prepare a second hit, so not only could he match Anthony's intensity, but surpass it as he was now the top dog. Hitting a million in chips in a matter of minutes.

He looked in the mirror and what he saw now was a different person. An infinitely better person. New and improved, with an unshakeable confidence he'd developed over the last few weeks. A man with a nearly unlimited amount of wealth, as long as he continued to play his cards right, which ironically he had been. The man in the mirror was the same man who had attracted an extremely successful and stunning top model, *and her friend*, which he couldn't wait to see again. He'd flown private jets, partied on a yacht in Monaco, driven some of the world's most expensive cars and stayed at some of the most luxurious places across the world. Three weeks, seven cities, five countries. This was the best time of his life.

He could feel the dopamine levels in his body rise and it made him more and more pumped for what was to come. He decided on a third hit, so he wouldn't have to excuse himself again for a while. As he tapped the vial, he was startled by someone flushing a toilet, so he quickly snorted what was in his hand and beelined towards the exit.

Once outside the restroom, Luis looked around for Jasmine and didn't see her right away. *Maybe she went back to her friends.* First, he checked his phone just in case and didn't see any messages. Then he looked up and saw Jasmine hugging a man with dark hair, a nice muscular frame and about half a foot taller than Luis. She stood very close to him as they held hands and the smile on her face told Luis this was something more than a friendship. As jealousy took over, he reminded himself of the confident man he was just staring at in the mirror and tried to quickly revert back to him. He approached the two and put his arm around Jasmine's hip as she looked up in surprise, and then in delight. "There you are. This is my brother Zhang, but he goes by John."

He was instantly relieved because the man was very handsome and the six inches of height he thought the man had on him felt more like a foot. The only resemblance him and Jasmine shared was their beauty because they looked nothing alike. But she had mentioned him being a half-brother, which made it more likely.

"Pleasure to meet you, John. Sorry, I've had a few drinks and I think the jet lag may be hitting me a bit. I'm sure you know what I mean," Luis shook his hand and patted him on his shoulder which was just as hard and muscular as he thought it would be.

"Oh yes, he just got in from Sydney. I'm so happy you made it out," Jasmine interjected.

"Yes, yes, Australia. I know exactly what you mean. I've just been so busy," he then lowered his voice and leaned into Luis and Jasmine, "But there's nothing a little blow can't fix, right?" John made the sign just as Jasmine had a few minutes prior by pointing at his nose and started laughing.

"Hey! Now we're talking! I'm starting to see the resemblance," Luis joked and reached into his pocket before Jasmine stopped him.

"Here take mine, I've got more than plenty," she insisted as she handed her brother a vial from her clutch. *More for me then*, Luis thought.

"Well hey man, it's really is nice to meet you. We're gonna have some fun tonight," John said as he once again grabbed Luis' hand for a firm shake and returned the pat on his shoulder, but with his much bigger hands. "I think I saw Anthony and the rest of the guys by the craps tables, meet you two over there?"

"Don't hit that too hard," Luis pointed at John's closed hand and winked at him.

John let out an exaggerated laugh before turning towards the bathroom.

The hours flew past as the seven of them engaged in some serious debauchery throughout the casino. They splashed chips and raised hell at the craps table until the croupier had had enough and kindly asked them to leave. Anthony tried reasoning with them but instead decided to grab the dice from the table and toss them across the room. His lady had to bribe the furious pit boss with a large denomination chip to calm him down, which must've worked because they were left alone to rampage through the rest of the casino, causing quite the scene. John quickly caught up to their level of intoxication as he approached the group with a tray full of cocktails he had convinced a waitress to sell him. They downed drink after drink and took shot after shot while other casino guests either joined them or watched in disgust as they had little regards for the people around them. Luis told jokes and the group laughed hysterically every single time, making him feel like he was now one of them. Part of the family.

John became quickly attached to Luis after their shaky greeting as Luis confessed his initial jealousy over him. "Hey mannn, I'm sorry I kind of…like… confronted you when I umm met you earlier. I was jealous! I thought you were gonna take my girl. My woman! I love your sister, man. That makes you my brother…bro-in-law, right?" Luis laughed out loud as he slurred his words to John, who stood erect next to him in the bathroom while taking another hit of cocaine. Luis splashed water in his face and looked in the mirror. "Holy shit, you look *fuuuucked* up."

"Yeah you do," John laughed out loud as he helped Luis stand upright.

"Wait, I said that out loud? Oops." Luis shook his head laughing and tried to regain focus but it was becoming harder and harder to do so.

"Sure did, *bro-in-law*. I think you might be quite pissed."

"Pissed? I'm not mad, I'm having a…a great time!" Luis responded and forced a smile that took more energy than usual.

"You're funny, mate. I mean *pissed* as in *drunk*," John laughed. "I forget you Americans have a different way of doing things."

"Actually—" Luis held up his finger to John. "I'm Puer-to Ri-can. *Y estoy muy muy bo-rracho!*" He spaced out the words and almost fell back before John caught him. "Wow, you're so *strong*." He hoped those words had stayed in his head so John wouldn't get the wrong impression. The room felt like it was closing in on him one second and expanding the next. Luis couldn't believe how John was so alert and seemingly sober and when he tried to focus on his face, John seemed to be smiling with a devilish grin instead of showing concern. They'd done about the same amount of drugs and kept up with each other shot for shot but he was losing all functions in his limbs.

"It's ok, Luis. I'm gonna take you to your room and you will sleep this off. I'll tell Jasmine…"

That was the last thing Luis heard before everything faded. John tossed him over his shoulder like a rag doll and took him away.

CHAPTER 32

*R*ing. Ring. Ring.

The tone pierced his ear canals and into his brain which felt like it had swollen to the point where his head was ready to burst. He wrapped another pillow around his head to try and stop the noise but the light beaming through the massive windows was enough to inflict the same amount of pain conducing his headache. *What a fucking night,* Luis thought to himself as it had all become a blur at some point late into it. Not wanting to escape from under the pillows and covers, he reached his arm over and felt around for Jasmine's usual naked body. He reached further and further but was only grasping at more sheets.

"Jasmine?" he muffled into his pillow, receiving no response. Then he turned his head towards the bathroom. "Jas? You in the bathroom? I've got the worst hangover of my life."

Still no response.

Maybe she went to get us some breakfast.

He found his phone on his nightstand and looked at it with one eye closed. Dead. *Shit.* He plugged it in and saw that the clock read 1:15 P.M.

Holy shit! Then he remembered Jasmine mentioning the dragon boat races being at 10 AM. That's where she must've gone. She must've seen how messed up he was and decided to let him sleep in. Awful nice of her but he felt bad not being there and participating in the family tradition she so badly wanted to introduce him to. But there was no way he'd been able to make it to the races that morning, he couldn't even remember what time they had gotten back or *how* he'd gotten back.

He rolled over in bed to see if he could begin to recover and then slowly made his way to the bathroom. His pants and jacket were tossed next to his bed, his luggage was still by the closet but something was missing. He opened the closet and it was empty. Then he went to the bathroom to find only his belongings. None of Jasmine's stuff was there. *Weird.* Then the hotel phone rang again, this time he decided to answer in case Jasmine had left a message.

A lady began speaking rapidly in Mandarin and he paused her, "Sorry, do you speak English?"

"Yes sir. Check out time twelve. It's one thirty now. We need room for next guests. Please come down to the desk and pay," she said assertively.

"But wait, I thought we had this place for the weekend? Can you extend our stay?"

"No sir, fully booked. You only book two night,

today is check out."

"There must be some kind of mistake, ma'am. Give me a few minutes and I'll call you back." He hung up. Then his cell phone turned on. He waited what seemed like an hour before the home screen finally showed and waited for some messages to come through. Nothing. He checked his recent messages and found nothing new there either so he dialed Jasmine's cell.

"This is Jasmine, please leave a message."

"Fuck!" he yelled as he started to get agitated. He texted her immediately after.

Jasmine, where are you? Please call me ASAP. Hotel says I need to check out now.

Luis looked around the room and nothing seemed out of place besides her luggage being gone. *Maybe she packed and took it all to her brother's?* All of his belongings were still in place. He picked up his coat and found a few bands of Yuan currency with some large numbers on the bills. Then he remembered winning a bunch of money playing blackjack. He picked up his pants and checked the pockets, where he found another couple of bands and his wallet. "Well, I didn't get robbed at least." He tried calling Jasmine again. Straight to voicemail. He hung up and yelled, "Fuck! Pick up the damn phone!"

Bits and pieces from the previous night were

playing in his head. The last thing he remembered was being in the bathroom taking drugs with her brother John. He checked his phone again to see if maybe he had taken any pictures or grabbed John or Anthony's information for any reason. No luck. Then he searched his pockets again for the vial of cocaine he had been hitting all night. That would fix him right up and get rid of his massive headache that had worsened over the last few minutes. He emptied all of the pockets and checked the coat. Not there. Maybe he'd given it to John. Or maybe it fell out of his pocket when John carried him up to his room. It was coming back to him. That was the last thing he remembered. Taking drugs with John, fading away and John saying he'd bring him up to his room. It started to make sense. He'd gotten so messed up in front of John, that Jasmine must've felt embarrassed and ashamed. Maybe she was so pissed at him, she left him there and went to the races with her brother. But she wouldn't just dump him like that in a country completely foreign to him and not try to contact him again, would she? They had something special. Not a lifetime's worth of special but he didn't think it'd be over this quickly. He did act a fool though. Between trying to one-up Anthony all night and impress her brother John, he'd forgotten to attend to Jasmine. He couldn't remember much else so maybe he did deserve to get dumped this way. But he hoped this wasn't it for them. *It can't end like this.*

After throwing all of his belongings in his luggage and stuffing his duffel bag with the cash, he made his way down to the lobby and approached the receptionist.

"Hi, um, do you speak English?" he asked.

"Yes sir, how can I help you?" the man replied.

"Look, I thought we had the penthouse suite for another few days but then I got a call saying I needed to check out. Can you confirm that for me?"

"Name?"

"Check Jasmine Li. If not, Luis Diaz."

The man typed quickly on his computer said, "Yes. Luis Diaz. Two nights. This morning was check out."

"But we just got here last night," Luis said confused.

"No it says you checked in two days ago. Jasmine Li and Luis Diaz. I have copies of your passports here." He checked in the drawer underneath the computer and pulled out two papers. He looked at them in confusion. "Wait I have a Jasmine Li and Zhang Li here, but the reservation was under your name and you are here now. My apologies on the confusion, Mr. Diaz but we have no more rooms available tonight because of the dragon boat races. I can check nearby casinos…" Luis heard the man's voice trail off as he started to think how and why Jasmine and 'John' had checked in a day prior. He thought John had just flown in from Australia but then he remembered Jasmine butting in the conversation saying he'd just flown in from Sydney as if John had forgotten the script. His mind started spinning again before the receptionist cleared his throat and asked, "How will you be paying, sir?"

Luis pulled out his wallet and handed the man his card, all the while trying to connect the dots without much success. Why would she lie about her brother flying in late that night? Was it actually her brother? Or were they actually lovers, like he'd thought initially when he saw them together last night? He'd always been an optimist, but right now he couldn't imagine a scenario where this was all a bad mix up and everything would turn out just fine. His intuition was telling him that he messed up. Big time.

"Sir, your card has been declined. Do you have another?"

Fuck.

"There's no way. Try again."

The man tried again, with no success.

"I'm sorry. Give me a few minutes, let me call

my bank. I didn't tell them I'd be traveling to China. Can I leave this here for a sec?" Luis grabbed his card back and left his luggage by the receptionist and kept his duffel bag. As Luis made his way towards the exit, he tried Jasmine again. This time he left a voicemail. "I don't know what the fuck is going on but I need you to call me back."

He then checked his banking app. *Error*. The app wouldn't open. He asked the bellhop for the wifi password and the guy typed it in his phone for him. He tried again. *Error*. "Damn it!" Then he reached in his wallet for Leon's business card. He dialed the number on it. A tone was followed by, "Sorry, the number you are trying to reach is no longer in service, please try again."

Luis felt like his world was crumbling. Jasmine was gone. John may or may not be her brother or lover. He had no access to his money. He was in China, as an American. He knew he would get no help. He then ran outside to see if maybe he could get better reception and then at a distance, he could see the driver from the night prior standing beside the same black Rolls Royce he and Jasmine had been riding in. When the driver noticed him, he waved Luis over. Maybe it all turned out to be a series of unfortunate events and he was freaking out for no reason. The driver waved at him as if he was expecting him. Did Jasmine have the driver on standby for when he finally woke up?

He approached the driver in relief. "Hey, sorry but did Jasmine send you for me?" The man nodded. "Will you take me to her?" He nodded once again and walked around the car to open the door for him. He motioned him in and Luis gratefully said, "Thank you. Thank you so much, you have no idea what I was—" The man cut him off as he shut the door on him. *Asshole.*

When he sat back in the massive backseat, he felt someone else sitting there. Luis looked left and saw John sitting there, shooting back some brown liquor from a glass with one hand and holding a black pistol in the other. "About time, Luis. You went pretty hard last night, huh?" John chuckled and patted Luis on the thigh, gun in hand.

Luis froze for a second as he took everything in, before calmly responding, "That was a hell of a time. You and your sister know how to party." He was trying to stay cool.

"Oh yeah, my *sister. Jasmine.* Nice name, fits her well." He grabbed a whiskey bottle with the same hand he held the gun and poured some more. He then offered it to Luis who downed the shot, hoping to find a friendly resolution to all of this.

"Is she alright?" Luis asked.

"She's more than alright. She just hit quite the

fortune actually and all it took was about three weeks worth of work," he said as he calmly poured another shot. "This is some good whiskey, huh? It's a tradition of mine every time we complete a job. Cheers mate." He raised his glass and took another shot.

"Another job?"

"Yes, *dude*! Another job! How stupid are you?! Really? Tell me, I'd love to know."

"I'm not sure what you're talking about, John. Please tell me what the hell is going on?" Luis started to fear for the worst as John played with the gun in his hand. He was stuck. He couldn't do anything. If he fought back, he risked getting shot. If he ended up taking the gun and killing the man, how would the Chinese treat him? He had nobody there. He'd probably end up in jail for the rest of his life, so he decided to stay calm and play John's game. Meanwhile the driver merged onto a highway and stayed focused ahead, ignoring what was going on in the backseat.

"Funny thing is, you weren't even supposed to be a job for us. But when Maya told us you'd confided in her about hitting the lottery, we knew you'd be an easy target. Throw a few flashy things at you. Private jets, cars, women. You enjoyed that little three-some, didn't you?" He laughed. "Oh you thought…you actually pulled them?! That is great. You were in love so quick! If I'm honest, I really thought it would've taken longer, Luis. Being a family man and all."

John tossed a manila envelope onto Luis' lap. He waved his gun at it telling him to open it. When Luis opened it, he saw pictures of his family. He knew they were recent because he could see Krystal getting in and out of the new Mercedes G550 that she'd recently purchased. As he scanned the photos, he started sobbing. He knew he had messed up before but he didn't imagine it'd turn out to be this bad. In one of the photos, he saw Victor getting out of the passenger side and hugging the kids. That made him boil slightly, except he had bigger problems at the moment.

"Please tell me they are okay," Luis pleaded with John.

"They're fine. And they will continue to be, if you play by the rules."

John handed him a passport with a plane ticket inside. Luis opened it and realized it was his own passport and a plane ticket bearing his name from Macau to Los Angeles.

John continued, "Like I said, if you abide, nothing else will happen. Call it a fair trade. We take your money, you keep your life *and* your family. And let me assure you, that is against my wishes. If it was up to me, I'd shoot you right here and dump you in the Pacific. But *Jasmine* felt pity. Maybe you are a good guy after all. But you're an idiot, so I agreed."

"You took all of it?" Luis asked, defeated.

"With the help of my guy Leon, yes. Everything. That was a pretty elaborate scheme, huh? He'd just rented that office room that morning. We couldn't find anything on that short of notice, but *Jasmine* got it done somehow. Clever, right? We make a hell of a team. Leon enticed you with his quick talk, got a couple signatures, made some calls and a few clicks later, two hundred million dollars in *our* accounts. Cha-ching!" He pretended to pull a slot machine lever. "It's not that much really, but enough to keep us going a while longer. You know, til the next job."

"But why bring me all the way to Macau?"

"We had to make sure you wouldn't talk. Plus we liked that necklace you purchased with our money. I can't believe you spent almost four million dollars on that! For a woman you barely knew! You really are a sucker for love. It's adorable, really. But hey, at least we left you with some of that cash from last night. You did bring it, right?"

Luis nodded and squeezed his duffel closer to him as the driver pulled into the departures lane at the airport.

"Maybe now you can buy a fancy cheeseburger

when you get back to America," John laughed hysterically. Then a switch flipped in him and he immediately changed his demeanor to a more serious and violent one as he grabbed Luis by the throat and pressed the gun up to his temple. "Leave my fucking country and forget any of this ever happened. Or I'll fucking kill you, Krystal, Mikey and Mia. All of them. Understood?" Luis nodded for the last time as John reached over, opened the door and shoved him out of the Rolls Royce.

As the car sped off, Luis stood in utter shock and disbelief as he looked around to see if anyone had witnessed what had just happened. Nobody seemed to care as everyone was either saying their good-byes or glued to their phones while making their way into the terminal. He looked down at the plane ticket and noticed the departure time was in about an hour. He didn't have anytime to think or process what the hell had just happened, he needed to get out of the country, as fast as he could.

CHAPTER 33

The long haul back to the states was as miserable of a time as he'd ever had in his entire life. Dealing with Chinese authorities as he tried rushing through security checkpoints had turned into a nightmare. Even more so, because he showed up at the airport for a trip across the world with only a duffel bag full of cash. But it was Macau, and things like that happened more often than not. After the government officials took their cut and after exchanging the Yuan back to US currency, Luis was left with about fifty thousand dollars. Maybe John and Jasmine had taken a cut of his blackjack earnings after all. *Greedy assholes.*

The near two-day trek across the world, allowed Luis to reflect on the last few weeks of his life while trying to mask the pain with endless amounts of alcohol. He knew he should've followed his intuition when it all seemed too good to be true. A short conversation on the yacht with Maya led to his eventual downfall. He felt like a fool. Why'd he confide in her about his lottery winnings? The answer was simple. He was trying to conquer her that night and because she was so out of his league, he tried to impress her by telling her his secret. *Idiot.*

Jasmine had done her part though. She enticed him to go to Monaco after a few spats back at home with his wife, which was nothing new in his marriage. They fight, they make up. That's what they had vowed to each other. *Til death do us part.* But he failed. First by being unfaithful, then by carrying on with the lies. This wasn't how he normally operated, and now he began to question whether this was his true identity. He allowed money and temptation to turn him the wrong way at the fork in the road. And if it wasn't for him being conned, how long would he have kept going in that path?

The more he tried to put the pieces together, the more questions it led him to and as much as he wanted to get the authorities involved, he knew he'd need to be patient. Something he was running out of, especially after Jasmine had gotten him hooked on uppers. Was that part of the plan as well? *Bitch!* Now he ¥as starting to experience light withdrawal symptoms while crammed in an economy class seat between two foreign passengers. His pride had been snatched away just like that. He considered how much time and money it would take to hire someone to get to the bottom of it all discretely. But would it be worth it? *Yes*. He had been humiliated. Embarrassed. The thought of explaining this to someone made him feel so stupid. He was a complete fool. He'd been broken. Emotionally and financially, and vowed to one day get his revenge.

After landing in LAX, he had a massive sense of relief knowing he was finally back in the U.S. Now he could begin to plot how he would get his money back, but as he had always known, it takes money to make money. He tried to access his banking app one more time, just in case it had all been a bad dream, and it finally opened. Only this time, the account read zero's across the phone. "Fuck!" he blurted out as people looked at him suspiciously. Then he opened his Instagram to see if he could find Jasmine. He looked through his messages, and not surprisingly, her account was deactivated. Then he looked up Maya's account.

"There you are," he whispered to himself as he scrolled through her pictures. A woman he once envisioned as becoming a close friend and part-time lover was the sole reason his life had turned to shit. He sent her a message.

WTF Maya?! You were in on this the whole time???

The message was instantly read and she was

typing back, much to his surprise. He waited anxiously.

There's more to the story. I feared for my life and still do. This is all my fault. I'm so sorry, Luis. They are bad people.

What else could there be to tell? And why did she fear for her life? He was going to try to get answers.

Tell me more! I can help you if you help me. How do I find Jasmine?

He hit send and received an immediate response. *This account has blocked you.*

"Shit!" he said in defeat. He was so close to getting answers and wondered if Maya was forced into helping Jasmine. Or was she still working the job? His gut told him Maya was being taken advantage of against her will and that she was holding the keys to him getting everything back.

Luis walked quickly through the crowded airport and made his way to the car rental booth. A heavily tattooed Latino man with a bald head attended him. "Hello sir, how can I assist you?"

"I need a car man. Something nice, but I've only got cash."

"Sorry sir, we'll need a credit card on file or I can't give you a rental. None of these companies will."

Luis leaned in to try and reason with the man.

"Look bro, I'm going through a divorce and my wife cancelled all of my credit cards. I need some help here. I'll slide you some cash under the table if you can hook a brother up."

"Man that sucks. I'm sorry to hear that but I just got this job and I'm trying to be good for once, you know what I mean?" the man responded, but after a few seconds he leaned in closer to Luis and said, "I got a homeboy that might be able to hook you up. But it's gonna cost you."

"Any chance your boy might be able to hook me up with some…*white?*" Luis whispered and grazed his nose.

"Damn bro, what the fuck? You a cop or something, *ese*?" the man was perturbed.

"I'm just asking man. I thought maybe because —"

"Because what? I'm Mexican and I got all of these tattoos? Man fuck you!" The man dismissed him and flipped him off. After being profiled so many times in his life, Luis actually felt bad as he walked away.

"Ayo!" the man called back. "Give me five minutes, *puto*."

While Luis waited for his ride, he decided to call Krystal. It'd been almost four weeks since he up and left. This was going to have to be the beginning of their reconciliation. Not the way he imagined it but if he was going to ever get revenge, he was going to need help from his wife, at least financially. He found a quiet corner in the lobby and dialed her cell.

"Hello?" a voice said on the other line after one ring, but not Krystal's.

"Mikey? Hey it's papi!" His eyes instantly watered as he heard his son's voice for the first time in what seemed like an eternity.

"Papi! When are you coming home?"

"I'll be home soon, buddy. I promise. Daddy had to go away for work but I'm almost done, ok?"

"Ok." Luis could hear the sadness in his son's voice and it broke his heart.

"But guess what? I met Lewis Hamilton while I was gone and I told him all about you! He even recorded a video for you! I have it here on my phone!"

"Really?!" Mikey's mood quickly changed.

"Really…" Luis could hear a woman in the back asking, *"who are you talking to? Give me the phone, Mikey."*

"Hello?" It was Krystal.

"Hey. It's me again." He normally called her *babe* and it felt weird not doing so anymore.

"Let me guess. You're done running off with your whore? Or did you already blow your money and you need my help to get out of a mess? Which one is it, asshole?" Damn, she was good. He was left speechless for a moment and she could hear him sobbing over the line. "You can save those fake tears because you're getting no sympathy from me."

"I...I can explain," he stuttered.

"I don't need an explanation anymore. Your kids do!" she yelled at the phone.

"I got scammed! They had this whole elaborate scheme and took everything! I was set up from the very beginning. The cocaine and everything!"

"What do you mean, everything?" she asked.

"Everything. All two hundred million."

He heard her laughing.

"Well, looks like you got what you deserved then. Thank you for leaving me with the other half at least. I'll make sure to not blow it all like your dumbass did."

Her subtle jabs were causing his anger to fester.

"Look I know I made a terrible mistake, but I'm gonna need you to send me some of that money so I can find a way to get it all back. I won't let them get away with this."

"Oh yeah, sure baby. Where would you like me to deposit it, my love? How much do you need? A million? Ten?" she said with a great amount of sarcasm.

"Stop playing with me," he said as his anger

was now boiling over.

"Screw you, Luis! You left us. You want the money? Come and get it yourself!"

She hung up.

"Fuck!" he yelled out loud as the car rental attendant waved at him from a distance.

An hour later, he was riding in a black Chevy Camaro ZL1 with the top down on his way to Las Vegas. The Mexican's homeboy fixed him up with a ride and an eight ball for some cash and collateral. He asked for the Patek watch on Luis' hand until he got the car back. Unfair trade, but Luis was short on options so he agreed. After taking a few hits and getting no response back from his wife, he'd decided he would drive to Las Vegas for the night to see if he could multiply the cash he had left. Maybe there he could make a shady connection that could help him resolve his dilemma. He was all alone now, with nobody that could help. He doubted his friends would send him money after painting himself as an enemy back home, even though it was *his* money to begin with. *Actually, Danny might,* he thought. So he called him.

"Hello?" Danny said, sounding a bit distant.

"Yo Danny, it's Luis! What you up to?"

"What's going on?"

"Man, more than I can tell you over the phone…"

"Oh yeah?"

"Yeah bro, you have no idea. I kinda need something—" Luis was cut off.

"That's cool. Because I'm in Puerto Rico living my best life and I can't come to the phone right now. So leave me a message and I probably won't call you back. Peace!"

It was his damn voicemail. Normally, Luis would've laughed, but he didn't have it in him to do so this time. He dialed Victor next.

"Luis?" Victor picked up after a few rings.

"Yeah bro, what's up? I'm sorry about the other day, it's been a crazy few weeks."

"It's all good man, I know you're going through some shit. It wasn't my place to interject but I'm really just trying to look out for you."

"I know, I know. I fucked up man. Jasmine set me up and took everything."

"What?! What you mean?"

"That account I opened in Switzerland, it was all part of the setup. I should've called you first."

"Please tell me you're kidding. She took all of it?!"

"Every last fucking dollar."

"You've got to be shitting me! That bitch! Where are you, you okay?"

"Yeah I'm okay. I'm on my way to Vegas right now. I don't know what to do man, I'm so fucked." Luis was crying again as he sped through Interstate 15.

"Have you talked to Krystal?"

"Yeah man, she's over it. She won't help me and I get it, but what she needs to understand is that money she has is still technically mine. You think you can go in there and get rid of my restrictions to the account so I can use my card again? I have nothing."

"It's Saturday man. Besides, I dunno if that's the right thing to do. I can wire you some money tomorrow to get by but you can't tell anybody I'm helping you."

"After all I've done for you, Vic? All you have to do is unblock me from my own account without anyone knowing. We'll deal with the consequences later. I'll give you another million," Luis pleaded.

"It's not about the money, man! It's principles! Something you obviously don't have anymore, leaving your wife and kids for some skank! Enough already, Luis! What the fuck happened to you?" Victor was furious after holding back long enough. "Did you know that your wife's—"

Luis cut him off. "You wish you were me, asshole! Don't let me catch you when I get home," he threatened and hung up. He pinched a little more of the cocaine from the small baggy and shoved it up his nose before inhaling it. Then he cranked the music all the way up as he passed a billboard sign that read, *City of Sin. 150 miles ahead.*

CHAPTER 34

Luis unloaded his duffel bag and tossed the cash in front of the cage cashier at the Bellagio without saying a word. As she ran the money through the counter, his phone buzzed in his pocket. He looked down at it as it read, *the watch is a fake puto*. He figured as much, which irked him even more knowing that Jasmine had been playing him every single minute of the time they had spent together. The deep conversations they shared were all for naught. *Love a hundred times? More like die a hundred times bitch!* He chuckled to himself in disgust as he relived some of those memories. He clenched his fist, wanting to punch something until the cashier got his attention.

"Fifty two thousand five hundred. What chips would you like?"

"I don't care, whatever," he replied dismissively. He looked down at his phone which received another text message. *You got til the morning to return the car.* He decided to ignore it and put his phone away. They had no way of knowing where he was at so he ignored it. The phone vibrated again. *Or my people will meet you in the lobby at the Bellagio.* "Shit!" He looked around for anyone that might be following him and then figured they must've put a tracker on the car. *Smart*, he thought. So he replied, *10-4.*

Luis took his chips, grabbed a triple pour of neat scotch at the bar and went straight for the high-roller blackjack tables. His luck at the tables had been incredible the last few times and he was ready to take full advantage of it once again. He sat next to an older man dressed in a business suit. The man was accompanied by a much younger blonde woman with piercing dark eyes and wore a black cocktail dress. *Another con in the works,* he assumed. She sipped elegantly from her martini glass and winked at him after making eye-contact. He hated to admit it, but it made him feel good.

"Welcome to the table, sir. Blackjack is the game, thousand dollar minimum," the dealer said.

Luis stacked his chips in front of him and passed on the first hand while he got settled in and gulped down his scotch. The old man seemed to be annoyed that Luis sat next to him as he tossed five thousand in chips in front of him. The dealer dealt him a losing hand and the man pounded the table and got up, frustrated. "Hold my chips, I'm going for a walk," he told the dealer. When the lady tried to follow, he waved her off so she stood back and sipped her martini as if nothing had happened. Luis made eye-contact with her again and she just shrugged, making him laugh and shake his head.

"He's had a tough night," the dealer said. "Let's see if your luck is any better, place your bet."

He looked down at his chips again. Out of almost two hundred million dollars, this was all he had left. A measly fifty two thousand dollars. He couldn't help but to laugh at himself, as he had blown the opportunity of a lifetime in less than a month. All those hypothetical conversations he'd had at work about being smart with the money if he'd won the lotto, and quitting if he'd hit two million because he would find a way to make it last. All bullshit. He'd proven the doubters right, and it wasn't a good feeling. He was going to have to find a way to bounce back. Take big risks or live the rest of his life in shame.

"Sir?" The dealer tried to bring Luis' attention back to the table.

"Sorry," he said as he pushed every chip forward. The dealer looked back at the pit boss for approval and he gave him a thumbs up.

"Good luck," the friendly dealer said. Luis liked his vibe. The young lady watched intently. He liked her vibe as well.

Luis was dealt a king of hearts. "No fucking way," he said to himself.

The dealer dealt himself a card face down.

Next card for Luis, king of spades. "Oh my god," he clasped his hands together and looked up at the gambling gods because he knew the other god would disapprove of this behavior. History had repeated itself for the third time. Kings again. Maybe it was a sign that he was meant for big things.

The dealer then dealt himself a queen of hearts. Fitting. King vs queen. Luis vs Jasmine. She'd taken him for all he had, would she do it again? He wanted to split like he had done twice before but he didn't have the money to do so. He waved his hands over his cards. *Stay.*

This was it. All or nothing. Good vs evil.

The dealer flipped a four of clubs. *14.*

Luis was a nervous wreck. He sat back in his chair and the lady massaged his shoulders, "You got this."

"I got this," he agreed as he loosened up and finished the last bit of scotch in his glass.

The dealer reached for the last card. He slid it across the table slowly and flipped it.

King of clubs. *Bust! Winner once again!*

Luis jumped out of his seat, spilling the lady's drink on her. She didn't seem to care though because she jumped up in celebration with him. "I'm so sorry ma'am, let me get you a napkin," he apologized as he looked around for one.

She wiped it off with her hand and replied, "Oh it wasn't much. I'm Jessie." She stuck out her other hand in a flirty manner for a handshake. "And please don't call me ma'am."

"Luis," he replied as the dealer pushed his winning chips towards him. He grabbed the cocktail waitress' attention and ordered another round before sitting back down. His focus was back on the card game, he had to take advantage of his hot streak. And a hot streak it was, indeed. In about a half hour of playing at the table, he'd gotten up to about a hundred and fifty thousand dollars. Jessie continued to flirt and claim herself as his *good luck* charm. She must've been *bad luck* for the other gentleman because he hadn't come back around.

The pit boss came by and asked Luis if he was staying as a guest. Everything was going to plan as he had now been comped a free room without being asked for a credit card. He felt like he was taking back control of his life but was starting to feel a bit lethargic, and only one thing could fix that. He asked the dealer to have his chips cashed and went to the bathroom with Jessie following closely behind. "You like to party?" he asked her while tapping his nose. She grabbed his hand and pulled him into the men's room and they went into the handicap stall. He opened the cocaine baggy and poured a some on the palm of his hand. "Ladies first," he said as she shamelessly brought her nose down to his hand and snorted the coke. He followed suit and they went back to the bar.

"What is it you do, Luis?" Jessie asked sensually as they sipped on their cocktails.

"A little bit of everything." He wasn't up for talks about life and such. Under any other circumstances, he'd sit and chat all night, but he knew what Jessie was after and he wouldn't fall victim to another whore again. She was extremely attractive though and she seemed like a fun girl, so he would enjoy her company for a bit longer. After a few laughs and a couple rounds of shots, she suggested going to the nightclub at the hotel, to which he agreed.

The techno music bounced from wall to wall as Luis and Jessie made their way through the thick crowd. Defeated just a few hours earlier, he now felt the as if the bass was pumping his heart back to life like a defibrillator. He stared at the lights and lasers illuminating the beautiful people in the crowd. People who were all escaping something. Everyone had problems. The resilient found solutions. He knew he would pull himself out of this hole but it wouldn't be easy and that was okay with him. Nothing good in life was ever easy.

He'd come to the conclusion that the only path forward was to go back home and prepare for a lengthy divorce process. Krystal made it seem like there was no way she'd take him back, and after thinking about what he would do with his cut of the remaining two hundred million, there was no going back for him either. It was settled. He was going to get his money, one way or another.

After a few hours of dancing and more substance abuse, Luis and Jessie stumbled back to his room. Both were way beyond the state of inebriation, as they sloppily kissed their way to the bed before ripping each other's clothes off. She jumped on top of him and as he watched her silhouette in the dark straddling him back and forth, all he could think of was Jasmine. He closed his eyes to try to think of something else, but there she was, telling him she loved him but that one day it would all be over.

"Is everything ok?" Jessie asked as she looked down.

"Get out," he replied calmly.

"Hey, it's okay. I can help you get back up, most of my clients are older," she said as she spit on her hand.

"Get the fuck out!" Luis demanded in a fit of rage and Jessie jumped off terrified.

She slipped her dress back on, grabbed her heels and purse and hurried out of the room before yelling at him, "Limp dick asshole!"

Luis paid her no mind as he stared up at the ceiling, wondering what to do next. He grabbed his phone and looked up private flight companies in Vegas and chose the first company that popped up. He dialed the number and reserved a Gulfstream for the next evening. Late enough to where the kids would be asleep.

Daddy was coming home.

CHAPTER 35

"Daddy?" his daughter said, with a frightened look on her face. She was supposed to be asleep, but here she was past 11 PM answering the door to a possible stranger. The thought of that pissed him off but he wasn't prepared for his daughter to be the first person he'd confront when he walked in the door, so he tried hard to look less intoxicated and more stable and loving. He tucked the Smith and Wesson revolver back in his waistband, crouched over and reached for a hug.

"Come here honey! It's ok, daddy missed you!" He pulled her in close as she nudged up underneath his neck. "It's ok baby, where's Mikey?"

"He's at Ricky's sleeping over," she said in a low sad voice. "Where were you?"

"Daddy had to go take care of some things with work…"

He looked up and saw Krystal darting inside from the back patio. He stood up tall as he rubbed

Mia's head to try and calm her down but as he stretched upwards, the gun fell out of his waistband. It made a loud sound as it rattled around on the tile floor but luckily it hadn't discharged as he thought it would. Mia looked at the gun in shock and ran towards her mother as Luis hurried to pick it back up off the ground.

"What the hell are you doing here?!" yelled a confused Krystal who noticed the gun a split second later. "Is that a gun?!" She reached into her pocket while Mia attached herself to her leg. "Here honey, call the cops like mommy taught you, okay?" She handed the phone to Mia, who ran quickly to her room.

"Don't do that Mia! Come back to daddy!" Luis tried to yell nicely but it hadn't worked. "You're making my daughter call the cops on me? What kind of mother are you?!"

"Oh look who's talking!" she snapped back.

"Okay, call the fucking cops! See what I care. I'll shoot anyone that dares enter my home." He pointed the gun towards the open door and made a firing gesture. His mood reverted back to the aggressive and anxious behavior that the drugs and alcohol had rose out of him. After taking a better look at him, Krystal's demeanor changed as well. She went from combative to concerned and fearful. Luis was a mess. He hadn't shaved in days, wore a loose tie around his neck with a wrinkled white button up shirt that had been discolored by sweat and a few other things. His face had a greasy gloss to it, damp with sweat and his bloodshot eyes looked like they were being kept open by tape attached to each eyelid.

She put her hands out to try to calm him. "You don't have to shoot anyone, Luis."

"Where is he?" he asked as he made his way around the house opening room doors, clearing them as if he was back in the military. "Where the fuck is he?! I saw his car outside. Vic! You better not be in my room!" He looked in the master bedroom, which was completely empty, furniture and all. Then he saw Krystal looking out back, motioning someone to leave. Victor ignored the warning and came inside.

As he walked in from the patio, he had his arms raised in an attempt to diffuse the situation. "I'm right here brother. Just calm down, everything is going to be okay." He tried reasoning with him and got a few steps away until Luis lifted the gun and leveled it to his face.

"Back up! Over there," he waved the gun towards Krystal who was now sobbing, fearing for the worst. "Calm down, huh? You want me to calm down?!" He paced back and forth, chuckling at the thought of calming down. Even if he wanted to, the amount of cocaine he had consumed in the last few hours was enough that his body was twitching every so often from built up energy he wasn't expending. "This guy! He's funny!" He twitched again and faced Victor and Krystal who were standing side by side.

"You guys actually look cute together. Let me take a picture and show you," he reached in his pocket for his phone. "Ah shit, I forgot I threw my phone out."

"It's not like that, brother. You know I would never—" Victor said.

"Shut the fuck up!" He pointed the gun back at him and looked at Krystal. "What is he doing here at 11 PM on a Saturday night?"

"He was only helping with the kids! He just dropped Mia off, I've been so busy handling the move!" she cried out while showing him the almost empty house which had been sold.

He paced while he tried to process the answer. "Sounds valid," he whispered to himself. Then he walked up close to Victor and stood face to face with him. He slowly rubbed the gun on his face and asked, "Is that the truth? Or are you trying to take my wife and kids from me? Two million dollars wasn't enough for you?" Victor stood tall, further infuriating Luis. "Tough guy, huh?" He pushed the gun on his forehead and tilted his head back and said, "BANG!", but didn't shoot. Victor then let a tear run down his cheek as he realized how close to death he had just been. Luis walked backwards, scratching his head with his gun. "My theory is that Victor here was going to play the nice guy. *In case* I didn't come back. Then you guys would build a romance. Next thing you know, you guys get married and boom! Just like that, you're two hundred million dollars richer! Fuck, that's actually genius Vic! I commend you." He laughed and clapped his hands while still holding the gun. Then his whole body twitched and his mood flipped again. "Both of you. On your fucking knees!"

Krystal and Victor were now on their knees crying uncontrollably and pleading with Luis, to no avail. He continued, "Let's make a deal. Give me half of what's left. One hundred million. You guys keep the other half and we all live happily ever after. I'll disappear. You won't *ever* see me again." *BANG!* He shot the gun into the ceiling. "That quick, that easy. I'll be gone. I'm serious."

"Take it all! I don't care about the money!" Krystal yelled back. Luis looked at her, she was defeated. "I'm pregnant!"

A wave of emotions rushed over his body. It wasn't a feeling he'd ever felt before. He was furious, excited, anxious and panicked at the realization of where he was and what he was doing. Luis had never been one to snap at anyone, much less his wife. Now here he was holding a gun to her and one of his best friends, with his daughter probably scared shitless in her room. He couldn't focus like he wanted to but managed to finally ask, "Why? Why didn't you—"

Victor replied, "I tried telling you yesterday but you—"

"Shut the fuck up, Vic!" Luis cocked back the gun and fired it twice.

BANG! BANG!

He missed his head by about a foot, on purpose, but it caused him to fall back on the floor and he curled into a fetal position. He stayed there covering his head just in case Luis decided to shoot again.

"How? Is it mine?" Luis asked in a lower tone but still waving the gun loosely as he spoke.

"Yes, of course it's yours!"

"But when—"

"Had to be that night after you won the lottery…" She wiped her tears trying to regain her composure. Luis thought back to that night. She had jumped on him after he asked her if she ever made love to a millionaire before. One of the happiest days of his life. He started weeping, reminiscing back to those beautiful days.

"I remember," he said as he sobbed, wiping his tears on his sleeve.

"We can figure this out baby," she kept pleading. "We'll get back to normal and start over. We can travel the world with the kids like we always dreamed of." She crawled towards him and he backed up, waving her back with the gun. "I'll forgive you! I promise!"

He paced around the house yelling at himself and banging himself in the head. "How could you be so fucking stupid?! Why?!" He pounded his fist on the dining room table as the glass shattered. "WHY?!" Then he pointed the gun up and shot the roof a few times in a fit of rage. Krystal screamed in fear as the ceiling was now raining debris down on Luis.

He then walked towards her. "Okay. Okay. I'm so sorry baby." He had given in. She said she would forgive him and he knew although it was an almost impossible task, she would be the one person in the world to give him a second chance. He'd have to go to hell and back to redeem himself but it didn't matter anymore. He would do it. Luis was a family man who got derailed by temptations but he was going to get back on the track. He put his head down in shame, then looked her in the eyes. "Would you really forgive me?"

She wiped the tears from her eyes and managed

to let out the most beautiful smile he had ever seen. The same smile that had made him *fall in love a hundred times*. Never mind, a million times. The last five weeks meant nothing to him anymore. If anything, it reassured him of how lucky he had been in life by marrying Krystal. His true prize. But her smile quickly turned into a face of dread. He was confused. Had she changed her mind suddenly? Was she bluffing? She let out a loud yell as she looked past Luis. "Noooooooooooo!"

Luis turned around to see an officer rush through the open front door and instinctively raised his gun at him.

BANG!

BANG! BANG!

Luis fell back onto Krystal, who was now crying out loud, checking on him. Blood was rapidly soaking though his already filthy white shirt. He'd been hit. Victor came over to try to keep him alert as the cop ran over to them.

"Man down! Several gunshots! Need an ambulance ASAP!" the officer yelled over his radio. "Are you guys okay? I heard shots and saw you laying like you were dead!" He asked frantically, attending to Luis and applying pressure to the wound on his abdomen.

"We're fine! Oh my god, is he going to be ok?!" Krystal was yelling frantically, rubbing Luis' head on her lap trying to keep him awake. "Stay with us baby!"

The officer tried calming everyone down. "Sir, you've been shot. Ambulance is on the way, can you hear me?"

Luis nodded.

"What's your name, sir?"

"Luis…Luis Diaz," he muttered, spitting out some blood while trying hard to keep his eyes open.

"Oh my," the cop leaned back in disbelief. "The same Luis Diaz that wrote me a hundred thousand dollar check?!"

Luis fixed his heavy eyes on the cop. It was Officer Jones. The nice man who had pulled him over minutes after he had read his winning numbers. The same man who he decided he would gift a hundred grand to because of his respect for his service and for being *one of the good ones*. Luis smiled at him. "Yeah," he chuckled, spitting up more blood. "That was me."

"Shit. Hang in there, Luis! What the hell happened to you?!" Officer Jones reached behind Luis' head to keep him upright and alert.

"I screwed up man," Luis answered. "I hit the fucking lotto."

His last bit of strength faded and his body fell limp onto Krystal's arms.

EPILOGUE

Two Years Later

The sun was slowly disappearing into the water as it provided the perfect backdrop for the small private ceremony on a beach in Rincon, Puerto Rico. It'd been two difficult and tumultuous years since the passing of her late husband, Luis, but there she was at the altar once again. Krystal was very nervous but she stood confidently and hopeful for the future as she grinned from ear to ear looking up at her fiancé and listening to his vows.

"…I promise to love you *and* your two beautiful children, Mia and Mikey who I miss terribly and wished were here. But ever since that day I strolled in to your coffee shop, I just knew you were the sugar *and* spice I needed in my life."

Krystal blushed and blew him a kiss, then she said her vows. "I know this has all happened so fast and everyone told me I shouldn't rush into this, but I'm a woman who's always stood up for what I wanted. And *this* is what I want. I choose you, because you make me feel so special. I love your free-spirited way of life. You constantly push me to be a better person. You're there anytime I need a shoulder to cry on. You're very understanding of my past and you've helped me ease my pain. I feel like a brand new woman when I'm with you. I love you, John, and I can't wait to do life with you."

The ceremony wrapped up soon after and the half-dozen friends they had invited, were now hugging and congratulating them. As they posed for a few selfies, Krystal caught John looking around.

"Everything ok, babe?"

"Yeah, I just really thought my sister was gonna make it. Maybe she got lost."

Just as he said that, his face lit up as he saw her carrying her heels in her hand, walking through the sandy beach on her way to them. Krystal looked at her and was very impressed by her beauty as the woman approached in a stunning body-hugging blue evening dress.

"I'm so sorry I'm late! The driver took me to the wrong beach," the lady pouted as she hugged her brother.

John then introduced the two, "Krystal, this is my half-sister, Jamie."

Krystal hugged her and replied, "You're so gorgeous, oh my god! And that necklace! Where'd you get that?"

Jamie placed her hand on the the diamond-studded necklace with red pigeon blood Burmese rubies and said, "Oh this? I got it from a fool I once dated."

ACKNOWLEDGMENTS

What a fun year it's been after releasing my very first novel and getting so much positive feedback! I can't believe I'm a published author. In case you're here for the first time, I previously released this novel with a different cover, not much marketing and a ton of slips in editing and proofreading. I'm new to this, so when I had finished writing the book, I just wanted it to be out there right away and rushed its release. But I'm glad it happened that way because I've been able to learn a lot about the self-publishing business and even had the opportunity to create my own company, Fly The World Publishing, that will feature all of my future works and will serve as a platform for other authors writing travel-related content.

First off, I'd like to give a special thank you to my original supporters. My family, friends, co-workers, local book stores, Bookstagrammers and anybody else that managed to grab an original copy, thank you sincerely. You gave me the motivation to continue writing and pursuing a dream that I didn't really know I had until a few years ago. I know in this day and age, we don't have much time to pick up a book and then keep our attention focused long enough to finish it, so when you tell me you read the book, I know how much of your time you've given me and I truly value that. My goal will always be to reward you with something you can get lost within and be entertained.

This year has been a special one because my wife, Krystal, and I welcomed our beautiful daughter Gabriel Rose into this world, making us parents for the first time. It's been the most joyous time of our lives and we're doing everything we can to cherish these moments where she's changing so rapidly every day. She's a big fan of books already and I can't wait to write her a children's book, since this one is not suitable for her just yet, or ever. Papi loves you and thank you for brightening my days, even when you want to start them at 4 in the morning.

Lastly, I'd like to thank my wife, Krystal, for doing all of this with me. She's my biggest supporter and a sometimes harsh critic, so I make sure I come correct when approaching her for some feedback. You're not only the best wife I could've ever asked for, but you are the best mother for our little Gaby. *Our story* will always be my favorite. I love you a lot a lot a lot a lot.

ABOUT THE AUTHOR

Luis R. Diaz is a Puerto Rican author residing in Fernandina Beach, FL. He currently works as an air traffic controller after serving four years in the Navy and contracting in Afghanistan and Guantanamo Bay for almost three years. He is a world traveler, having visited over 25 countries and loves to learn and embrace other cultures while also being very proud of his Puerto Rican heritage and representing it across the globe. He is married to his high school crush, Krystal Diaz and they just welcomed their first child, Gabriela Rose, in April 2022. Their family is also accompanied by Rocky, a golden doodle who also loves books…as chew toys.

After releasing *WHAT'$ ¥OUR NUMBЄR?* in March 2022, the reviews and feedback were incredibly positive, causing him to change gears and start his own publishing company, *Fly The World Publishing*. A year later, with a fresh cover, some original music and new advertisements, *WHAT'$ ¥OUR NUMBЄR?* was re-released with plans for the highly anticipated sequel already under way. But first, you can expect his psychological thriller novel, *The Connected*, by summer 2023.

WHAT'$ ¥OUR NUMB2R?
Coming Soon...

To read about The Making of WHAT'$ ¥OUR NUMB€R? and for a sneak peek of the sequel, please visit Lrdiazblog.com.

Don't forget to leave a review on Amazon or any other reading platform. Reviews are essential to Indie authors and helps us gain exposure amongst other readers. If you loved my book, share it on your social media with friends & family and be a part of this journey with me!
Follow me on Instagram @wheres_luigy and give me a shout!